THE THRILL OF THE LIFE

Johnnie looked to the north and then to the south, at the two posses closing in on us, then he looked at me for a few short seconds in silence before saying, "Keep a tight cinch, amigo."

We pointed Big Track and Chip west, touched our spurs to their bellies, gave them their heads, and leaned over on them. They were running wide open in nothing flat, neck and neck, ears laid back and heads stretched out. Then Chip gained a little and Big Track's head fell back to my stirrup.

I heard shots ring out from the posse coming from the south and instinctively ducked a little as the horses jumped small bushes and deep trails.

I glanced back at Johnnie as he reached back and tapped Big Track's butt with the ends of his bridle reins and smiled.

More shots.

Johnnie pulled his hat down and yelled, "Powder River be damned!"

Books by Sam Brown

THE LONG DRIFT

SAM BROWN

HarperPaperbacks
A Division of HarperCollins*Publishers*

HarperPaperbacks *A Division of* HarperCollins*Publishers*
10 East 53rd Street, New York, N.Y. 10022

Copyright © 1995 by Sam Brown.
All rights reserved. No part of this book may be used or reproduced in any manner whatsoever without written permission of the publisher, except in the case of brief quotations embodied in critical articles and reviews. For information address Walker and Company, 435 Hudson Street, New York, N.Y. 10014.

A hardcover edition of this book was published in 1995 by Walker and Company.

Cover illustration by Tony Gabrielle

First HarperPaperbacks printing: June 1996

Printed in the United States of America

HarperPaperbacks and colophon are trademarks of HarperCollins*Publishers*

10 9 8 7 6 5 4 3 2 1

This book is dedicated to Verna Mae and Ray Brown, mother and father, for life and a lifetime of love. It is also dedicated to the memories of Billy Peters, Bill Gudgell, R. C. Chism, and Brent and Ken May—all good Panhandle cowboys and all safely across the river, but much too soon.

There came a time when I no longer craved to see new country from between a cow pony's ears. To be a truly successful drifting man, you've got to be able to keep yourself from formulating plans. You've got to be like a coyote—he needs less to be more content than any creature I know of. Give him a sunny rock in the winter and a little jag of creek-bank shade in the summer, and he's convinced God is on His throne and all is well with the world. On the rare occasion he gets to feeling melancholy and the sun and shade don't seem to fulfill him like they ought to, a quick romp along a moonlit creek with a cute little tawny-haired trollop will restore him to his former nap-taking, all-is-well self.

Johnnie Lester was as much like that as any man I've ever met. Maybe Ab Deacons and I should have been more like him.

I had drifted a long time. It had been nearly twenty-four years since I'd left the banks of the Little Kanawa River in West Virginia. When I left home I didn't have much of a plan, and I guess that's what made me so successful at roaming for so long. But then, somewhere and sometime, something began to change. I can't pick out an exact time or place when it happened. Some things change so slow that for a long time you're unaware of any change at all, then all of a sudden you see it and you have the feeling that the change must have occurred while you slept the night before, but somewhere inside you know better.

For years and years you're just a carefree young cow-puncher, one of the "kids" around whatever chuck wagon, bunkhouse, or cow camp you're calling home at the moment. Then one day maybe some cowboy good-naturedly lets you get in the chuck line in front of him and he says something about respecting his elders. Or maybe you hear someone grumbling about some cranky old fart and you realize he's talking about you. All of a sudden you're past forty, though you don't see how it could be. One morning at the crack of dawn you look around and take a quick inventory of the men standing around the rope corral with their bridles: They're calling out the name of the horse they want for the morning's circle and it strikes you—*they're all kids!* Then you realize some of them are a quarter century old, even though they weren't even born until the time you started punching cows.

Exactly how I arrived at this point in my life, I'm not sure, but there came a time when I found myself longing for more than the sun and the shade. Oh, I still wanted them—I just wanted something else to go along with them. My dissatisfaction was something that even a moon-light romp with a tender trollop wouldn't quell.

The wagon boss of the HV had sent me to the mouth of Coyote Run Canyon to block any cattle that might try to sneak inside the canyon and hit the steep trail that would take them back out on top and behind the day's gathering. Lots of cattle in that country were masters at that kind of game. You would usually hear them scattering rocks or popping brush long before you could see them, so you had to keep your ears cocked and keep watching your horse's ears, too.

I calculated it would be an hour or so before any cattle were pushed my way, so I stepped off my horse and loos-ened my cinches so he could breathe a little easier—we'd had a hard ride getting there and he was pretty winded.

Then I dropped down on one knee and pulled out my sack of Bull Durham. I hoped the cigarette smoke would keep the gnats and cedar flies away from my face, because in the hot mouth of that canyon there sure wasn't enough wind to blow them away—or to dry the sweat that was already sticking my shirt to me, for that matter.

I licked the cigarette paper, twisted the ends, and put it between my lips. Then I put the makin's back in my pocket, lifted my hat off, and wiped the sweat from my forehead with a shirtsleeve, struck a match on the top button of my Levis, inhaled deep, and blew out the match with a puff of gray Bull Durham smoke.

I stuck the burnt end of the match into the sand and leaned on my knee while I smoked. When the cigarette started to fry my lip I dropped it to the ground, picked the match back up, and tamped the cigarette into the sand with it.

I rolled the match between my fingers and cocked an ear toward the brush, and heard nothing but locusts. Then I absentmindedly drew a short, crooked line in the sand with the match, angling it down and to the right—a line that meant nothing. Then, for some reason, it came to represent a river to me. Not a slashing, roaring mountain river, though. This was more of a gently winding river, one that murmurs instead of roars. It was a plains river. Of course it was.

It could have been the Platte or the Canadian, the Brazos, the Arkansas, or the Red, or a dozen other meandering plains rivers, but I didn't think it was, because I had seen and crossed all of them, and I had never seen or crossed this particular river.

I chuckled at the thought—the possibility of there actually being a plains river that I *hadn't* seen or crossed in twenty-four years of cowboying from Kill Deer in Dakota Territory to Del Rio, Texas. From Sweet Grass, Montana, to Nogales, Arizona.

Next I drew some trees on the north bank of that river right where it turned down and angled to the right, toward the southeast by my map in the sand—not brush, just a few trees, and so thick that cattle could hide in them. Be a good place to take a nap, I thought, underneath those trees by the river. I could almost hear the water murmuring and feel the cool of the shade. I put the match in my mouth to chew on and stood up and looked across my horse's neck to the lava rock and the thick, head-high cedar brush.

I hated this country. It was hot and dry, and just seemed to bake and mash you into the ground. The cattle were spoiled and the horses were a bunch of inbred, chicken-boned, no-hearted lunatics. They were apt to pitch when they were fresh and even more apt to quit you when they weren't.

I had the quits—I knew because I had had them before and I knew what they felt like. But I'd stick it out till the outfit was finished branding, then I'd be rolling my bed.

Suddenly my horse jerked his head up and pointed his ears toward the cedars. I listened for a few seconds and heard what sounded like a hoof slipping on rock.

I reached down and jerked my cinch tight just as the bush popped no more than a rock's throw in front of me.

As I stepped onto the sorrel, an old wrinkled-horned reprobate stuck her head out of the brush. She was standing in a dim trail, and by the look of her I could tell she was sure surprised to see me and the sorrel blocking the trail into the canyon. "You better rattle your hocks the other way, mama," I said. Then I yelled and she boogered and swapped ends and disappeared in the brush again.

That night as we lay sweating and smoking cigarettes on top of our bedrolls, I said, "I'm tolerable close to havin' my fill of these rocks and cedars."

"Got the quits again, don't you, Wills," Johnnie said. "You ain't never going to amount to a goddamn thing."

"The king of quitters has spoken," I said.

Ab laughed.

None of us said anything for another cigarette, then Johnnie said, "That streak-faced bay that Marvin was ridin' today is undoubtedly the most ring-tailed bastard God ever created. I'd be embarrassed to ride 'im."

"What about the gap-mouthed, head-slingin' roan he usually rides?" I said.

"If I was wagon boss on a big cow outfit like he is," added Johnnie, "I'll be damned if I wouldn't have the best string of horses in the remuda."

"The sad part about it," Ab said, "is that Marvin *does* have the best string of horses in the remuda."

We all laughed, because what he said was true.

"That doesn't say much for the horses that pack us around, does it?" I said.

"If they were killin' cow horses, there wouldn't be a single goddamn head to perish on this outfit," Johnnie said.

After a short silent spell, Ab said to Johnnie, "So I guess this *ain't* the perfect cow outfit you said we were going to find?"

"Just the thought of quittin' makes me feel better," Johnnie said.

"Was there ever a time you thought we *wouldn't* quit?" I asked.

Johnnie laughed. We never stayed in one place very long. Punchin' cows was just something we did between journeys. He was still in love with drifting, too, and I knew he wasn't lying about feeling better by just talking about quitting.

I was as ready to leave as Johnnie was, but my blood didn't get to pumping by just talking about it the way his did. I wanted to leave because I didn't like anything about the outfit, but Johnnie wanted to leave just for the sake of leaving. I had no craving to see new cow country from between a cow pony's ears, either. Leaving, to me, was just something that had to be done, like pulling a rotten tooth; to Johnnie, it was a source of excitement.

Not that I faulted Johnnie. In fact, in spite of some fights we'd had, I always admired him. There wasn't a name better known in cowboy circles than his and not a better cowboy. I'd never seen a man who had so many cowboy skills honed to near perfection. Some cowboys who could ride a really rank pitchin' horse weren't too talented with a thirty-foot catch rope, and some who could throw a nearly perfect loop every time couldn't set an even half-rank bronc. There were some who could rope and ride as well as he could, but they couldn't handle cattle half as well as he could, couldn't sense what the critters were going to do next. But above all else, God never made a man who loved cowboying more. Or who loved quitting one outfit and going to a different one more.

"So where are we going to go when we leave here?" Ab asked.

Me and Ab both knew what Johnnie's answer would be and we weren't wrong. "We're gonna find the best cow outfit in the world, Ab." he replied. We'd just met Ab at the XIT the fall before, but he'd fallen right in with me and Johnnie—which might or might not have said much for the caliber of company he chose to keep. That would depend on who you were talking to, I guess. George Findlay, the Chicago bookkeeper for the XIT who sat a horse like a two-by-four and who fired us for violating "ranch rules," would have said we were irresponsible and undependable. But of course, George Findlay wasn't a cowpuncher, so his views didn't count for much in our estimation.

Anyway, we met up with Ab at the XIT and he fell in with us and we were glad he did. Ab was about fifteen years younger than me and Johnnie but he was a good hand and he was from Dixie. He never said much, even less than I did, but sometimes he could say something that made everyone laugh till they cried. He'd only been cowboying about five years and was already talking about going back to his Dixieland home to raise cotton and kids with the sweetheart he left behind—talk that could send Johnnie into a long oratory telling Ab what a mistake that would be and expounding the benefits of the cowboy life, especially when compared to that of a married cotton farmer. I figured it was Ab's decision and I never tried to talk him into it or out of it. I just told him what I knew from experience—the longer you wait to go home, the harder and harder doing it becomes, and the men who keep talking about it seldom end up going home.

So it was decided, as if there were ever any question to

the contrary, that we would quit the HVs. I lay in my bed-roll, listening to Johnnie tell Ab about the perfect outfit they would find someday, until I dozed off. When I woke up a little while later they were both asleep. I lay there, listening to the coyotes and the crickets. I began to think about that unknown river I had drawn in the sand that morning. Just before I dropped off to sleep again I envisioned a cabin in the trees I'd drawn where the river angled to the southeast—it was a log cabin—and that was when I realized the trees weren't cottonwoods but pines, maybe cedars, tall, cool pines growing along a plains river.

Three weeks later we drew our pay, rolled our beds, and left the HVs. We could have stayed and back-prowled and branded calves that were missed during the works, but we had all tolerated that outfit as long as we could. By then it was the first of June, 1888.

"What do you say we go to the Black Range country?" I said. The Black Range was in southwestern New Mexico, some four hundred miles west. It was a big, rough, wild country, home of cinnamon bears, elk, lions, a few reservation-jumping Apaches, and wild cattle.

"Hell, yes," Johnnie said instantly. "I hear they struck gold and silver all up and down Percha Creek and that Kingston is boomin' like a firecracker. And I've heard there's a street called Virtue Avenue that has some of the most refined and cultured whores there are, and the truth is I've been lookin' to extend my own culture for some time."

Thus are the decisions of drifting men made.

We were camped underneath a cottonwood along a little creek at the edge of the Guadalupes in west Texas. The creek had a seep in it, and by scooping out a hole in the sand with our hands we had been able to water the horses as well as ourselves. Now the sun was about down and the horses were all hobbled and grazing. Ab and Johnnie had been talking about what kind of women they preferred, as if the opportunity to choose one over another presented itself on a regular basis. They agreed on most of the most critical aspects of conformation—they both liked straight legs, round hips, a good jaw, big breasts, and clean teeth. Johnnie preferred black hair and Ab was partial to red. Johnnie didn't care if the woman screamed like a panther or sang "Bringing in the Sheaves" while he was hoeing cotton in the short rows, as he said it, but he did not like for her to just lie there like a piece of cold granite stone. Ab said he thought noise or movement by a woman was not only distasteful but downright unnatural. Johnnie laughed like hell at that.

Then they debated over who was the best forefooter they had ever seen. "I think Casey is," Ab said.

"Naw—he picks up one leg too often and cripples too

much stock," Johnnie said. "Feller named Whit Milton is the best I've ever seen or heard of."

I listened to them and grinned. I was leaning against a big old dead branch and doodling in the dirt with a twig. Had I been voting, I'd have voted for Whit, too. He loved nothing more than to spur up alongside an old renegade who was headed for the tules and thought she was getting away, roll that loop over her right shoulder, pick up both front feet, turn off, and crack an egg in her. No doubt about it, he *was* the best at it I'd ever seen.

"What do you mean I cripple too much stock?" I said when the voting was over.

"Well, you do."

"Like hell!"

"You do, Casey," Johnnie insisted. "If you'd use a bigger loop and more handle you wouldn't miss the left leg so often and cripple so much stock."

"What in the hell are you talkin' about?" I said. "I can't even remember the last time I crippled anything by forefootin' it."

"What about that old high-horned, red-necked cow that hooked Shug's horse in the butt and then broke out of the roundup last fall?"

"You mean that day up on that flat above Minneosa Creek?"

"Yeah. Didn't she come up with a broke shoulder?"

"Well I sure as hell didn't cripple the bitch or forefoot her, either one. I roped her slick around the horns and laid it behind her ass just before she bailed off the rimrock . . . and you weren't even there! You were late gettin' in that day. But Ab was there, weren't you, Ab?"

"Yeah," Ab said. "He never forefooted that old cow, Johnnie—or crippled her. I helped him lead her back to the herd and turn her loose. Just before you came in she hooked Shug's horse and broke out of the roundup again. When she did, Nick forefooted her—*that's* how she got the broken shoulder."

Johnnie didn't say anything for a little bit. He hated worse than anything to lose an argument, but he could see he didn't have a chance with that one. "Well, when I came in I saw her shakin' her head and draggin' that leg and I heard someone say something about Casey roping her and someone else said something about a forefootin' loop that just picked up one leg . . ."

"That should have been enough to tell you that it couldn't have been me they were talkin' about. Hell, I use a big loop with a lot of handle!" I said. Now Ab laughed like hell.

Johnnie got up and stretched. He was grinning, but I knew he was also thinking hard, trying to remember sometime—anytime—I'd crippled something that I'd forefooted.

"Dug yourself a hole, didn't you, Johnnie," Ab said.

"He wouldn't do that, Ab," I said. "It takes work to dig a hole, and one thing Johnnie's never been found guilty of is working."

"Never been found guilty?" Johnnie came back. "Hell, I've never even been accused of it. The truth is, I'm allergic to work—it makes me break out in a sweat and makes sores on my hands. A doc told me one time that the only kind of work I could do without putting my life in jeopardy was the kind you do with your feet hanging on either side of a cow horse." He walked over to where I was sitting and looked at my dirt-doodling. "What'n the hell's that?"

I looked down at my drawing in the sand and pointed with my twig to the crooked line that ran across and then angled down and to the right. I thought about it a minute, then said, "This is a river right here . . ."

"What river?"

"Don't know . . . not for sure. . . . Anyway, this is a river right here . . . and over here on the north side is a stand of timber—pines . . . maybe cedars, tall cedars."

"Casey, what in the hell are you talkin' about?" Johnnie asked.

"I'm talkin' about something I got in my mind and can't get out, Johnnie."

"Are you talking about some place you've been before, Casey? Are you tryin' to remember—"

"No, this isn't some place I've been. As far as I know, it

only exists in my mind. Just something I've been drawing in the sand. Maybe I'll find it for real someday."

"Why?"

"So I can file on it."

"File?"

"Yeah. So I can file a claim on it."

"A mining claim?"

"A homestead claim, Johnnie."

"A what?!"

I nodded my head and pointed to the pines drawn in the dirt with my twig. "And right here I'll build a little cabin . . . right here a barn . . . here a set of pens . . . and right here'll be my bronc pen."

Now it was Johnnie's turn to laugh. "You're tellin' me you're gonna turn homesteader?"

I looked up at him and grinned, because I knew what was coming next. And it did: "Just like you were gonna file on a homestead in Rana Canyon last winter when you lost your goddamn head over Lillie?"

I was still looking up at Johnnie and still grinning, but I didn't have a comeback for him, not one that made any sense anyway. I knew I'd just as well get ready for the razzing I got every time Johnnie even *thought* about Lillie Johnson.

"Hey, Ab . . . Casey's got the homestead fever again!"

"He has?" Ab asked. "He in love again?"

"Must be—but God if I can figure out who with this time."

"You wantin' to raise corn and snotty-nosed kids again, too, Casey?" Ab asked.

I had sense enough to just keep grinning and not anwer either one of them.

"What're we gonna do about it?" Ab asked.

"Well," Johnnie answered, "I think I still got a few of those Dr. Chaise's Brain and Nerve Pills. I reckon we could poke a couple of them down his throat and keep 'im tied to a tree stump till he's out of heat and the home-steaditis passes."

"I gotta go pee," I said.

"Don't let him outa your sight, Ab," Johnnie said quickly. "I'll get the pills and my rope." While they were laughing I went a long ways down the creek. I knew Johnnie would have a hard time understanding what I wanted and why I wanted it. By then I was wishing I'd had sense enough to have never told him to begin with what I was drawing in the sand. Whoever it was who first said silence was golden must have known a lot of cowpunchers like Johnnie Lester and Ab Deacons.

3

So we rode to the Black Range country and into Kingston, located on Percha Creek and surrounded by rocky hills. It was booming like a firecracker, exactly like Johnnie had heard it was. It had boomed into the biggest town in the territory.

The last time I'd been there it had been just another little cow town with twenty or thirty permanent residents, one store, one bar—the Union—and one practicing whore. Now there was a sign at the edge of town, odd-length slats nailed to a crooked cedar post. Kingston boasted one opera house, three hotels, twelve cafés, fourteen general stores, twenty-two saloons, and—so at least the bottommost and the most recent and crudest-painted slat proclaimed—⚔ 37 whores.

Ab whistled. "Reckon there's really that many?" he asked.

"I don't know," Johnnie said. "Maybe we ought to throw 'em all together and take a head count. And while we've got 'em throwed together in a herd, I'll do some cullin' on 'em. After all, you and Casey need some fun too."

"An which ones do we get, Johnnie?" I asked. "The culls or the keepers?"

"Why, I'm surprised you have to ask," he answered with a grin. "You get the culls—you've always been satisfied with 'em before."

"What do you suppose happened to number thirty-eight?" Ab asked.

"More 'n likely," Johnnie surmised, and with great humor and self-satisfaction, "some love-struck cowboy filed a claim on a homestead along a river and moved her onto the goddamn thing."

The muddy streets of Kingston were jammed with men, wagons, horses, and mules, and with the discarded shipping crates and the saloon and hotel garbage that goes with boomtowns and the people who populate them. Wagons rumbled, horses nickered, mules brayed, dogs barked, men shouted and cussed from the boardwalks, and women screamed and laughed from inside the saloons, accompanied by barroom pianos. In a couple of hotel windows whores leaned out to display and hawk their barely covered wares.

We decided to tie up at a hitching rail and partake of a little of Kingston's sin and wickedness.

The first place we stepped into was the Percha Gold Saloon. We stopped just inside the swinging doors to let our eyes and nostrils adjust to the dim light and the fine barroom aroma—a combination of working men's bodies at midweek, stale beer, and cigar smoke.

To our left was the longest and one of the most crowded bars I'd ever seen. Every chair at every table was occupied, too. And all occupied with miners, which should have come as no surprise, since Kingston was a mining town and not a cow town any longer. Behind the bar was the longest mirror I'd ever seen, and above the mirror was a big picture of a curly-haired damsel lying on a table with one arm and one leg up in the air. She wasn't wearing clothes, but she held a flimsy veil—just not flimsy enough—over the most prized parcels of her anatomy.

It was the first bar we'd been to in nearly three months, and on top of that, this being such a big, busy place, we just stood inside the door and looked around for several minutes.

"Let's have two or three shots of whiskey in here and then go see if we can find Virtue Avenue," Johnnie said.

"Look around in here, Johnnie," I suggested. "Notice that you don't see hardly any weak and lanky old cowboys like us. These are miners—a fact you can tell not only by their dumb-lookin' faces and ugly brogans but by their thick chests and big hairy arms as well. These men swing picks and shovels all day long, Johnnie. . . . Look at the hands on the one drinking whiskey out of the bottle at the bar—it would take a side of leather to make him a pair of gloves. He could probably knock a jack mule to his knees with one blow."

"What'n the hell are you sayin'?"

"Just that maybe we ought to go see if the Union is still open. They'll have the same cheap whiskey and maybe there'll even be some old weak and lanky cowboys in there like there used to be. That way if any trouble gets started after we've had a couple of drinks, like it's been known to, we might not . . ."

Johnnie seemed to weigh this for a few seconds and then said, using hand gestures for emphasis like he did a lot of times when he thought what he was saying was more important than usual, "Now, *we're* here and the *whiskey's* here, so we might just as well drink."

Johnnie headed for the bar; Ab looked at me and shrugged his shoulders. I shrugged mine too, and we followed Johnnie.

We had three quick drinks apiece and should have left, and I think *would* have left if Teresa had not sidled up between me and Ab, told us her name, and asked if either of us would like to buy her a drink.

Teresa was a plump Mexican girl with long, dark hair, dark eyes, a dark mole on her plump cheek, and white teeth that all slanted in the same direction. It was part of her job at the Percha Gold to sidle up next to patrons and ask them to buy her a drink, and it was part of her job to smile and put her warm hand on a man's shoulder when she asked him to buy her that drink. When a man is stone sober he has no trouble seeing the business aspect of it, but after three drinks of cheap whiskey, and especially if it's been weeks and weeks since he's hardly even seen a woman at a distance, much less been close enough to smell her perfume, feel the warmth of her hand on his shoulder, and even see the wonderful hollow of her throat and the wonderful way the hollow fades into a soft flat and then the way that soft flat becomes a valley between two wonderful mounds of the type of flesh, as revealed in a low-cut saloon dress, that men have been known to kill for in a more savage age . . . well, in those circumstance a man tends to see the transaction as being a lot more personal than it actually is. He even feels flattered to be asked to buy her a drink and in fact cannot buy her one soon enough. The fact that her drink is probably only colored water, that he pays full-liquor price for, is of monumental insignificance.

I was older and more experienced in such matters than Ab was, of course, so I was not as easily taken in by the ploy. I let Ab pay for her colored water, which he was falling all over himself to do, but we were crowded close enough together at the bar so that I was able to reap most of the same benefits he did—same perfume, same plump cheeks, same teeth all slanted in the same direction, same wonderful hollow, flat, and valley as revealed by the same low-cut saloon dress.

Of course, Ab, being a southern gentleman, would never have been so rude as to let a young, plump Mexican maiden drink alone, so each time she threw down a shot of colored water Ab threw down a shot of fine Kentucky bourbon. He'd started out with the cheap cowboy stuff like me and Johnnie had, but Teresa had ordered the fine Kentucky stuff, so he naturally had to make the switch. Saloon girls are a hard lot to impress at any rate, and especially so if they're drinking a better brand of liquor than you are, even if theirs is colored water.

"Let's go find Virtue Avenue," Johnnie said.

"Y'all go on," Ab said. "Think I'll stay here."

I didn't think it was my responsibility to protect Ab from the sins of demon rum or the flesh. He could partake of all the sins he wanted to, but at the rate Teresa had him downing liquor, if he ever got a chance to partake of sins of the flesh he wouldn't be able to remember them, and a sin you can't remember is a sin wasted.

Ab drank too much too fast. He needed fresh air and a chance to clear his head and be able to make an honest, calculated effort at deciding which sins he wanted to succumb to.

"Let's go, Ab," I said, putting my hand on his shoulder.

"He's gonna stay with me, ain'tcha, honey," Teresa said, rubbing up against him and playing with his ear.

"You're crowdin' him too much, honey," I said. "He needs some air and a chance to make a break for the rimrock. Everything deserves that much." She still didn't unwrap herself from him, so I put a hand on each of her arms and pulled her loose. "Get'im, Johnnie," I said.

Teresa started struggling and kicking. "You dirty, stinking, gringo son of a bitch!" she screamed. I picked her up until her feet were dangling in the air and let her kick and scream and cuss.

"Put her down, cowboy!" the miner who had been standing on Johnnie's left said.

"He will in a minute," Johnnie said as he reached for Ab.

"Right now, goddammit!" the miner yelled.

"In a goddamn minute, gopher face!" Johnnie yelled as he pulled Ab away from the bar.

You should never refer to a miner as "gopher face" unless your kind outnumbers his kind, and you especially should not do it in the irritated tone of voice Johnnie used.

4

It could be said we three weak and lanky cowboys gave a good accounting of ourselves in a brawl with a barroom full of thick-chested, hairy-armed miners. Or it could be said that we merely prolonged our misery and suffering in a war as short as it was dirty—and one that had a fore-gone conclusion. However it is said, the fact remains that in an embarrassingly short amount of time we were un-ceremoniously cast into a common mudhole, the consis-tency of a hog waller, in the street in front of the Percha Gold.

If it had to be my lot in life to find myself sitting in a mudhole in a street filled with curious, condescending, laughing, pointing passersby, alongside assorted cigar butts and garbage, with alcohol on my breath and blood and mud on my face, then I was glad it was far removed from the banks of the Little Kanawa River in West Virginia and my God-fearing folks. Still, I swear I could all but hear my mother crying and calling out: "Casey Wills, Casey Wills! . . . Oh, what in God's name has become of you?"

"Where's what's her name?" Ab asked on my left, the effects of fine Kentucky bourbon not having been completely pounded out of his brain. His muddy hat was perched on the left front corner of his muddy head.

I looked at him. "We got our butts kicked . . . and you can't even remember her name?"

"Them sonsabitchin' rock-lovin' bastards!" Johnnie said on my right, pulling himself up out of the mud and blood. He tossed his muddy hat aside and headed for the door of the Percha Gold.

"We goin' with him?" Ab asked.

"I'd just as soon wait right here," I said. "I don't think he'll be gone long." Then, still sitting in the mud and thinking out loud, I said, "Forty years old . . ." I turned to Ab again and said, "This is exactly what I'm talkin' about, Ab!"

Ab looked at me, blinked his eyes, and snorted mud out of his nose.

Just then Johnnie arrived back in the mud on his back. The boys inside the Percha Gold, though, had been accommodating enough to knock some of the mud off his face.

"Them claim-lovin', rock-gnawin' bastards!" he said.

"Think about it, Johnnie," I suggested. Just then something caught my eye. There was a newspaper in the mud, so I pulled the paper out and began reading it as he went back inside.

Not ever having been sure how things such as fate and destiny work or even if they exist, I can't say that I was meant to one day find myself sitting in a mudhole in a busy street in what should have been, and until that moment was, one of the most embarrassing moments of my life, totally engrossed in reading the newspaper. But there I was, with the paper resting on my knees, and me wiping the mud off one line after another as I read, suddenly and completely oblivious of the mud and the blood and the garbage and even of the haughty stares and banal remarks of the already dispersing boomtown public—not that it hadn't been fun for them for a few moments, but their attention spans were short and unless someone had died or there was some disgusting animal-like act of passion on display they could not long be engaged.

Shortly after Johnnie's arrival in the mud once again, this time headfirst, I said, "Ike Holt's in town."

"Ike?" he said, spitting mud, the stuff dripping off his chin, his eyes and teeth looking extraordinarily white. "What for?"

Before I could tell Johnnie what little I'd been able to gather from the newspaper, a voice behind us said, "Lookin' for men who savvy wild country and wild horses and are full of piss 'n vinegar and pride."

We all turned our heads, and there standing grinning on the sidewalk was Ike Holt, still tall and slim, but the years beginning to tell on him.

"Hey . . ." Johnnie said, sitting in the garbage-rank mud like a hog, holding his hands up and grinning, "that's us!"

I couldn't help but laugh. Johnnie could make me laugh regardless of what we'd gotten into. He could make me laugh when there was nothing to laugh at.

"And I'm lookin' for some men who are willin' to work their butts off for a lot more than cowboy wages."

"Oooh . . . that's *not* us," Johnnie said. "Cowboy wages have always suited us just fine." But I said, "Tell us about it, Ike."

Ike looked up the street before stepping to the edge of the mudhole and pushing his hat back with a thumb to expose the pale forehead common to the breed. He knelt down and said, "I've got a hell of a horse deal to offer somebody, boys, but so far I haven't found anybody that I wanted to offer it to—nobody I thought I could trust or that I thought could do it . . . but I think you boys are both. As a matter of fact, you may not believe this, but I was wishin' I knew how to get aholt of you.

"Now, I've got a ticket right here in my pocket for a seat on a stage that's a couple of hours late but that just now pulled in, a stage takin' me back to Texas. If you're interested in hearing what I've got to say, though, I'll go right over to the stage office and tell 'em to roll that stage on out of here without me. Then I'll meet y'all at the Union in an hour—that'll give you time to clean up a little. What do you say?"

"We'll be there," I said.

"This don't involve any shovels or axle grease in *any* way, Ike?" Johnnie asked skeptically.

Ike laughed and shook his head. "No shovels and no grease, Johnnie."

"Picks or wire pliers or plows or—"

"No, Johnnie . . . this involves horse sweat and saddle leather and workin' with your feet hangin' down, but it'll take a lot of ridin' and a lot of sweatin' by men who know how to handle wild horses."

"We'll be at the Union in an hour, Ike," I told him.

Ike stood up and pulled his hat down. "Okay. Before I cancel that stage ticket, though, do y'all have any engagements or commitments that'll get in the way if we come to an agreement?"

I thought, *That's a joke!* but I said, "Naw."

"What about . . . what's her name?" Ab asked.

"I'll be engaged on Virtue Avenue just as soon as I can find the damn place," Johnnie said.

I grinned. "We'll meet you at the Union, Ike."

Ike was a cowman Johnnie and I had worked for twice in the past. Actually, Johnnie had known him first and introduced me to him. He ran cattle over a pretty good scope of country in south Texas, and although he was a pretty big operator, he was nothing like George Findlay, the Chicago bookkeeper who'd had us fired from the XIT. Ike was a cowman, but he was also a cowboy himself and saw in cowboys a lot more than a cheap source of labor. His would have been the "perfect" outfit to work for that Johnnie was always going to find, except for the heat, brush, and ticks in his country. It was always a mystery to me why the men you really wanted to work for never seemed to be in a country you really liked, and why the country you really liked always seemed to be operated by men who wanted to work you to death and charge rent on your grave.

Anyway, Ike Holt was our kind, and I, for one, was more than a little interested to hear about the "hell of a horse deal" he had to offer somebody.

* * *

Hotel rooms were a luxury we usually denied ourselves because of money, or rather, a short supply of it. So immediately after leaving the mud we rode to a spot just outside of town and made a quick camp—hobbled the packhorses and unstrapped our bedrolls from them, stripped our muddy clothes off and rinsed them, and ourselves, in the cold waters of the Percha Creek.

"I'm hungry," Ab said while splashing in the cold Percha waters.

"You know it's plumb frightening," Johnnie said, stepping out of the water and wearing nothing but his pale skin and a set of goose bumps, "how much cold water is like a sharp knife."

"Go to hell," Ab said.

"A knife will change a bull's mind from ass to grass and this water's done the same thing to you. A few minutes ago you weren't thinkin' about nothin' but mammyin' up with that gal who was rubbin' all over you at the bar, but now this water's drawn your little wavels up and all you're wantin' to do is eat."

"I can have that gal any time I want," Ab said in defense, "and after I eat, I may just do that . . . but *I'm* in control of my wavels, Johnnie. I take them where I want to go—not the other way around."

"Casey? Did you know ol' Ab takes his wavels ever'where he goes?"

"I heard," I said. "That's good news, Ab."

"Goddammit, Johnnie," Ab moaned, "that ain't what I said."

"The hell . . . wait a minute, Casey . . . take that back—he *don't* take 'em ever'where he goes."

"Where do you go without 'em, Ab?" I asked.

"Go to hell," Ab said again. "Both of you."

5

The Union hadn't changed much since Johnnie and I had
seen it. The dust and soot on the lantern globes was probably not the same, but the eye couldn't tell the difference;
it still had a packed-dirt floor and smelled more of wet dirt
and less of men's dirty bodies than had the Percha Gold.
Francisco was still behind the bar, but his hair had gotten
gray and his jowls and belly had dropped. Rosetta was still
there, too. She had been the single practicing whore in all
of Kingston the last time we were there. Since then she
had become Francisco's wife and made the change from
soiled dove to cook. Now she looked nothing like a dove at
all, soiled or otherwise. She looked as old and blank and
saggy as Francisco did.

Ike Holt was sitting at a table in the corner with a bottle
of whiskey and was the only patron there. We shook hands
with him and introduced Ab to him. Then we dragged up
chairs around the table and Ike asked Rosetta to bring us
out a big bowl of beans, a plate of beef, and a pile of bis-
cuits. Then he tossed the bottle of whiskey across the table to Johnnie, who uncorked it and took a drink and
started it around the table.

"Figured old Josh might be with you," Ike said.

Johnnie wiped his lips on his shirtsleeve and said, "Josh got hung-up to a horse last winter on the XIT—got the thunder stomped out of him. Feller named Tatum Stagg hired a girl to get him drunk, and hell, you know how Josh was . . . The doc said him layin' around drunked-up right after the stompin' caused the pneumonia to set in. . . . We buried him in Endee."

"I'll be damned," Ike said, looking down at the table, no doubt remembering some cowpunching experience or other involving Josh. Then he said, "I've heard of Tatum Stagg."

Johnnie nodded. "When Josh and Casey were at Trujillo Camp, Stagg figured they'd look the other way while he cut the fence and stole cattle. They wouldn't do it, but he figured it was dealer's choice and he was the only one tough enough to deal."

"Casey killed 'im," Ab said bluntly.

Ike looked at me, held the bottle up, and said, "Here's to Josh Smith." Then he took a drink and passed the bottle. Then me and Ab and Johnnie all took a silent drink to Josh, too. I suddenly saw him hung-up again and being kicked and stomped by that goddamn stupid horse. A picture of Lillie came into my mind, too, uninvited, but I was getting better, because that was the first time I'd thought of her in a couple of days.

We talked about Josh and what all happened on the XIT for a while, along with some other cowboys we knew and of course some horses and outfits, until Rosetta brought the beef and beans out. The food pretty well put a stop to the talk for a while, and it wasn't until we'd pushed our plates back, rolled smokes, and sharpened matches into finishing sticks to pick our teeth that Ike said:

"There's some country on the west side of the White Sands that's got a bunch of horses on it—and I don't mean mustangs either—and they can pretty well be had for next to nothin' by somebody who can get 'em gathered and gone. Here's the story.

"A rich easterner by the name of Banister came to New Mexico in eighty-four, lookin' for a place to locate his son, who wanted to start a horse ranch—at least the son *thought* he might like that. They say the boy was wild an' never could buckle down to nothin', that he'd never stick and see a thing through, and the old man thought that starting him in the ranching business would help tame him. Mister Banister already had an interest in some mines around White Oaks and decided to locate his son in the same country. The range was all open, so he bought a ranch site at a good watering hole and turned it over to the boy, who registered a Slash B as his brand.

"The old man even stocked the place with four hundred head of Old Mexico mares and a carload of standard breed trotting studs from the East, called Hambletonians." Here Ike grinned big, like any cowboy would when he thought about trying to make a cow horse out of such a cross.

"The boy didn't take much interest in the horses, even while he was livin' at the ranch," Ike continued, "but the country east of the ranch itself is good horse country and they bred and multiplied on their own.

"After a while the boy evidently couldn't take it anymore and went on a tear for a couple of years—gamblin' and drinkin' and runnin' whores. After he'd gone through all his cash he wrote his old dad a farewell note and shot himself deader 'n a by-god.

"After the boy's death, the old man forgot about the ranch and the horses for a couple of years—until the county assessor wrote and reminded him that back taxes was pilin' up on his ranch. That's when old Banister contacted a banker in San Antonio to ask him to dispose of the ranch for him. That banker is also *my* banker—James David. Mister David has bought the Banister and other ranch holdings and asked me to come out here and see about the Banister horses—he'd heard there were so many of them there wasn't room to run cattle on the range, which he intends to do. . . . The horses and what to do about 'em is up to me."

"And you've been out there?" I asked.

Ike nodded. "Just got back into Kingston yesterday."

"And how many horses are there?"

"Oh, hell . . . It's hard to say. They're scattered all

the way from the head of Three Rivers to Salt Creek on the west side of the White Sands. I counted over five hundred head, not counting colts at mares' sides, and I figured I couldn't have seen much more than half of 'em.''

"And all of 'em as worthless as tits on a boar hog, ain't they," Johnnie said.

"To us, Johnnie, they probably sure as hell are," Ike said, and then he struck a match and lit his smoke, drew the smoke deep into his lungs, and blew out the match. "Looks like before most of 'em decide to break into a run they have to first walk a spell and trot a piece." Which would make them nearly useless as far as cow work went in nearly anyone's book. No matter what else a horse could do, if he couldn't be running wide open no later than the second jump after you threw him his head and called on him, he wasn't much use for handling cattle, at least not the kind of cattle we knew anything about, the kind that loved their freedom and were always waiting for just the right time to put their tails over their backs and head for the tules or the nearest high rimrock.

"So why in the hell would anyone want to go to the trouble of gatherin' em?"

"The best reason in the world," Ike said. "Money."

"But how is there any money in 'em?" I asked.

"Like this . . . I'm sure I can offer James David two dollars a head for everything, say, that's not a suckin' colt—that's two dollars a head for all the mares, studs, yearlings, cripples, and sounds that can be gathered. Hell, that's two dollars a head profit for him . . . He'll go for it.''

"And you want to hire us to gather 'em for you?"

Ike shook his head. "No . . . I don't want to hire you at all. I want to *sell* you the Banister horses, range delivery—four dollars a head for everything above a suckin' colt.''

I was disappointed. For some reason I thought opportunity had been knocking. But now . . . "Ike, that's crazy as hell," I said. "We don't have that kind of money, and even if we did, why would we give anything for a bunch of horses we couldn't sell?"

"Who said you couldn't sell them? Just because they aren't worth anything to us doesn't mean they're not worth anything to anybody."

"But who—"

Ike pulled a folded-up piece of paper out of his back pocket and began unfolding it. It was a page out of the *San Antonio Optic*. He spread it out on the table, put his finger on it and said, "That's who." The headline underneath his finger read: INDIAN TERRITORY LANDS TO BE OPENED FOR SETTLEMENT IN APRIL! He said, "The people who'll be pushin' and shovin' to file a claim when they open up the Nations for settlement will want *any* kind of broomtail nag, and I'm bettin' they'll be willing to pay good money for 'em too.

"All you boys have to do is get the horses gathered, do some sorting on 'em, get the better end at least halter broke and even put a few saddlin's on the better end of the better end, and have them all at the border of the Nations a few days before they open 'er up on the twenty-second of April. When you sell 'em, you give me my four dollars a head plus repay me for what I'm going to advance you to operate on—you'll probably need to hire another hand or two and you'll need a cook and a wagon. The horses won't be easy to gather, 'cause if they were, I'd hire a couple of ranahan boys for a few days and make the big money myself—but I don't have the time to put into a deal like this.

"I figure you shouldn't have much more than five dollars a head in the horses by the time you get 'em to the Nations; I think that with any luck at all you could average fifteen a head—a ten-dollar-a-head profit. If you get there with, say, five hundred head, that's five *thousand* dollars to split between the three of you—close to seventeen hundred apiece. How long's it been since you had seventeen hundred dollars in your pockets?"

"Wait a minute," I said. "You'll advance us some operating money *and* sell us the horses on credit—and we'll settle up after we sell the horses?"

Ike nodded.

"What about us havin' to pay for the cripples?" I asked.

"We oughta get to cull some of 'em, looks to me like. What about the ones too crippled to make the drive to the Nations? And the ones that're too old?"

"What head count do we use to pay you on?" Johnnie asked. "Do we pay you on the total number we gather, the number we start toward the Nations, or the number we get to the Nations with?"

Ike grinned and looked at Ab. "Give your compadres a chance to make a buck and they turn into gouge-your-eyes-out businessmen."

Ab started laughing. "By god, y'all *did* sound like a couple of Chicago bookkeepers!"

"I guess there's a little George Findlay in all of us," I said. Johnnie grinned and pointed his finger at his temple like he would shoot himself if that were true.

"But you've brought up a damn good point," Ike said, scratching his nose, "and one that needs to be settled to everyone's agreement. We don't want any misunderstandings.

"Okay . . . Here is the number I expect to be paid on, and the number I'll pay my banker on—the number of merchantable head, not counting sucking colts, you have *before* you start foolin' with 'em. In other words, you won't pay for any horses you gather that for some physical reason—crippled, blind, old, creepy, whatever, except for stupidity—you don't think will sell, even at the Nations. But anything that comes up crippled or dead *after* that point will be paid for at four dollars a head. I'll go by your head count all the way. If I didn't trust you, I wouldn't be sittin' here tellin' you about it."

"How long's it been since any of 'em were branded?" Ab asked.

Ike shrugged. "I couldn't get close enough to many of the ones I saw to read a brand, but I'll bet less than half of 'em are branded. They're not hard to tell though—once you see 'em you'll know what I mean. If I was you, I'd damn sure road-brand 'em before I head 'em toward the Nations—that is, *if* you boys are game."

I thought for a few seconds, then said, "Hell, yeah, I'm in."

"If Casey is, I am too," Ab said, tapping on the table with a finger.

We looked at Johnnie, who let a slow grin come across his face. "Why the goddamn hell not?" he said. We stood up then and sealed the deal with Ike Holt and finalized our contract with him in the most binding of ways—by reaching across the table and shaking his hand.

Suddenly we were no longer drifting cowboys; now we were cowboy businessmen. If that fact had any effect on Johnnie you sure couldn't tell it, because as soon as he had shaken Ike's hand, his spurs were jingling across the dirt floor and he was saying, "I've wasted all the time on these trivials I can afford, gentlemen—I've got important matters to attend to on Virtue Avenue." Just before he reached the door, he stopped and turned and tipped his hat to Rosetta and said, "That was mighty larrupin' eatin', ma'am."

Ab stood up too, tipped his hat to Rosetta, and thanked her for fixing us a fine meal. Then he said, "I think I'll just . . . uh . . ."

"Just remember, Ab," I said, "I don't think that mudhole in front of the Percha Gold is there by accident." Meaning that I thought it was there specifically for hairy-armed miners to chuck cowboys into. Ab grinned and nodded his head. "Her name was Teresa," I said.

"You're not going too, are you, Casey?" Ike asked. "I need to draw one of you a map where you'll find the Banister horses. Let's have a couple more drinks."

The next thing I know the sun is beating down on our camp and I'm stretched out on top of my bedroll with my boots and spurs on, feeling like I'd been kicked in the head by a mule and forced to drink that mudhole in front of the Percha Gold dry. I'd been rimfired by Ike Holt's whiskey.

I heard some animal-like noise and lifted my head. The noise was coming from Ab's bedroll. Teresa was in it with him. They weren't asleep. They weren't even discreet.

Johnnie wasn't in sight. I fell back on my bedroll with the gnats swarming around my face. A hell of a way to run a business, I thought. Here I am sick and probably not plumb sober yet, one partner's in his bedroll with a barroom whore, and the other didn't even make it back to camp.

I felt something in my pocket and reached into see what it was. It was the map Ike had drawn me and four hundred dollars cash for operating money. I guessed we were still in business.

6

God equipped the cowboy uniquely to deal with the rigors of far-off and lonely places. He could handle wild cattle, snorty horses, rattlesnakes, wolves, blizzards, prairie dog holes, bog holes, treacherous trails, deep canyons, and wide rivers—just to start the list—with grace and stoic dignity. However, it was a rare one of the breed who was able to show even the slightest trace of dignity or grace when it came to handling the rigors of civilization: the honky-tonks, cheap liquor, and painted women. There are other elements of civilization I am aware of—churches, recitals, theaters, schools, and teas—but they usually arrived after the farmers and storekeepers, who came after the cowboys, who came after the noble red man—each one less "civilized" than the one after but much more free. Which is all a fancy way of saying that we were better off once we got out of town because, as we had proven over and over, the battles we waged against the temptations of the flesh and demon rum were notably short and historically unsuccessful. Our only saving grace was that out in the sagebrush, cactus, and rimrock, we were different.

And as we pulled out of Kingston we had a nice little outfit that consisted of a wagon and chuck box and two sets of harness we bought for $120, $60 worth of chuck, a Chinese cook whose name none of us could start to pronounce, so we called him Squint, and a young Mexican kid of about fourteen or fifteen we called Help, who said he savvied horses. We hired Squint and Help for $25 a month apiece. We also bought $65 worth of grain for the horses.

Ike said there were work mules that were running with the Banister horses that we could use and then tally in with the horses when we got to the Nations. So we put Ab's and my extra horses in the harness to get the wagon to the ranch and didn't have to buy a team.

Using Ike's map, we found a place called Milagra Springs where there was not only good water and a little shade but a nice set of corrals and a barbed-wire horse trap that had about thirty-five hundred acres in it. The first thing we did after setting up camp was to put our horses on full feed—two big baits of oats apiece, twice a day—and to get them walking on steel. No barefooted horse could last more than half a day in that lava-rock country without getting too sore-footed to use.

Then we went to work on the barbed-wire fence around the horse trap. There were many places along it where the wires had been broken or stretched so badly they were all on the ground. There were also places where posts were either broken off or leaning over so bad they had to be dug out and reset.

When I saw "we" were working on the fence, I was not referring to an absolutely all-inclusive sort of "we." I was referring to a "we" that included me, Ab, Help, and even sometimes Squint, but never Johnnie.

"You don't know how much I've been lookin' forward to getting to do a little fencin'," he had said immediately after breakfast on the morning we were to begin the project—but I noticed it was a rope and a bridle he was holding in his hands and not a hammer and a pair of wire pliers. "But *somebody's* got to start scoutin' the Banister horses and try to locate them work mules."

"So I guess that'll be you, huh?" Ab said.

"Well, Ab . . . ," Johnnie said with a shrug, "yeah, hell, I guess I'll do 'er."

"We could flip a coin or take turns," I said.

"Aw, it's gonna be hell out there, scoutin' around in this hot, rocky godforsaken, son-of-a-bitchin' country. So, I'll just do it ever' goddamn day for a while."

"At least until *we* get the fence fixed anyway, huh, Johnnie?" I said. He started to come back with something real quick, but instead he just smiled and said, "At least."

Me and Ab could have thrown a fit and said that if we were going to all three be full and equal partners in the deal then we all three would work on the fence. But we didn't because we knew Johnnie Lester, and we knew that it would be easier to just go ahead and do the work by ourselves than it would be to have to put up with his whining *and* still do 95 percent of the work ourselves. But on top of that, and even more importantly, we also knew that when we had the horses gathered and started in to breaking the ones we decided to break, it would be Johnnie volunteering to step astraddle of the rankest ones.

One afternoon as we were working between two rocky hills and it was so hot that when you kicked a lizard out of the shade of one post he would scurry across the sun-seared ground to the next one and stand in its shade with his mouth gaping, picking up two feet at a time off the hot ground, Johnnie rode up and stopped his horse a few feet away, leaned on the saddle horn, and said, "God'll send you to hell for this, you know."

I pulled my hat off and wiped the sweat from my forehead with a shirtsleeve, cocked a hateful eye toward him, and said, "For what?"

"*This*," he said firmly and with a sweep of the hand. "Fencin'."

"Well, I guess you're safe then," I said.

"What about drankin' and whorin'?" Ab asked.

Johnnie smiled. "Why not?"

"I mean, don't you figure the Lord frowns on them things at least as much as he does fencin'?"

"Oh no," Johnnie said quickly. "Drankin' and whorin' are transgressions, Ab, and atonement for transgressions is done by us gettin' bucked off or stomped like an ant. But this"—the big hand-sweep again—"this is *sin*."

"Throw me your rope," I said, "and see if you can straighten up this damn post so we won't have to dig it out and reset it."

Johnnie smiled and tossed me the end of his rope, and I slipped the loop over the top of a post that was leaning at a 45-degree angle. He turned his sorrel around, took three or four dallies around his saddle horn with the other end of his rope, and put the sorrel into it.

The post barely moved.

"Hell," Ab said, "that sorrel son of a bitch couldn't pull the hat off your head!"

"I'll be damned if he can't!" Johnnie said as he backed the horse up a few steps and then drove the steel into his belly.

That woke the sorrel up, and this time he drove to the end of the rope so hard that something had to give. What gave was the post—it broke off even with the ground and with a crack that sounded like a .22 rifle.

The sorrel lunged forward so hard that the post couldn't just fall peacefully over like a dead post ought to, but landed on its top, somersaulted, and bumped his—the sorrel's—hocks, making him clamp his tail, lunge again, and kick with both hind feet while he snorted, bugged his eyes, and flared his nostrils. This all happened in the bat of an eye, but even then, Johnnie, being the kind of hand he was, wasn't in any trouble at all. He had his hands full—the left one full of bridle reins and the right one trying to get the dallies off the saddle horn—but he wasn't in any trouble of losing his seat.

That is, until I sailed my hat underneath the sorrel's belly and he jumped straight up like a bobcat with a bow in his back and sucked straight back, pawing over his head and squealing as soon as he came back to earth. Then he shot forward again like a cannonball.

That's when Johnnie and the sorrel had enough of each other's company and went their separate ways.

Johnnie sat on his butt in the lava rock and watched in stunned disbelief as the sorrel pitched on down the draw without him. Then he looked at me and said, "You son of a bitch."

"Me?!" I could barely talk, I was laughing so hard. "Why I was just a mere tool in God's avenging hands." Me and Ab sank to our knees, laughing. It was an unexpected blessing for which we were enormously grateful and one that confirmed our belief in a supreme being of benevolent spirit.

It was the middle of October when we began gathering horses, just about the time it started to cool down. The gathering didn't go fast, but we kept at it steady, sometimes getting fifty or sixty head a day and sometimes only two or three. Some days would pass where we would not gather a single head, but those days were few. Ike was right when he said we wouldn't have much trouble telling the Banister horses from any others. Their trotting blood made them carry their heads and move in a way that a man could tell from a half mile off.

The range was unfenced, so the horses were scattered a long ways. We didn't have enough hands to hold anything under day herd, so each day's gathering had to be driven to Milagra Springs and thrown into the fenced trap even if it meant driving horses twenty miles after sundown.

We started out at Salt Creek, then moved to the old SLY Ranch country, then on to Mound Springs. From those three places we gathered a total of 146 head of horses and the four work mules.

Then we worked the Tularosa, Nogal Creek, and Three Rivers country, where we gathered another 173 head, including seven that had saddle marks on their withers and turned out to be usable saddle horses. Then we picked up 117 head from the waterings at Duck Lake, Red Lake, and Indian Tanks.

Most of the four-year-olds and up were branded with the Slash B on the left thigh, but hardly anything younger than that was branded at all. Sometimes we would gather a horse that was branded with something other than a Slash B, and these we would try to separate from the rest and leave them where we found them.

It was a good time for us. We were horseback all day long nearly every day. The fall weather was cooling down and crisping up and we had no bosses other than ourselves.

Somedays I would look at the horses we'd gathered that day, and I found it hard to believe that they were actually ours—at least in a way they were—and that each and every sound one represented a possible profit. Nearly every night I wasn't too tired I'd figure up how much money we stood to make on the horses we already had thrown in the trap, and I'd figure it from every possible angle. Even when I tried to be realistic and conservative in my figuring, the possible payoff at the end of the venture at the Nations was hard to believe. Cowboys hardly ever get a chance to make that kind of money, at least not for honest work.

I also found myself drawing the layout of a ranch in the dirt again and more often.

Then we ran into the Rawhiders from hell.

7

We were working the country that drained into Nogal Creek. Of course nothing drained into Nogal Creek except after a rare hard rain, and the creek itself was usually dry as a chip, as were most of the rocky hills, gulleys, and narrow canyons that were offshoots of the creek. The fall of '88 there were none of those rare hard rains—or any rains at all, for that matter. We'd been there nearly a month by then, and it had not so much as sprinkled the whole time. But instead of being a hardship for us, that dryness was actually a blessing—the less rain that fell, the less water holes there were for the horses to water from and the easier they were to find.

Most of the sandy bed of Nogal Creek was not even damp as I rode down it one day, but there were a lot of fresh horse tracks in that sand; I saw that the tracks were going into a narrow, rocky canyon that cut toward the west. There was also a deep-cut trail on the west side of the creek bed that went into the canyon.

After studying the tracks for a few seconds I decided that there must be a spring in that canyon, and I'd come at just the right time of day to catch some of the Banister horses watering there.

When I trotted around the first bend in the narrow canyon I saw that I was right. But I saw something else, too, besides the fifteen or twenty head of horses gathered around a little seep of a spring—I saw that they were trapped in the canyon by a two-board fence.

The horses could go up into the canyon, but couldn't come back on the same trails because somebody had set up a trigger the horses had to pass through in order to get to water.

A "trigger" is a simple device used to catch wild horses or cattle at water holes. We'd talked about setting some up at different water holes, but so far we hadn't needed to. You put up a fence around a water hole where you have seen tracks—or, if the water hole is in a box-end canyon you just put the fence across the mouth of the canyon— and you make only one narrow opening in that fence. No matter how wild or spooky the stock is you're dealing with, if you are in a barren, dry country they will start to pass through that narrow opening in a few days, depending on how spooky they are and how hot and dry it is. After one or two of the bravest of the bunch gets up the courage to pass through the unobstructed opening to get to water and nothing happens to them, the others will slowly start to do the same. In a few days they will get used to the fence and pass through the opening with no more concern than they would have when passing between two rocks.

When they reach that comfortable point, you slip in late some night or early some morning and set the trigger. All it takes is one pole set chest high across the opening that opens to the inside and is held closed by a weight tied to the other end with a rope passing through a harness ring that is tied to the fence. A horse or cow can push the pole to the inside and get to water but after they get inside, the pole swings back across the opening because of the weight tied to it and they can't push it the other way to get out. They think no more about having to push the pole aside to get to water than they would pushing against a small tree branch or weed that's across the trail—it's a natural thing for them to do, just like going to water is—and many times the whole bunch that's been watering at the little spring will be found inside the trap the first day after the trigger's been set.

Inside this trap, I counted fourteen mares, eight colts, six yearlings, and a blood-bay stud that was shah of the harem.

Of course, fences and triggers don't occur naturally or accidentally but are results of human activities, done on purpose. When I saw this fence and trigger I got mad. The Banister horses were ours—mine and Johnnie's and Ab's—and now somebody else was building triggers around water holes and trapping them? *Not for long,* I muttered to myself as I dropped a loop over one of the spindly posts, took four dallies around my saddle horn and jerked that section of the fence down. I dragged it back and out of the way.

We always went well-armed when we left the camp to go horse hunting, not because of horse thieves, but because of studs. All studs, when they have a band of mares with them, are protective of them to some extent and will always get in between their mares and another horse. A horse carrying a cowboy is even more threatening, and a lot of studs will back their ears and run at you. Most can be turned away with a swinging rope and a menacing yell. Sometimes they'll get so close to you that you can hit them across the nose with the rope; that'll usually turn them. There are some studs, though, that aren't bluffing and have no turnback in them. They'll wade right into you on a full run with their mouths gapped open and can be as dangerous as a mad grizzly. They'll clamp down on anything they can, an arm or a leg or whatever, and not only can they take a hunk out of you, but they can drag you out of the saddle and kill you. More than one cowboy's had the opportunity to meet his maker that way, but I didn't care to be one of them, so when I rode through the hole I'd made in the fence I slipped my old '73 Winchester carbine out of the scabbard underneath my right leg and levered a .44-40 shell into the chamber.

As I started to circle that little bunch of horses, a voice behind me yelled out in a not-so-polite voice, "Hold on there, goddammit!"

I stopped my horse and wheeled around to see three

riders standing in their stirrups and long-trotting toward me. One of the riders was carrying a rifle. That's when I noticed how terribly hot of a day it was.

Although I had not come through the trigger, I suddenly felt as trapped as the stud and his mares were. Two things about those three riders were obvious—they were the ones who had put up the fence and they didn't know that I had legal right to the horses—or if they did know, they didn't give a damn.

Not that I would have run even if they had not been between me and the only way out of the canyon; under the circumstances, though, it would have been a comforting thought to know that particular option was available to me. But it wasn't.

It was a dangerous time. A man could just tell it was. Danger was in the air, and I think the horses could sense it, too. I could hear the bay stud slapping the ground with his forefeet and snorting behind me, but I didn't have an eye to spare for him and at the moment it wasn't four-legged critters that were making me nervous.

The riders rode up close—too close—and stopped.

They were sweaty and dirty and unshaven, just like I was. The one in the middle was older, in his fifties, and the others were ten or fifteen years younger. They wore floppy hats and weren't dressed like most cowboys, but they were riding decent saddles. The one on my left was the one carrying the rifle, an old long-barreled, cap-lock muzzle loader with a hole in the end of the barrel that looked, at least from the angle I had, big enough to stuff a shoat down—at least fifty caliber.

"What'n the goddamn hell do you mean, mister," the older one said, "by tearin' down our fence? If I didn't know better, I'd say you was fixin' to steal them hosses yonder, too."

"They're Banister horses," I said, "and I *am* fixin' to take 'em, but not steal 'em. We got an outfit that's got a right to 'em. I got a paper at camp that says so."

"Papers ain't worth nothin' out here. Besides, most of these horses ain't even branded and they're on free range—they belong to whoever can gather 'em. You're welcome to what you can gather too, but we ain't gonna tolerate stealin' what we done got gathered."

"Branded or not," I said, "they're all of the same breedin'—Banister breedin'. And my outfit's got an agreement with the legal representative of the Banister holdings to gather *all* the Banister-bred horses."

"You ain't nothin' but a common goddamn horse thief who's tryin' to talk like a Philadelphia lawyer," he said. "Now git out'n our way or we'll step on you like you was a bug . . . NOW! MOVE!"

Words enough.

The heavy hammer of the big fifty and the lighter hammer of my Winchester started toward full cock together. It wasn't something a man thought about—it was just something done by instinct when the will to survive takes over.

Our hammers started back together, but mine bumped against its sear first and then fell toward the firing pin, igniting the primer and exploding the cordite gunpowder behind the 200 grains of .44-caliber lead.

I was aware only that my cordite had exploded first, that the man holding the big fifty had been knocked backward at the same time his cordite exploded in my face, and that the horses had gone beserk with panic from the sudden gunfire.

When I came to, I had a terrible headache and was tied to a wagon wheel. The bullet from the Sharps had not touched me, but the butt of another rifle had.

The wagon I was tied to was one of seven wagons that were camped together at a small green lake on a desolate flat of rocks and scattered prickly pear. The wagons were circled, forming a corral of sorts, and inside the wagon corral were several horses—Banister horses. Many more horses were hobbled or picketed on the outside of the wagon circle, and again, most of these were Banister horses.

There were woman and kids and men standing in a semicircle around me, eyeing me, and whispering.

It didn't take but a few seconds of looking through a bloody eye to figure out who I was among—Rawhiders.

They were called Rawhiders mainly because of their

reliance on rawhide to fix or make so many different things, but I also think they were called that because of the way they lived. They were usually dirty, not only the men but the women and kids too. They were drifters, but unlike cowboys, who usually drifted alone, they traveled in clans, with sometimes as many as twenty wagons. They were gypsies, but they weren't. That is, they lived a lot like gypsies, but they weren't gypsies by true breeding. And in some ways they were like cowboys—they could rope and handle horses as good as anyone—but they weren't cowboys, either, and I never heard of one ever leaving the clan to drift alone or work for a cow outfit.

Where these people came from was a debatable subject, especially among Texans, since it was in Texas after the War where they started showing up, or at least where westerners first began to notice them. Most people believed they originally came from the mountains of Tennessee or the Carolinas, where they lived by hunting and trapping. They were not slave owners, and most slave owners considered them white trash. When the War started they refused to be conscripted by the South or join the Northern army; they drifted westward, where they found plenty game and thousands of wild horses and unbranded cattle.

They never put down roots or stayed put. A pack of them would light somewhere and brand all the unbranded cattle they could find or run wild horses and then move on.

It was said that nearly every woman in a clan of rawhiders had at one time or another been married to nearly every man in the clan and they had trouble remembering which men had sired which children and by which women. I don't know how much of what I'd heard about them was true, but they were a tough bunch who asked no quarter in a scrap and offered none.

Remembering the look on the face of the Rawhider I shot, I shifted uncomfortably under the gaze of the Rawhiders gathered around the wagon wheel to which I was tied.

In a few minutes several men pushed their way through the onlookers to stand above me. Among them were the two I'd had the run-in with in the canyon.

The older of the two men walked up in front of me and asked my name.

"Casey Wills," I said, looking up and squinting my right eye because of the sweat and blood seeping into it.

"Casey Wills, I am Lon McDaniels. Devon Wilburn is the man you shot, but it is not much more than a flesh wound. You are both lucky. You will be flogged with your own doubled rope for attempted murder and horse stealing. When we put you on your horse, Casey Wills, keep riding until you are two days gone from here."

"How many Banister horses have you got here?" I asked. "And what right do you have to them?"

"As many as we want but not as many as we will have, and by the right of the range, Mister Wills.

"Now stand him up and turn him around and strip him to the waist. Casey Wills, you will do well to remember this."

8

After I was whipped by McDanials, he and some of his men put my shirt back on me, set me on my horse, wrapped the reins around my saddle horn, and slapped the horse on the butt. I never lost consciousness, but I was in a dazed sort of pain. I remember feeling, above and beyond the pain, grateful that they hadn't killed me, because that meant I'd still be able to come back and get the Banister horses—*our* horses—they had gathered.

We'd been camped at Milagra Springs for more than a month, and it was home not only to me but to the horse I was riding. All I had to do was let him have his head and stay in the saddle. Sometime after dark he threw his head up and nickered and I knew we were almost to camp.

I laid around camp for a few days without a shirt on while Squint kept bacon grease on my back. While I was healing enough to wear a shirt and to ride, Johnnie and Ab located the Rawhiders' camp and kept a watch on them in case they pulled out of the country or moved camp to another part of the Banister range. They did neither. They just stayed by the little spring with the two trees and keep making circles and checking their triggers and each day throwing a few more Banister horses into their growing remuda.

"They musta figured we'd booger easy," I said.

"Kinda arrogant bastards, aren't they," Ab said.

"I got a feelin' there's gonna be war," Johnnie said as we rode out of camp before daylight one morning a week after the Rawhiders whipped me.

"Surely they're reasonable enough men to leave once they see we got proof of our right to the Banister horses," Ab said.

"They're Rawhiders, Ab," Johnnie said, and then he grinned. "They ain't no more reasonable than we are."

"Somebody don't come back," Squint warned, "I don't take less money for cook the food."

"Squint," Johnnie said, "you're overpaid as it is, and if none of us come back you're fired."

"Ah-so. Ah-so," Squint said with a smile and a nod. "If none come back, big day for Squint. Take rest of life off from cook and be in horse business."

We told Help that he was going along with us only to help drive back the horses we liberated from the Rawhiders. If, as we expected, there was a serious difference of opinion regarding the liberation, he would wait a safe distance back until the negotiations were concluded. We insisted and he objected, but somehow the closer we got to the Rawhiders' camp, the more ceremonial and the less heartfelt his objections became. "Help ain't no fool," Johnnie said under his breath. "This goddamn thing's gonna be like ropin' a bear—a hell of a lot more fun to talk about than to do."

But we never talked about turning back. We lived by a stern code where the greatest fear is not of pain and death, but the fear of giving up, of taking the easy way out, of slipping the bridle off a humpy remuda horse and catching a gentle one instead.

The spring where the Rawhiders were camped was in the middle of a wide draw, and the two trees growing beside that spring were the only two trees, the only things more than stirrup high, for as far as you could see. And since you could see those trees from four or five miles away, the Rawhiders saw us trotting out of the shimmering horizon half an hour before we got there. Surprise is hardly a factor in a daylight approach to a camp like the Rawhiders had, but the *lack* of surprise was hardly a factor either, as we'd never planned on a strategy any more elaborate than trotting straight into the camp in broad daylight.

When we were within three hundred yards of the camp we stopped to drop off Help and slip the long guns from our scabbards.

"Company's acomin', Paw," Johnnie said as he jacked a round into his rifle's chamber and watched four mounted riders trotting out from the Rawhiders' camp toward us. Before those four had covered a quarter of the ground between us, two more riders loped out from the camp and caught up with them. "And if they keep comin' we'll have to throw another pullet in the pot."

"I need to pee," Ab said.

"Well . . . good gawd, Ab!" Johnnie said.

I looked at them and chuckled. Then I levered a shell into my rifle's chamber and looked at the riders coming toward us. By then I could see that most of them had their rifles out, too.

"You know what I'm thinkin'?" Johnnie said.

Ab looked at him. "Probably some stupid shit about it not matterin' how many of 'em there are."

"No . . . Actually, Ab, right now I was thinkin' what difference should it make to us if a bunch of stupid Rawhiders want to gather a few head of worthless high-steppin', Hambletonian-bred, slew-footed, thimble-brained horses?"

That was probably one of the smarter things Johnnie ever said, but the truth was we either didn't have enough sense or else we had too much pride to fully adopt that attitude. So we all just laughed and trotted out to meet the Rawhiders, instinctively spreading out a little.

We were traveling east, with our shadows nearly all the way underneath our horses and a hot wind hitting us in the back. I was riding my good gray horse who kept blowing his nose and tossing his head like he had face flies. I jerked on his bridle a time or two to make him quit. I sure as hell didn't want those Rawhiders to think I didn't know how to make a good horse.

The Rawhiders all had their rifles either in hand or laid across the fronts of their saddles, and McDanials was in the lead. They spread out as they came closer and stopped twenty feet away. McDanials looked me hard in the eye for a few seconds and leaned over to spit tobacco juice past his stirrup. Then he looked at Johnnie and Ab and wiped his mouth with the back of his hand. He looked back at me and said evenly, "I figured you for a thief, Wills . . . but I never figured you for a fool."

"You must not be much of a hand at figurin'," Johnnie said to my left. "Hell, most everyone we meet figures Casey for a fool first thing."

McDanials glanced toward Johnnie as the breeze picked up our horse's hoof dust and carried it into the Rawhiders' faces. "And you?" McDanials said.

"He's even worse," Ab said to my right, the beginning of what was to be about the longest oration I'd ever heard from Ab. "What kind of men would ride right into twice as many guns just to prove a point? Nobody but fools would do that. I figured y'all are reasonable men, and once you saw proof of the deal we had with Ike Holt on behalf of James David of some bank in San Antonio that gives us legal right to the Banister horses we could work out an agreement of some kind. . . . But hell no, not with these two. So now there's goin' to be some good men killed on both sides. Damned if I can see the sense of it, but I guess it must be better to be dead than to give even a cunction of an inch. Let's get started so we can tell who lives and who dies."

McDanials worked a twig in his chewing tobacco to the front and spit it out. He looked to be thinking about what Ab had said—just like I was. Then McDanials straightened up and said to me, "You got that paper on you?"

I dug it out of my vest pocket and walked my gray forward until I was close enough to hand it to him. He took the paper, unfolded it, and looked at it for a few seconds.

Handing it back to me, he said, "Paper don't mean squat out here."

Especially to someone who can't read squat, I thought as I put the paper back into my pocket with my left hand. At the same time I eased my right thumb onto the Winchester's hammer.

Suddenly it got quiet. Even the horses stopped shaking their heads or stomping their feet or switching their tails at flies. Men and horses, bridles, spurs, and saddles were quiet—deathly quiet—and I felt sweat popping out on my forehead.

Then, surprisingly, McDanials said, "We'll leave"—I let out a long-held breath—"and we'll take the horses we done gathered with us."

"You'll pay seven kinds of hell, too!" I said, gathering my breath again.

Ab cleared his throat.

"You're a hell of a hard man, Wills," McDanials said in a low voice. "I guess all of you are—and I'll bet you fancy yourselves horsemen too, huh?"

I didn't say anything, and neither did Johnnie or Ab. The fact was, I fancied myself much more of a horseman than I did a hard man, not that I'd spent any great amount of time thinking of myself either way, especially since I'd gotten old enough to realize that whatever a man spends a lot of time considering himself to be is something he usually is not.

"But are you gambling men too?" McDanials asked.

We didn't answer.

In a few seconds McDanials said, "We caught a five- or six-year-old pig-eyed blue stud a few days ago that's a pitchin' bastard—the boys have yet to cover him even once. If one of you can ride him to a standstill, we'll leave here without takin' a single horse we've caught. If you can't ride him, we leave with all of 'em."

"How many head have you gathered?" I asked.

"Eighty-four, not countin' suckin' colts."

I looked at Ab and he smiled. I looked at Johnnie and he shrugged.

"I reckon you're on, McDanials," I said. The Rawhiders

reined around and started trotting back toward their camp beside the two trees.

Me and Johnnie and Ab sat on our horses without saying a word. Mayhem and destruction seemed inevitable only a few seconds ago, and now the Rawhiders were riding away from us, laughing. It was an incredible turn of events. Finally, Ab stepped off his horse to pee.

Johnnie and I looked at each other for a second and then we got off to pee, too. Ab looked over his shoulder at us and said, "Well . . . good gawd!"

"I don't care what you say, Ab," I said, feeling suddenly carefree and lighthearted again, "this is just about the most enjoyable pee I ever took."

As we were getting back into our saddles the topic of who was going to ride the blue roan stud came up.

"Casey, you're probably still too sore," Johnnie said, "and, besides, you'd probably get farted-off anyway. And, Ab, you're a hell of a hand at settin' a pitchin' horse, that's for sure, but this ain't gonna be no ordinary rough-string bronc ride. There's gonna be lots of people watching and lots of money riding on this—hell, eighty-four head of horses at ten dollars a head is—"

"Eight hundred and forty dollars," I said.

Johnnie whistled. "Right . . . damn!"

"That's why Ab's gonna do the ridin'," I said.

"You don't think I could ride the son of a bitch?"

"Yeah . . . ," I said, "I think I could too, but when it's all said and done, I think Ab can come nearer covering any horse than either one of us."

"And if he don't ride 'im?"

"Then I'm sure we'll have to listen to you bitch and say 'I told you so' till hell won't have it."

"You can count on it," Johnnie said.

"How come nobody's asked me what I think?" Ab asked.

"What do you think, Ab?" I asked.

"I think it's a hell of a fine, beautiful day, and I think that Teresa gal I met in the Percha Gold was a fine, *fine* lady."

Johnnie grinned. "Why, I'll bet she was almost a virgin, if it hadn't been for all them men she diddled before you."

I said, "Now, Ab, if you don't mind, I'd like for you to forget about Teresa and concentrate on that blue stud."

"It's done, Casey," Ab said. "Ain't nothin' but tight cinches and pitchin' horses in here." He tapped the side of his head with a forefinger and smiled.

"Why, I bet you can't even remember that gal's name now, can you, Ab?" Johnnie asked.

"No," Ab answered as we trotted toward the Rawhiders' camp. Then he smiled and added, "Or how soft the inside of her thighs were or how her hair smelled when I buried my face in it."

"Pitchin' horses, Ab," I said, tapping my forehead and looking at him. "Buckin', bawlin', sonsabitchin' pitchin' horses."

9

The Rawhiders had their wagons, about a dozen of them, circled a few yards behind the two trees, and inside the circle of wagons, running loose, were about half the horses they'd gathered. The rest of the horses were either staked on either side of the wagons or picketed between the two trees. The Rawhiders had put some time into halter-breaking the horses.

All the Rawhiders, men, women, and kids, were naturally curious about us and anxious to see one of us crawl on the blue stud. All the men were gathered in a cluster off to one side and were talking and laughing and, no doubt, were making bets between themselves about which one of us cowboys was going to get his head stuck in the rocks by the roan. Most of them were armed, but that didn't bother me much by then. Of course, me and Johnnie had never put our rifles in our scabbards but still carried them in hand. I carried Ab's rifle too, as his hands would soon be occupied with other things and he didn't want the thing banging around underneath his knee during the pitchin'.

McDanials met us in front of the circle of wagons near the two trees. He had a halter on the blue stud and was leading him. "He halter-broke real easy," he said with a grin.

I reached out and took the lead rope and McDanials said. "We've picked up the rocks from inside the circle of wagons—you can ride him in there if you want to." Then he smiled again and said, "That way you won't get so bruised when you fall off."

"Out here in the rocks is fine," Ab said as he stepped off his horse and started undoing his cinches.

"Cocky bastard, ain't he?" Johnnie said with a smile directed toward McDanials.

Help came up to hold the horse Ab had rode in on while I snubbed up the blue stud by dallying the halter lead rope up short on my saddle horn, so short the stud's head was all but in my lap. Johnnie came in on the right side and ran a hand along the stud's neck until he could grab an ear. The stud slung his head, but Johnnie held on to the ear and squeezed and twisted as hard as he could. The stud froze for an instant, giving Johnnie time enough to lean over and get the tip of the ear he was twisting between his teeth. Johnnie twisted and bit down until the stud gave out a little halfhearted squeal and started peeing a little.

I nodded to Ab, and he eased up to the roan's left shoulder with his saddle and swung it smoothly and gently onto the roan's back and reached underneath his belly with his foot until the toe of his boot could bring back the front cinch. He ran his latigo through his cinch and pulled it gently against the blue's belly, which made him squeal again and squat lower. Then Ab pulled the cinch snug and fastened his flank cinch the same way.

Ab pulled the front cinch tighter, reached up and grabbed his saddle horn, and pushed the saddle back and forth, trying to get some of the swell out of the stud's belly. He finally pulled the latigo tight.

With his saddle screwed on tight to the blue's back, all that was left for Ab to do was to screw his hat on tight, pull the belt on his chaps up a hole, say "Whoa now, you worthless blue bastard," slide a boot into the oxbow on the get-on side, and ease up onto the middle of the blue, all in one smooth motion.

I undallied the lead rope from my saddle horn and eased it over to Ab while Johnnie kept his hand and mouth full of blue ear. Ab quickly took what he thought would be the right rein, one that wouldn't be too short or too long when the blue bogged his head down between his front legs and went to kissing his butt.

With the halter rein held tightly in his left hand, Ab nodded at Johnnie.

Johnnie spit the blue's ear out of his mouth, but before he released his grip he cocked an eye at Ab and said softly, "Show this counterfeit son of a bitch the difference between a goddamn Rawhider and a cowpuncher, Ab."

Ab smiled and nodded again and said, "Count on it, Johnnie."

As soon as Johnnie turned the blue's ear loose, he shot straight up on his hind feet.

He didn't get his head down and kiss his butt or even lunge forward—the son of a bitch just shot up toward the sky on his hind feet.

Usually when a horse does that he comes down on his butt and falls over to one side or the other.

But that blue wasn't going to come down on his butt, you could tell that pretty quick by the way his belly kept rolling up toward the sun.

I heard Johnnie say to himself, "Holy shit! You sorry bastard . . . Get aloose from him, Ab!"

But there was no way Ab was going to get loose from that blue stud, not with him falling over backward like he was. Even though it seems to be happening slowly, when a horse is falling into you like that there is nothing you can do to get away from him.

When the blue quit rolling his belly toward the sun and started falling toward the rocky ground, all four of his feet were straight up in the air and both of Ab's feet were still deep in the oxbows and his toes were turned out.

I couldn't force myself to watch them hit, so I turned my head, gritted my teeth, and closed my eyes.

But I couldn't stop my ears from hearing them hit,

couldn't stop them from hearing Ab gurgle as the saddle horn crushed his chest, driven into him by a thousand pounds of horseflesh.

By the time me and Johnnie could get off our horses and get to them, the blue had rolled off Ab and gotten to his feet.

There was already a growing blood bubble at Ab's nose and frothy blood was coming out of his mouth.

I kneeled down beside him and he looked up at me and grabbed my sleeve. Then the bubble coming out of his nose stopped growing and his eyes rolled to the top of his head.

I put my hand over the hand holding my sleeve and said, "Ab! Goddammit, Ab!"

But Ab was gone.

I kept looking at Johnnie and then looking back down at Ab, expecting to see him wink at me and get up.

But men crushed to death underneath a counterfeit blue stud do neither of these things. They do what dead men everywhere do—turn quickly cold, and bring heartache and doubt to those who cared for them.

I pulled Ab's hand off my sleeve and looked up at Johnnie again. Johnnie looked at me and shook his head slowly, as much at a loss as I was.

Ab couldn't be dead!!

But if he wasn't, how did we explain the lifeless body stretched on the ground between us?

"Casey . . . ?" Johnnie said.

But hell, what was there to say?

I laid Ab's arm down at his side, closed his eyes with my hand and put his hat over his face. The blood had stopped gushing from his mouth and nose, but there was a big sticky pool underneath his head.

I got up and walked away from him, went to my horse, and rolled a smoke, looking across my saddle seat into the far horizon as I held a match to the end of the cigarette. I inhaled deep and said, "I wonder if it tore Ab's saddle up."

"That's a goddamn stupid thing to say!" Johnnie said.

"What the hell difference does it make if his saddle's tore up or not?"

Help came up to us then, cautiously leading Ab's horse. "Is Ab hurt bad?" he asked.

"No, Help, goddammit, Ab ain't hurt bad," Johnnie said. "But he's sure as hell bad dead."

"We'll have to tie him across his saddle, Help," I said, "and take him back to camp." Then all of a sudden I thought of something. "Do you reckon McDanials knew that blue son of a bitch might do that?"

That's nearly as stupid a thing to ask as wondering if Ab's saddle's tore up," Johnnie said. "Hell, yes, he knew it! That sure as hell wasn't the first time that blue son of a bitch threw himself over backward like that!"

I looked over to where the Rawhider men were. They were drinking whiskey and having a ball. They seemed to have even forgotten we were even there, and I couldn't help but remember what Ab had called them—arrogant bastards.

Everything had happened so quickly that I don't think the Rawhiders realized Ab had been killed. I think they knew the roan had come over backward and had gotten up without Ab, but I think that's all they really knew. Probably all they really cared, for that matter.

Then I saw Johnnie walking toward them with his rifle in his right hand.

"Help," I said, "get Ab's saddle back on his horse and get him tied across it as quick as you can and get ready to ride." Then I picked up my own rifle and followed Johnnie toward the Rawhiders.

The Rawhiders were so busy settling the bets they'd made, and I guess celebrating the fact that they would get to keep the horses they'd gathered, that they didn't see Johnnie coming until he was almost on them. When they did see him, I guess there was something about the way he was walking that made them quiet down and take notice almost at once. McDanials stepped out from the knot of men with a bottle of whiskey in his left hand.

"Never got your name, cowboy," McDanials said, "but

you're welcome to a drink . . . after losin' as many horses as you just did I'll bet you need one, too."

Johnnie stepped up and took the bottle and took a drink out of it. By then I was standing only a few feet behind him. When he lowered the bottle he said, "You knew that blue son of a bitch would fall over backward, didn't you?"

McDanials smiled cockily and shrugged. "Well, hell, horses are liable to do anything, you know that. Besides, I said he was rank and none of us had ever covered him . . . I sure as hell wasn't surprised when I seen him trotting around with an empty saddle. Anyway, a bet's a bet and you boys lost."

Johnnie tossed the bottle back to McDanials and said, "You lose, too, McDanials. The Bible says an eye for an eye. Ab is dead and you're sure as hell fixin' to be."

"What'n the hell are you talkin' about?" McDanials said, the smile refusing to completely leave his face. "I ain't fixin' to be dead at all. I outsmarted you and you lost a bet, but don't think you can come in here and start pushin' your way around. Hell, we won't put up with it! Take that rifle away from him, boys, before he gets himself hurt with it."

I raised my Winchester to my shoulder and cocked the hammer. I didn't need to do anything else or to say anything. A cocked Winchester hard on a shooting shoulder usually does its own talking.

"The only question remainin'," Johnnie said, his own Winchester still hanging in his right hand, "is whether you're gonna die going for that Colt on your hip or not. That choice is yours, but it's the only one you got left."

"You ain't serious, are you?" McDanials asked. "You ain't that crazy." Then he saw Help struggling with Ab's limp body, trying to get it across the saddle. Suddenly, and I think only then, did he see the seriousness of the moment. "Hell . . . is he . . . hell, I didn't know. You can't blame me . . ."

"I can and I do," Johnnie said. "Just as sure as if you'd put a gun to Ab's head and pulled the trigger, you killed him. Now I'm killin' you and we're ridin' out of here with *all* the horses."

"You ain't doin' shit!" McDanials said. "And you're sure as hell fooling with the wrong feller if you think I bluff easy."

Johnnie stuck the butt of his Winchester under his arm and fired toward the ground.

McDanials yelled, "GODDAMN, YOU CRAZY BASTARD!" and picked up his right foot. Blood was dripping out of the bullet hole near where the little toe was, or at least where it should have been.

"The thing is, McDanials," Johnnie said, "I ain't bluffin'. I aim to kill you, and I aim to do it right now. Now, I'm holdin' a rifle, but it's got an empty chamber, and you've got a Colt, but it's on your hip. I'd say we're about even. When I get the next round in the chamber I'm killin' you with it. What you do is up to you."

McDanials hesitated a second, then his hand went for his Colt.

Johnnie jerked the Winchester's lever down and slammed it up, driving another round into the firing chamber.

By then the Colt was clearing leather.

But it was the Winchester that spoke first, and it did so with a loud BAA-OOOM! and fire and smoke.

The range was short, almost point-blank, and the heavy bullet that plowed through McDanials's breastbone and took out part of his backbone lifted him off the ground and slammed him backward. He was dead before his body crumpled to the ground.

I was watching the rest of the Rawhiders over the barrel of my rifle, ready to kill anyone making a move I wasn't sure about. But none of them moved. They just looked at McDanials's body in disbelief.

I kept my rifle on the Rawhiders while Johnnie got our horses and opened up the circle of wagons to let the Banister horses out and cut loose the horses that were staked and picketed.

In a few minutes we were leaving the Rawhiders' camp. It would take several days for me to fully realize that what

I had seen happen in the past few minutes had actually occurred. Just before Ab's ride, we had been laughing and razzing each other, really glad that the bloodshed that seemed unavoidable *had* been avoided.

Now, just a few minutes later, we were leaving the Rawhiders' camp with McDanials lying in a dead heap on the ground, driving eighty-four head of horses and leading one with Ab's limp body tied across his saddle and flopping like a rag doll. I couldn't even look at him until we rode into our camp at Milagra Spring and had to take him out of his saddle for the last time.

10

Ab's death stayed with me for a long time. I'd buried friends before and I'd seen men killed by horses before—why, old Josh hadn't even been in his grave a year yet—but I'd never had as close a friend killed as quickly as Ab had been. He didn't live thirty seconds after the blue came over on top of him, and he never said a word, just gurgled, looked me in the eye, and died while I was holding him.

We dug Ab a grave there at Milagra Springs, wrapped him in a blanket, and lowered him into the ground. After shoveling dirt over him we stacked rocks over the grave to keep out the coyotes who rendered the only sermon he got by howling from the nearby hilltops as the sun set. Other than standing over his grave with hats in our hands and singing the few words we knew to "We Won't Have to Cross Jordan Alone," it was all we could do for Ab and it seemed like a hell of a sorry and lonesome ending to a man's life.

Death always seemed close at hand out where we made our living, but for something so common, it remained a great mystery—the final mystery.

During the next few days I made Ab a tombstone by

carving his name and some words into a slab of rock and standing it upright at the head of his grave:

> *AB DEACONS*
> *BORN 1861*
> *CROSSED OVER JORDAN*
> *OCT. 23, 1888*

"That's kinda nice, Casey," Johnnie said when he read the tombstone. "Too bad coyotes can't read."

Johnnie and I never talked much about Lon McDanials. If he hadn't killed him, I would have, and I never once felt remorse or guilt for my part in his death and I know Johnnie never did either. There was no law way out there where the Banister horses were running wild and free, except right and wrong as dictated by the code of the Big Lonely. It was an honest code, but, like the Big Lonely herself, it was not a merciful code.

After Ab's death I was even more intent than ever on having a place of my own. There was some comfort in the thought that once I had a place that was mine, I would have a place to be buried—not just anywhere that I had happened to drift to when I died.

While Ab's death had that effect on me, it seemed to have just the opposite effect on Johnnie. "Just goes to show you," he said, "that a man's a fool to even *think* about tomorrow. Damn if I can see why a man would want to waste any of that precious time building up something that death's gonna rob him of anyway. Death's a son of a bitch waitin' for all of us, and there ain't no avoidin' him. It's dust to dust for sinners *and* saints—and precious little time in between for the pleasures of life."

Even though Ab's death cast a melancholy shadow across our camp and seemed to widen the gap between our views of the future, Johnnie and I continued to work as well together as we ever had, even though some days we would argue endlessly about the meaning and purpose of life—as if either one of us actually had a clue.

We kept gathering new Banister horses and working with some we had already gathered, halter-breaking many and putting a few saddlings on some. By the middle of March, through some of the longest, the hardest, and at times the coldest, days of work I'd ever known, we had the following behind barbed wire at Milagra Springs: 195 mares of breeding age of which we halter-broke 50 of the best-looking and put five saddlings each on half of those; 99 head of yearlings and two-year-olds; 61 sucking colts; 149 studs of which 60 head we castrated and rode under the saddle five times each. That made a total of 504 head.

I was thinking we should have had more, at least six hundred total head, but I guess if we'd had six hundred, I would have thought we should have had seven hundred. But it was the middle of March and the grass inside the barbed wire trap was grazed dangerously short and the soil was beginning to powder. The important thing by then was to get however many we had out of the trap and to the Nations border a few days before the official opening of the land rush, which President Harrison had set at high noon on the twenty-second day of April.

By the time we were actually ready to leave Milagra Springs our total head count was down to 501, as the night before we left, two studs had been killed in fights, which, with that many studs and mares thrown together in a relatively small space, were constant. I'd also had to shoot a nice-looking bay mare who had gotten tangled up in the barbed wire and cut the tendons in her left hind leg.

"These sonsabitches are going to give us hell for a while," Johnnie said as we were saddling up on the morning we were set to leave. "They're sure as hell not gonna want to leave the country where they've been runnin' wild and free most or all of their lives. They're gonna try to quit the bunch and stick their tails in the air and circle back to the south . . . and I reckon me and you would do the same if we was thrown in with a bunch of other people and taken away from all the places we've roamed and known."

"Let's tie all the saddle horses we've got that lead good to Squint's wagon and put him out in front," I said. "Maybe some of the horses will follow him enough so we can get the rest of them started." Then I looked at Squint and added, "When you leave here, Squint, you put your team in a lope and hold 'em there. Once we get 'em headed north, we need to keep kickin 'em in the ass until they're damn good and winded and several miles north of the nearest Banister range."

It was a good plan and after a while it began to work. The trouble was, when it finally began to work we were several miles south of Milagra Springs instead of north. The horses we were riding were used up, and we had lost fourteen head of horses to the canyons and rocks of the Banister range, with not enough help or time to try to bring them back. Once we did get the whole bunch headed north we didn't dare stop them or even give them time to slow down and look back to their home range. If something couldn't keep up, we dropped it.

By noon we were passing within sight of Milagra Springs again, this time headed north, Squint in front with ten horses tied around his wagon, me and Johnnie on each side, yelling and waving our coats, and Help yelling at the drags in Mexican and popping the rawhide snake he carried. He had actually started to make a decent hand.

I pulled up just long enough to turn in my saddle and look at the leafless trees in the distance that marked Milagra Springs, Ab's burying place, in the far distance. I nodded one final time toward him and rode on, choosing to think about what lay ahead—more than six hundred miles of mostly open range between us and the northern border of the Nations, where the land rush was to begin—instead of what lay behind.

In eight days, we reached the Canadian River between Fort Bascomb and the Texas/New Mexico boundary, and there, for two cold, wet, miserable days and nights, we held the horses underneath a red bluff until the waters of the Canadian subsided enough for us to cross.

After crossing the Canadian, we angled toward the northeast until we struck the fence line that marked not only the Texas/New Mexico boundary but the western boundary of the XIT Ranch as well. Memories came rushing in as we rode through that country again. Memories of not much more than a year earlier. Memories of Josh and of Ab and of Lillie . . . Memories it did no good to let into the brain, but ones impossible to keep out, too.

By letting down the fence and cutting across the XIT range we could have saved ourselves a lot of miles, at least two days' worth of traveling, but we didn't want to take a chance that by trespassing we'd invoke some highbrow law we'd never heard of and possibly end up losing our horses to the XIT. This was one time we decided the long way would be the quickest, and we stayed on the outside of their fence until we reached the northern end of the XIT range and angled northeast again across No Man's Land.

Once we crossed No Man's Land into Kansas we turned the horses due east, and to our surprise—and also to our financial delight—by the time we got to Caldwell a week later we were among an almost continuous camp of home-steaders. We'd never seen anything like it, nor could we have imagined anything like it. There were thousands and thousands and thousands of them, in wagons, tents, and buggies, their campfires flaring all night, all waiting for noon of April 22. It was that way all the way from Caldwell to Arkansas City, Kansas, a distance I estimated to be thirty miles. Thirty miles of humanity. All waiting for a chance to get a piece of land.

"You ought to be right at home here, Casey," Johnnie said. "You can just line up and go with 'em when they shoot the gun. Yes, sir, a driftin' cowboy at eleven-fifty-nine and a respectable homesteader at twelve-oh-one."

"No sir, what I'm looking for can't be found at the end of a race, and it can't be found with neighbors on all sides close enough to see, either. I'll not be joinin' this circus."

If we'd had a thousand head of horses I think we would have sold them all.

As it was, we got there with 481 head on the eighteenth of April and sold the last one on the twentieth. Many people were desperate for horses, having arrived at the border by train, by wagon, or by walking. But when the gun went off and the mad scramble began, the best pieces of land would go to whoever got there first, and nobody on foot was going to beat anybody who had a horse. On top of that, most of the people wanting land were farmers, and once a homestead was secured the grass had to be plowed under, which would require even more horses.

When the last horse was sold on the twentieth and all the tallying was done it looked like this: the 420 head of horses, yearlings, and above—the sucking colts were sold with their mothers—averaged $21.30 per head for a total of $8946. Out of that we owed Ike Holt $4 per head for the 420 head plus $400 to repay him for the cash advance he gave us, which came to $2080. When that was taken out of the total and deposited in a bank in Arkansas City in an account with Ike Holt's name on it, we had $6866 left, and when the $175 each we owed Help and Squint was taken out of that, we had—finally—a grand total of $6516 left—$3258 apiece.

Although the money had been earned with blood, sweat, and tears, I couldn't help but feel incredibly wealthy. Ordinarily, during the seven months we were gathering or working with or driving horses, I would have made $175 total in wages, just like Squint and Help did, and would have felt lucky to have the work. But suddenly I had eighteen times that much!

And so did Johnnie. "Let's go invest some of this," he said, shaking his money back and forth in front of me.

I looked up at him from where I'd been lying on my bedroll, counting my own money for the fifth or sixth time. "I aim to," I said. "But not in whiskey and whores—not this time, Johnnie."

"I never thought you'd turn out like this, Casey . . . By God and for the life of me, I *never* thought you'd turn out this way. Hell, you might just as well not have any money at all! Three thousand two hundred and fifty-eight dollars. Five of those will get you wah-whooin' drunk *and* get that little old shriveled up tallywhacker of yours dipped in some fine midnight oil, and you'll *still* have three thousand two hundred and fifty-three dollars!"

"Johnnie, I have full faith in your ability to drink and whore up every last cent of that money faster than any other living mortal could do it, and not only that, but to feel absolutely no regrets afterward.

"But I know I'll never have this much money again, and I want to do something else with it. Hell, I'm forty-one years old . . . I'm tired of driftin', Johnnie."

"So . . . bein' a cowpuncher ain't good enough for you anymore, huh? What do you want to be, one of those goddamn cattle barons or a gentleman farmer? I've seen you like this before—hell, remember when that XIT wagon pulled in and we all went to town? You said you was savin' your money then, too. But did you? Hell, no, you didn't, you . . ."

I laughed and shook my head. "I'm not goin' drinkin' and whorin' with you tonight, Johnnie. As a matter of fact, I'm rollin' my bed and leaving here now. There's some country I've heard about that I want to see. . . . You go on by yourself, Johnnie, and have a good time."

Johnnie looked at me like I'd lost my mind. Maybe I had. "I've made up my mind," I said. I stuck my hand out to him and he grasped it.

"Take care, amigo . . . and good hunting—for whatever it is you're hunting for. I don't think it exists, but if it does and you find it, let me know. Rosie will probably know where I am."

"Take care, yourself, compadre." I grinned. "You're lucky. You know exactly what you're looking for, don't you. And exactly where to find it."

Johnnie shrugged and smiled. "Unless they've invented a new hiding place on a woman since we were in Kingston . . . See ya, Casey. May your cinches always be tight."

"And yours too, amigo."

For two months after selling the Banister horses at the Nations' border and splitting company with Johnnie I continued to drift. Only now I traveled with a purpose—to find the place where I wanted to start my ranch. I was not searching for just any place to graze a few head of cattle. Those places were easy to find. They could be found from the San Simón in Arizona to the Milk River in Montana and a thousand places in between, but I had a picture in my mind of how I wanted my ranch to be and I didn't want to settle for anything less.

While I was visiting with some cowboys in the South Platte River country of northeastern Colorado, talk swung around, as it always did when I mentioned what I was about, to what some of their favorite cow countries were. The sand hills country of Nebraska was mentioned favorably by at least two as the place most likely to make a fine home for a cow brute, so, since it was not many days' ride from there, I decided to go look around. I had heard of the sand hills country of Nebraska for years, but had never had reason to pass through there. Now I had reason enough.

A few days later, I topped a long, sandy ridge in the far western fringes of the sand hills and looked down upon the

Niobrara River from the south. I could see a tall stand of cedars growing along the north bank at a point where the river turned toward the southeast. Above and to the north of the cedars was another long, high sandy ridge that would offer protection from the north wind without blocking any of the warming rays of the south-leaning sun in wintertime.

From my vantage point I could see the river winding through the grass-covered hills with scattered patches of cedar and pines along its banks. Dark patches of green marked stands of timber up on the hills, and now and then a rock outcrop jutting up through the tall grass, fresh and green after two days of June rains. The land went on forever with no towns or farms in the way. And the waters of the Niobrara flowed unhurriedly but steadily below me.

This was cow country. And it looked so much like the place where I'd been building a ranch in my mind that it sent a tingle up and down my spine and brought a smile to my lips.

"Boys," I said to the good gray gelding I was riding and to the three I was leading, "looky yonder." The horses didn't say anything, as if they didn't care.

"Shiftless sonsabitches," I muttered as I started them down the sandy slope.

I forded the sandy waters of the Niobrara River and tied the horses among the cedars, dug my hand ax out of one of the packs, and immediately set out marking the trees that would have to fall to make way for my house, barn, and corrals.

And just like that, after all those years of drifting to places where I knew I'd only stay a little while, I started building a home in a place I figured to stay forever. I could already see how the place would look when I was finished, and it would look exactly like I'd been planning all this time. I never really believed in the guiding hand of Providence, but as soon as I topped the ridge on the south side of the Niobrara and looked down on the land, I believed that somehow and someway I had been led there.

As I was marking trees and picturing the place in my mind I was also contemplating the simple one-man furnishings I wanted in the house—a cookstove, a real bed, a table, and a mirror for sure.

I would have no trouble getting enough timber from the stand where I was for at least half of the building I planned to do, and the rest could be gotten from any of the other stands I saw from the top of the ridge. I straightened up and stretched my back and smiled—what did I know about building? I could build a loop—and pretty damn good, too—and I could build a fire, but beyond that I hadn't had much experience at building anything.

"But, by God," I said, looking at the horses tied to the trees, sleeping on their feet with their hind legs cocked underneath them, "I reckon I can learn."

I would build the house just inside the cedars with only a couple of trees to the west of it. It would be connected to the barn by a dog run. The corrals would be built east and south of the barn, one big corral and two smaller ones. The barn would open directly into one of the smaller corrals. Just south of the corrals, but with a gate connecting them, I would build a round corral out of tall logs standing shoulder-to-shoulder in the sand where I would start my colts—and I would have *good* horses, too. Horses that I'd make myself that would look a hole plumb through a cow and be as honest as the day was long. No more remuda riffraff that were as apt to run off as they were to pitch for me, not anymore.

As I was marking the trees, it struck me that before I did anything I should go to the nearest land office and file a claim or else I might be proving up someone else's land!

Although it was a thirty-mile ride north to Chadron, Nebraska, I was there the next morning, waiting for the land office to open.

On a big map nailed to one wall in the land office, I put my finger on the spot where the Niobrara bent toward the southeast and where I'd already started notching the cedars. "I'm buildin' my ranch right there," I said to the land agent.

"Then what you should do, Mister Wills," he said, "Is to file a homestead claim on that quarter-section. Is that what you want to do?"

Not too long ago, I would never have believed that I would one day be filing a homestead claim, and even now, although I knew that's what I wanted to do, the term "homestead claim" coming from the agent's lips was a little unnerving.

"Do you want to file a claim, Mister Wills, or not?"

"Yes, sir," I finally said. "I do."

"You do know you are required by law to build some kind of structure on the property and to live on it for five years before you receive a clear title to it?"

"Mister Agent," I said, "if you'll show me where to sign, you won't have to worry about nothing else."

The agent looked at me over his wire-rimmed glasses. He looked at my hat and then he worked his way down to my boots and spurs. Then he said, "A cowman, huh?"

"Naw," I said, "just a cowboy."

"Do you have the five-dollar filing fee, Mister Wills? The government don't extend credit to no one."

I smiled, thinking I've got a lot more than that, but I just said to the agent, "I got the cash."

"Then give it to me and sign right here," he said, and just like that I had the official beginning of my ranch.

When I came out of the land office I saw the Chadron State Bank across the street. I thought about putting my money in the bank, but almost immediately decided against it, knowing I could never rest easy with my money in the hands of people I didn't know. I'd take care of it myself; that way I'd always know where it was, and anytime I wanted to, I could look at it and count it, a pastime I'd grown more than a little fond of.

So I bypassed the bank and walked to Brewer's Mercantile to get some necessities—Bull Durham tobacco, beans, flour, and molasses—and some carpentry tools.

"Mister Brewer," I said, "I'm building a barn and a house, and I'll have to admit there's a lot about carpentry I don't know. I don't have any tools to speak of, either."

Mr. Brewer cleared his throat and wiped his hands on the bib apron he was wearing. "Well, now, let's see . . . I've got most of the individual tools you'll need, and then

I've also got a couple of sets of carpentry tools in wooden chests."

"Let's look at the sets," I said.

"All right, I've got a really fine set called 'Artisan's Choice' and another called 'The Wood Butcher's Set.' "

I grinned and said, "I expect that 'Wood Butcher's Set' would come nearer fillin' my bill."

"All right. Here it is, right over here, Mister Wills . . . You see it's got a twenty-two-inch hand saw, a two-foot rule, a tri square, combination pliers and wire cutters, a bit brace and all these bits, a nail hammer, a draw knife, three wood chisels, two files, a jack plane, and a good carpenters pencil—all for five dollars and twenty-eight cents."

"I'll take it," I said, reaching for my money. "I also want your best double-bitted ax."

"The best costs seventy-eight cents, Mister Wills."

"I want it anyway," I told him, "and two extra handles for it and a half-dozen handle wedges. I'll need two four-pound chopping wedges, too; ten pounds of nails of different sizes, and a crosscut saw."

"Do you want a two-man or a one-man crosscut?"

"Well, being as how I don't think any of my drifting cowboy friends are going to drop by and offer to grab one end of a saw, I reckon I'd better get the one-man rig."

"What about a level?"

I nodded. "I expect I ought to have one."

"All right," Brewer said, as he pulled the pencil from behind his ear and started figuring on a pad. "That'll be nine dollars and forty-six cents."

I paid him and said I'd go get my horses.

"I'll get all your things together and have them out front for you," Brewer said.

It was on that very first trip to Chadron, that I saw Miroux Sevier for the first time. It happened while I was packing the things I'd bought from the mercantile on my packhorse as Mr. Brewer handed them to me one at a time. She was a small woman with tan skin, wearing a long, gray calico dress with puffy sleeves and little blue flowers in the cloth. She also wore a white sunbonnet with the brim buttoned to the crown.

She was walking straight and proud and, I thought, a little stiff, not glancing left or right or offering the slightest smile or nod as she passed by and stepped up on the boardwalk.

My eyes must have followed her as she disappeared into the mercantile. "That's Miroux Sevier," Mr. Brewer said. "Her and her husband live down toward the Niobrara, same as you. Strange folk. You ever spend any time around 'em you'll see what I mean. I expect she's part Injun. Talks damn strange sometimes. Pretty fine figure of a woman, though. I understand they don't have cattle and they don't farm. Don't work in town. Don't see 'em much. Been out there several months—maybe a year—but you hardly ever see 'em."

My plan was to file a homestead on the place along the Niobrara and use my money to buy cattle. The cattle could water in the river and graze out in the hills, where open-range rules were in effect. I wanted to get some cattle on that Nebraska open range with my brand on them—I'd decided to brand a /C on the left hip—as soon as possible, but knowing that winter can arrive in northern Nebraska anytime after the first of September, I decided the first thing I should do was to build a barn. A barn would mean that both the horses and I would have shelter—and with any luck we'd have it by first snow.

I worked every day for three weeks straight, daylight till dark, and by that time had all the trees felled and stumps dug out where the barn would be; the barn itself was already two logs high. The blisters on my hands had turned to callouses and my back was brown as a berry from working without a shirt. I wasn't carrying an ounce of extra flesh or fat on my body. Building a homestead is much harder physical labor than a drifting cowboy is accustomed to, and I was using muscles I'd never used before. But I wasn't bored, and I wasn't wondering what I was doing or what I was going to do. I thought about Johnnie from time to time, and about Ab and Josh and a lot of other things, but nothing I thought of ever made me wish I was any place but along the Niobrara River, building my ranch.

One afternoon I decided I ought to kill a deer and hang it in the shade of the cedars and have it there to cut deer steaks from for a few days and then dry the rest of it. It wasn't too soon to start thinking about putting provisions away for winter.

Six or seven miles upriver, standing at the edge of another growth of timber, I saw a spike buck. Game wasn't spooky in that country, so I stepped off my horse right where I was and slid my Winchester slowly out of its scabbard. I knelt down and aimed, and when the buck's chest was balanced on the front sight I started to squeeze off the shot. Just before I finished the squeeze, though, a shot rang out downriver, causing the buck to jump.

I shot anyway—I was too far into my best-aiming squeeze to hold it back. But luck was with me, and I smiled as I watched the spike run twenty yards and collapse in the sand of the riverbank.

A figure carrying a rifle stepped out of the timber on the same side of the river the buck was on and started toward him.

I mounted quickly and started across the river in a splashing trot.

Before I was halfway across the channel I could see that the figure was a woman. She walked slowly up to the fallen buck and nudged him with a foot. Then she cradled the rifle in her arms and stood there, watching me.

When I came out of the water on her side I saw the rifle she carried was an old .52-caliber Sharps carbine, and I saw that her small thumb was resting squarely, and I had a feeling not by accident, on the Sharps' heavy hammer.

She was a small woman in black braids and a buckskin dress with no sleeves, two rows of small turquoise beads across the front, and fringe around the bottom. A knife in a sheath and a leather bag hung on the beaded belt she wore. Her skin was tan but not brown, and the arms sticking out of the buckskin were slender and feminine. When I looked at her face, I knew she looked familiar, but I couldn't place her.

Maybe she wasn't strikingly beautiful, but for a woman coming unexpectedly out of the Niobrara timber alone and standing over a dead spike buck wearing a buckskin dress and cradling a .52-caliber carbine, she was unexpectedly handsome, to say the least—especially to a man who hadn't seen a woman at all in quite a while.

She looked like neither the typical work-worn haggard-looking pioneer woman nor an Indian squaw. There was nothing work-worn or haggard-looking about her at all. Her dark eyes were bright and fresh, and she stood straight and proud . . . and then I recognized her as the woman I'd seen going into Brewer's Mercantile in Chadron.

"Hello," I said, tipping my hat to her from atop my horse.

She looked up at me with dark eyes that held little expression other than pure business.

"*Bonjour,*" she said in a soft voice. "It was your shot I heard, *oui?*"

I was so surprised I raised my eyebrows and smiled.

"French?" I asked.

She did not return the smile. "*Oui* . . . Yes. French." Then she said, "What do you want, Monsieur Wills?"

"How do you know my name?" I asked.

"Monsieur Brewer told me who you were." She spoke English very well, though with an accent, pronouncing each word with much greater care than cowboys generally exerted in the undertaking.

"And you're Miroux Sevier, aren't you?"

"*Oui,*" she answered. And then she asked again, "What do you want?"

"What do *I* want?" I said. "I want to gut this deer and take him back to camp."

"*I* am the one who killed the deer, Monsieur Wills," she said, "My shot was first."

"And spooked this spike," I answered, nodding my head.

She reached out and down with the carbine's barrel to the bloody spot on the deer's rib cage and spread apart the coarse hair. "This is your wound, Monsieur Wills? No. This is the wound of a big Sharps. *This* is your wound here, *oui*?" She moved the carbine's muzzle six inches toward the rear of the deer, dead in the middle of the paunch.

I smiled again. There was no doubt but what she was right—and I was a little embarrassed.

"Excuse me, ma'am," I said. "The deer is yours. I'll gut him for you while you get your horse."

"I hunt the river afoot."

"Afoot? Then how—"

"I will sling him over my shoulders. He is not large and I live . . . not far."

And you weigh maybe a hundred and fifteen pounds, I thought.

"He's a small buck, I'll grant you that, Mrs. Sevier, but he'll still weigh close to a hundred pounds even after he's gutted . . . I'll carry him for you on my horse."

"No. *Merci*, Monsieur Wills, but I do not need your help."

"Won't be any trouble at all, Mrs. Sevier," I said as I pulled out my knife and carefully began slitting the hide over the deer's belly. "I'll just gut 'im for you and sling 'im behind the cantle of my saddle. It won't booger this ol' horse any and . . ."

I glanced up just in time to see her buckskin dress disappear in the cedars and chokeberries.

"Hey!" I yelled, but she was already out of sight.

"Well . . . hell," I said to no one, then leaned over and finished gutting the deer. If Mrs. Sevier didn't want him, I did.

As long as I could cut the logs I needed from trees in the stand of timber right where I was working, my barn construction progressed at a nice pace. But once I had to start going upriver or downriver to get the logs I needed and drag them to the barn site one at a time, horseback, the pace slowed considerably. On top of that, the weather got terribly hot and sultry during the first part of August and the mosquitoes and deer flies were a constant aggravation.

But I kept at it, daylight to dark almost every day, interrupting work only when necessity demanded it for such things as killing another deer, catching fish out of the Niobrara, or washing myself and my clothes in its waters. I was goaded on in my relentless work by the knowledge of two simple facts—if Casey Wills didn't build his own barn it wouldn't get built, and winter would set in soon whether it was finished or not. I was too busy and too tired to think about much else. However, at times I couldn't keep from thinking about Ab's sudden death underneath that blue stud in New Mexico, or thinking about Johnnie, probably holed up in some hotel doing nothing but drinking whiskey and frolicking with the ladies. Johnnie would have a good laugh if he could see me, I thought—working harder than I'd ever worked in my life and hoarding my horse money in a buried lard can. My money hadn't brought me happiness yet, but I knew it was coming, once the hard work was behind me and my own cows were grazing out on the range and I didn't have much to do but fish in the morning and sit out on the porch in the evening. By then, Johnnie's money would be gone and he would be drifting from one cow outfit to another for twenty-five dollars a month and living in his bedroll again.

Finally, one day in late August, the walls of my barn were a little higher than my head, which was as high as they were going to be. The barn was fifteen feet long and twelve feet wide, with double-wide doors in the south wall that opened into the southernmost corral. The cracks between the logs were chinked with mud, and there was a window in the north wall and one on the south wall just west of the doors. The windows could be covered by lowering the wooden shutters over them on their leather hinges.

It was time to go to town again. I wanted to get metal hinges for the barn doors. Also, I'd had enough leaky, sod-roofed barns and line shacks to do me for a lifetime. I wanted the latest word in roof construction for both the barn and the house—corrugated tin complete with ridge caps, just like I'd seen in a Sears and Roebuck catalog. And even though I hadn't even started on the house yet, I figured it was time to order the furnishings I wanted, just to be sure I had them when I wanted them.

I left camp two hours before daylight the next morning and stepped up to the door to Brewer's Mercantile just as Mr. Brewer was unlocking it.

"Well, hello there, Mister . . . uh . . . Mister—"

"Wills," I said. "Casey Wills."

"Yeah! Sure . . . I remember you," Brewer said. "Have you learned how to use those tools yet?"

"Well, I've sure been using 'em," I said. "I need some tin for my barn, Mister Brewer. Do you have any?"

"How much do you need?"

"Well . . . I'm not sure. My barn is twelve by fifteen feet, and my house will be the same size and I want tin roofs for both—plus I'm going to have a ten foot dog run between 'em that I want to cover too."

Brewer was figuring with his pencil in a notebook and mumbling. "Let's see . . . That'll be a total of forty feet—barn, house, dog run, and all—by twelve feet wide, and you'll want a foot overhang on both sides, won't you?"

I nodded.

"Are you going to have a pitched roof?"

I nodded again and then said, "But not *too* pitched."

"Then we'll have to make that fourteen feet wide by forty feet long, which means you'll have a total of five hundred and sixty square feet to cover. Tin is sold by the square—which is a hundred square feet—which means . . . Well, I would say you ought to get six squares of nine-foot lengths, and that would allow for the overlapping and the overhang and enough to make the roof pitched . . . Do you want the ridge caps to cover the cap where the tin meets at the peak of the roof?"

I nodded. I didn't know buying tin was so complicated.

Brewer figured a little more and then looked at me and said, "The cost per square is three dollars, so six of them would cost eighteen. You'll need six ridge caps, and they cost twenty-two cents each . . . I'm afraid the total cost will be nineteen dollars and thirty-two cents, Mister Wills."

I whistled. That was more than a good young cow would cost.

"I suppose I could open an account for you, but—"

"No thanks," I said. "Cash."

Brewer smiled. "Yes, sir! And is there anything else?"

"I need the stuff to put in the house," I said.

"You mean like—"

"I mean like a stove and a bed and a table and chairs . . ."

"I don't keep much of that kind of merchandise in stock."

"I won't be needin' it now, but I'd like to have it here when I get ready for it—say, in three months?"

"I could have it here by then, I'm sure, but I'll need to know exactly what to order for you. And I'll have to—"

"I'll pay cash for it all today," I said.

"Yes, sir!" Brewer said. "Let's look in this catalog and you can pick out what you want. . . . Now here is a fine, fine stove right here."

It was called the Acme Regal King Range with a big 45-inch top, nickel-plated teapot holders, and a nickel-plated towel rod. It also had burnished edges, weighed 475 pounds, and cost $13.75.

"I don't think so," I said. "I need something a little smaller and plainer, probably without the nickel-plated teapot holders . . . What's this one down here?"

It was the Monarch Wonder Cookstove, four hole with number 7 lids, a 21- by 24-inch top, weighed 148 pounds, had a kicker for opening the door when it was hot, and cost $5.14 complete with lifter and rake.

"I'll take that one," I said.

"Okay," Brewer said as he wrote. "Number 22R200."

I ordered a bed with a six-foot-tall headboard for $2.75 and a combination washstand and dresser with a mirror for $6.20. It was the first furniture I'd bought in my life.

I'd seen a felt mattress one time and made up my mind that if I ever bought a mattress that's the kind it would be. The catalog said it would not get lumpy, and this particular one was sewn inside a tick and "warranted against being infested by vermin." It cost a lot—$7.95—but I'd slept on the hard ground so long I wanted one no matter what it cost. I didn't want any springs underneath it though, just the felt mattress on the bed slats.

A small kitchen table and two chairs cost $2.25. A wall lantern cost 38 cents and a table lantern was ten cents cheaper.

A six-foot-high, four-foot-long, twenty-eight-inch-deep kitchen cabinet with divided compartments and shelves for canned goods cost $7.45. I thought about that one, but finally nodded my head and told Mr. Brewer to order it.

"This is runnin' into money," I said. "What does all this come to?"

Again Mr. Brewer took down his pencil and began figuring. In a minute he said: "With the freight, which will be three dollars and ninety-one cents, the total for the order comes to thirty-six dollars and thirty-one cents."

I puckered. "Add the cost of the tin to it."

"It all comes to fifty-five dollars and sixty-three cents."

I counted out the money. "A man nearly has to be a banker to start a homestead," I said, complaining.

"I agree," Brewer said. "I remember when you coulda bought that little Monarch stove for three dollars! Now it's over five and I don't make as much on it as I did when it cost three."

"Will you haul the tin for me?" I asked. "I don't have a wagon."

"But it's a day out to your place along the Niobrara and a day back, Mister Wills. I simply can't spare the time. Maybe you can buy or rent a wagon at the livery. Or"—an idea obviously just came to him as the door opened— "maybe you can get your neighbor to haul it for you."

I looked at the door and saw Mrs. Sevier coming in. Instead of buckskins and braids like she'd been wearing a month earlier when we'd both shot the same deer along the Niobrara, she had on what I guessed must have been her "town dress"—the same one she was wearing the other time I'd seen her in town, the gray calico with little blue flowers. She had on the same bonnet with the brim buttoned to the crown, too, only now she also had a triangle fringed black shawl over her arms.

She came into the mercantile and started toward the counter, not looking left or right or at anybody.

"Hello, Mrs. Sevier," Brewer said. "Mister Wills here needs some tin hauled out to the Niobrara, and I thought that since you folks live out that direction too—"

"No," I said. "I don't want to be a bother. I'll rent a wagon at the livery."

"If you're going to rent a wagon," Mrs. Sevier said, "then you'd just as well rent from your neighbor." She was all business, and cold business at that.

"Much obliged, ma'am," I said, "but maybe we'd better talk to Mister Sevier about it first."

"*Mons* . . . Mister Sevier is away on business," she replied.

"I'll just get a wagon at the livery," I said.

"My wagon is for rent, Mister Wills, and it is going back out in your direction anyway. I will haul whatever you have back to your place—for money."

I looked at her a minute. I didn't want to be beholden to her, but it did make more sense to hire her to haul my tin than to rent a wagon that I'd have to bring all the way back to town.

"What does that tin weigh, Mister Brewer?" I asked.

"Well, it weighs roughly seventy pounds to the square and you're getting six squares, so that's about four hundred and twenty pounds."

"What kind of hitch did you bring?" I asked Mrs. Sevier.

"A two-horse," she answered.

"I guess they could handle it," I said. "Unless you've got quite a bit of stuff too?"

"I have little . . . I'll haul yours for five dollars, Mister Wills."

It wasn't exactly a bargain, but I figured it would be about the same if I hired a wagon from the livery.

"Okay," I said. "You have a deal, Mrs. Sevier."

"My wagon is in front of the mercantile," she said. "Load your tin on the bottom. In thirty minutes we will go."

In twenty minutes Mister Brewer and I had my tin loaded.

After she loaded her things on top of my tin and climbed up on the wagon seat, I mounted my horse. I followed her wagon as we left town, neither of us saying a word. For twenty miles and four hours we maintained that distance and that silence.

We finally stopped at a spring to get a drink of cold water from a barrel buried halfway in the ground. The spring fed directly into the barrel before overflowing into a small pond for livestock to drink from. Before Mrs. Sevier leaned her head over to drink from the barrel she took off the bonnet and let her black braids fall down over her shoulders. After she had her drink she unbuttoned the top button on her dress so she could dip her hand in the water and rub it on her neck and in the hollow of her throat.

"It is hot," she said.

"Yes, ma'am," I said. "It sure as thunder is," and then I got my drink and we were off again.

Ten miles later, and with no help from me, she topped the ridge on the north side of the Niobrara directly above my homestead.

"I'll start a fire and put some coffee on to boil before I unload the tin," I said. "Then . . ."

"*I* shall start the fire and put the coffee on, Monsieur Wills."

By the time the tin was unloaded the sun had sunk beneath the rim of the ridge above the river and the air was beginning to cool off. I pulled five dollars out of my pocket and handed it to Mrs. Sevier. "Much obliged," I said.

"*Merci,*" she said and handed me one of my tin cups filled with hot coffee.

"You're welcome to pull up a log," I said. She hesitated a couple of seconds, then sat down in front of the fire.

I reached underneath my bedroll tarp and pulled out a rolled-up piece of oilcloth. I unrolled it and held it out to her. "Dried venison . . . deer," I said.

She looked hard at me for a moment, then looked at the dried meat.

In a few seconds the barest trace of a smile crept over her face, and she took a piece of the dried venison out of the oilcloth.

"Why did you run away the other day?"

"I did not run . . . I left."

"Yeah," I said. "Quick as a cat and quiet as a mouse."

"It is a good way to travel, *oui*?" I couldn't tell if it was supposed to be a joke or if she was making fun of me.

"You travel Indian, dress Indian, dress American, talk French *and* American . . ." I said.

"Is a question?" she asked.

I smiled. "No . . . no, it's not a question."

We chewed on jerky and drank coffee in silence for a few minutes before she stood up and said, "I must go."

"Thanks for hauling the tin," I said as she climbed into the wagon.

"*Merci*, Mister Wills." Then she clucked to the team of tired horses and slapped them on their rumps with the lines and started back up the long north slope.

13

Early the next morning, as I was putting my coffee on the fire to boil, I saw the money that I'd paid Miroux Sevier for hauling my tin lying on the ground almost out of sight underneath the log she had been sitting on the night before.

About midafternoon I stuffed the money in my pocket, saddled a horse, and set out to locate the Sevier place.

The country the Niobrara cut through was a big country with few people in it. It was just one grass-covered sand hill after another with a few scattered patches of timber. The wagon tracks I was following led to one of those scattered patches of timber two miles north of the river and about seven or eight miles from where I was building my place. There was a small spring among the trees and a ramshackle frame house in the shade at the east edge of the timber. The house was small, seemed to lean a little to the east, and had cracks between the boards wide enough to throw a cat through. It reminded me of some of the line shacks I'd lived in over the years.

A horse nickered from the corral behind the shack, and almost immediately Miroux appeared in the doorway, cradling the Sharps carbine in her arms.

"*Bonjour*, Monsieur Wills," she said. "What are you doing here?"

She was wearing a brown linsey-woolsey skirt and a white muslin shirtwaist. Her hair was not braided this time, but pulled back and tied loosely at her neck with a blue ribbon.

"I found your money this morning underneath the log you were sitting on last night, Mrs. Sevier—it must have fallen out of your pocket."

"*Oui*," she said. "I did not know until I got home that I had lost it."

I held the money toward her. She leaned the rifle against the inside wall of the shack and stepped out to take it.

She took the money and walked the few steps back to the doorway. Once in the doorway she stopped and turned and said, "*Merci bien*, Monsieur Wills."

I tipped my hat toward her and said, "Yes, ma'am." Then I reined around to head back to camp.

"Monsieur Wills?"

I stopped and reined toward her.

"Would you care to stay for *souper*?"

"Supper?" I said.

"*Oui*—supper."

I studied it. "Yes ma'am," I said. "I would."

"It will not be so much . . . Rabbit and camas stew and chokeberry preserves."

"Next to jerked venison and cold tomatoes, rabbit and camas stew and chokeberry preserves sounds like a banquet. . . . I'll just hobble up and wash in the spring."

The inside of the house was as simple as a house could be and also as clean. There was only the one room, furnished with the barest of necessities and no luxuries. There was an iron-frame bed covered with a quilt and an old trunk at the end of the bed, a cookstove, two tables—one for working on and one for eating on—and three chairs; there was one small window in the south wall and another on the east wall beside the door. Hanging on the wall on the other side of the door was a mirror about the size of my hat, and beside that hung an old fiddle. The only other thing on the wall was a white sampler with small red flowers and birds stitched into it along with the words MIROUX BARDEAUX, AGED 13, 1872.

The rabbit and camas stew was a welcome change in diet, and the chokeberry preserves were the first sweets I'd had in weeks; when all of that was washed down with hot coffee it *did* seem like a banquet.

Miroux ate the way she spoke—gracefully and distinctly—and with one hand always in her lap. She didn't lean over her plate and she took very small bites, each of which she seemed to chew completely and to swallow before eating the next small bite.

"You eat the way my mama always tried to get us boys to eat," I said.

"And you eat the way my father ate. He worked hard at everything he did, even eating—like you do."

"Yes, ma'am," I admitted, "I guess it's the only way I know."

"I do not criticize. It is good to see a man hungry from a day's work, a man who enjoys eating as much as he does working. When I cooked for father he would eat in such a way."

When I was rolling a cigarette after supper my eyes fell on the old fiddle hanging on the wall again.

"Does Mister Sevier play?" I asked.

"No, DuPont does not play . . . *I* play."

"You play?"

"It is so strange?" she asked.

I got up and took the fiddle and bow carefully off the wall. I smiled and said, "If you don't mind me saying so, *you* are strange, Mrs. Sevier. . . . Now, how do you say 'please' in French?"

"Please? *S'il vous plait.*"

I handed the fiddle and bow to her, bowed politely, and said, "Do me the honor . . . *s'il vous plait.*"

She grinned slightly, a rare occurrence indeed, and cradled the fiddle in her neck. She raised the bow, but before she placed it on the strings she said, "My father taught me to play. . . . His name was Dijon Bardeaux, a French-Canadian trapper in the north woods of Quebec.

"In the winter of seventy-one he suffered an accident—a broken leg—while on his trapline. The cold and the snow that winter were as hungry as a snow-bound lynx—and as merciless. I found his body after the spring thaw and buried him alongside my mother in the front of the cabin where we lived. . . . This was his favorite tune and the last he ever played on this fiddle."

Then in her hand the bow began to glide across the old fiddle's strings, effortlessly and gracefully.

Miroux played the fiddle the way Johnnie handled a rope or Ab sat a pitching horse. She drew more feeling out of an old fiddle than I ever knew it could contain, and she did it with a passion I could only guess must have been gained from too many long nights and silent days spent in a northwoods trapping cabin.

The tune she played was slow and rich. Sometimes she closed her eyes.

I didn't know the tune, had never heard it before. Although the melody was played on an old fiddle, the feelings it stirred in me came from places and times outside the shack, from the darkening timber and the sand hills just outside to lonesome cowboy graves and the unfulfilled dreams they contained, of the loves they had lost or had never known.

Feelings came, too, from a place rarely spoken of by men like me—the place tucked deep inside where lonesome lives its well-concealed but ever-gnawing life.

There was all of that in the tune Miroux played—the lonesomeness, the sadness, the unfulfilled dreams—but there was also a sweetness in it, something not quite complete, like a single coyote howling from a hilltop at sundown. Howling. Howling. Alone. Lonesome. Until far in the distance, from a hilltop somewhere unseen, the coyote's mate answers.

When the last strains of fiddle music died away, the shack grew silent—only the evening wind could be heard as it prowled through the timber in which the shack stood.

I was on my feet, looking out the small east window and

wrestling with emptiness and loneliness and a sad acceptance of such things in life, when I turned and looked at the wisp of a girl in the white shirtwaist with the dark hair and tan skin. I looked into her black eyes and felt a sudden and unexpected peace. Strangely, I was drawn to her, and I walked over to her in silence and touched her hair, gently rubbing the softness of it between my fingers.

Then I suddenly realized what I was doing and dropped the hair and moved away—embarrassed.

Miroux stood up and hung the fiddle back on its pegs on the wall as if I had never touched her hair at all. "My father called it 'The Waltz of the Pines,'" she said.

"Thank you . . . I had better get back to camp now."

"Yes."

I put my hat on and opened the door. "Where is your husband, Miroux?" I asked. "Where is DuPont Sevier?"

She hesitated. "I . . . am not sure."

"What? How long has he been gone?"

"Seven months."

"Seven months! But why?"

"Casey . . . thank you for bringing the money. Thank you for the company. It was the first time in a long time that I have wanted to play the fiddle. But now . . . *s'il vous plait* . . ."

I nodded, pretending to understand something I did not understand, looked at her for another moment, then went out to my hobbled horse.

14

As I left the Sevier place behind and rode toward my own camp I made up my mind to also leave behind everything that had happened there, especially the feeling Miroux had unexpectedly stirred inside me—the way she looked, the way her eyes looked into mine, the way her hair felt on my fingertips, the way she smelled.

But telling your mind to leave something behind is not the same—not nearly as simple—as getting on a horse and riding away from it.

I thought about all the things I told myself *not* to think about. I even wondered about DuPont Sevier—what he looked like, where and why he had gone, and if he had come back yet. I pictured him as a tall, good-looking Frenchman with a black beard and quick smile.

Crazy things to think about and all things I never once invited into my mind. But still they came, usually when a hard day's work was over and I was lying in my bedroll listening to the Niobrara murmur, the coyotes howl, or the cedars moan in the night wind.

But Miroux wasn't all I thought about. Just two mornings after eating supper with her, I threw back my bedroll tarp and found a light coating of frost on it. Fall had arrived, and with it cooler weather and an almost constant flight of geese and cranes high overhead on their way south for the winter.

It was the first time since I'd left West Virginia that I wasn't punching cows on some outfit when fall came, and I missed it in a way. I missed being around good cowboys like Ab and Johnnie and Early Monroe and Jim Bob and Jesse Cabe and Booger Waters and old B.D. and all of his cowpunchin' boys and ol' Frank and Bunk and a hundred others that I suddenly started thinking about. I missed the humor and good-natured ribbing of those kind of men, and I missed the sound of a big cavvy of horses coming into camp before daylight and the singing of the cowboys and the snorting of cold-backed horses as cinches were snugged against tight bellies.

But with fall in the air and winter not far behind, I didn't have time to think about old friends and snorting horses much. I'd set out to build me a ranch and have my own cows and I wasn't backing off from that or wishing I was somewhere else. And what I sure wouldn't miss was what was bound to happen after the works were over—the moving on, drifting, hoping to find enough work to see you through the winter, not knowing where you'd find it or how you'd survive the winter if you didn't.

No, although I was missing some things about cowboying, I had no regrets about working alone like a mule along the banks of the Niobrara, because I was working for myself and I didn't have to worry about how or where I'd winter out. And just to put myself at ease, every now and then I'd dig up the lard can in the northwest corner of the barn and count my money.

By the time the first light dusting of snow covered the banks of the Niobrara, I was finished with the barn. I had worked on it for two and a half months and it wasn't the best-looking barn in the world, but I stepped back, looked it over, and said, "By God . . . it'll sure enough do." And it sure enough would do, too. And it was mine—cut, hewed, nailed, sawed, sweated on, and cussed by no one but Casey Wills.

But it had taken me longer than I'd planned to

complete the barn. I'd thought that by the middle of September, which it was now, I'd have bought some cows and had them grazing out in the hills wearing my Slash C brand. Now I decided it would be better to wait till spring to get the cows.

With that decision out of the way, I started right in—the same day I finished the barn—building my corrals, all but the round pen where I'd ride my broncs, as I figured it could wait. Since the corrals were made out of poles, all it took to make them were enough long, straight trees cut down and trimmed of all branches and tied to the posts with rawhide. Since all I had were my horses, I decided two poles tied to each post would be enough.

The weather held. It got steadily cooler but stayed dry, and in ten days of hard work the corrals were finished.

The day after I'd tied the last pole up for the corrals I started on the house. I was now an experienced builder of log buildings and planned to put that experience to use in the house and to get straighter walls and squarer corners than I'd been able to get in the barn.

After that first dusting of snow, I moved my bedroll into the barn, but I still had my fire outside, although I stacked a lot of wood inside the barn in case of a bad storm.

There was plenty of grass along the banks of the river for the horses to eat, and I usually led all but one out each morning and hobbled them so they could graze. The other horse I kept in the corrals and fed grain.

Overall, things were going good. My ranch was coming together even if I didn't have any cows yet.

And then one afternoon as the tall cedars were standing motionless and I was busy notching out a log, my eyes unconsciously, I guess out of habit, lifted toward the river to scan the grassy bank and . . .

Miroux was standing on that grassy bank, as motionless and silent as the cedars overhead.

By then it had been close to a month since I'd seen her, at least in any place other than the unguarded regions of my mind, and I stood there as silent as she for a few seconds, looking at her with my hand resting on the ax handle, the ax head buried in the log.

Finally she smiled and said, "*Bonjour*, Casey."

She was in a buckskin dress again, a different one with fringed half-sleeves, a wide row of beads on both sides of the neck running off the shoulder, and a half-dozen polished elk ivories sewn in a semicircle between her throat and breasts.

"*Bonjour*," I returned, then noticed the fish she was holding on a twine, four catfish. "Looks like the fishin's been good."

"Yes . . . just around the bend in the river . . . Your barn is finished and your house is begun. You are building a fine home, Casey."

"Haven't really thought of it as home yet," I answered. "It's still just camp to me."

"But you *are* going to stay, no?"

"I'm sure plannin' on it. Hope to be in the house by Christmas and have cows bought by spring. Then maybe *I* can fish once in a while."

"A place you stay is a home, Casey—a camp is only temporary."

"I'll work on it," I said. "Say, you want me to cook those fish on a spit? I'm almost done for the day."

"No," she said, and she walked up from the riverbank and stopped where I was working, pulled the ax out of the log, and handed it back to me. "You work—I will cook the fish."

I looked down at her, smiled, and reached for the ax. But though it was the ax handle I reached for, it was not the ax handle I felt. I had accidentally covered Miroux's hand with mine.

Neither of us jerked our hands away. Neither of us did anything for a few seconds.

Then I felt my hand squeezing hers, felt her small sharp knuckles pressing against the palm of my hand, felt the warmth of her hand in mine.

I was still looking down into her face, uplifted and a foot from my eyes, eyes that I let explore the details of that delicate face slowly and strangely without any embarrassment—the smooth forehead, the dark hairline and eyebrows, the sharp outline of her jaw and cheekbones, the strong chin, and the smooth skin turning into the soft, pink skin of her lips.

I looked into calm black eyes again and let a fingertip of my free hand gently run the length of her slender nose from a spot between her eyes, over the hard crest, and off the soft tip.

"Are you Blackfoot?" I asked, as I moved my hand away. "The Blackfoot are beautiful people with beautiful noses."

"The blood of their northern cousins courses my veins." She was still talking softly.

"Assiniboin," I whispered. "Your mother married a French trapper?"

"Yes."

And then almost as naturally as my hand had encircled hers, her hand was out of mine, I was holding the ax alone, and she was walking away from me toward the circle of rocks in front of the barn containing the cold coals of morning.

"Where's your horse?" I asked.

"Horses are for waging war and counting coup," she turned and said with a smile. "I came for neither."

"But it's eight or nine miles to your place," I said.

"Cowboys are afraid to walk, Casey—not the product of Assiniboins and northwoods trappers."

"And is that product generally sassy too?"

"*Oui*," she flashed. "Now build your home, Casey Wills, while I build the fire."

"Can you speak Assini too?" I asked later as we sat on logs on opposite sides of the fire and ate spit-baked fish and drank strong black coffee.

"Some words . . . but I have to search my head for them," she answered. "And only a handful of Assini ways do I know. When I was three years old my mother died in childbirth along with a baby boy. From then until I was twelve and the winter claimed my father, I spoke only French and knew only the ways of a northwoods trapper. It was my father who taught me to hunt and fish and trap, and to make jerky and pemmican, and to make buckskin from deer and decorate it with beads, elk ivory, and porcupine quills."

"But then who taught you English and how to stitch pictures and words on samplers and how to be a lady in the white way?"

She looked only into the fire. "After my father died I left the lonely cabin along the Chicoutini River. For the next four years I lived at a mission school run by Anglican priests and sisters. It was there I was taught English and how to be a 'decent lady with civilized manners'. . . . Why are you smiling, Casey? Do you not think I have the ways of a decent and civilized lady?"

"Oh, yeah . . . sure . . . decent *and* civilized . . . but"—there was also something wild and untamed, although for sure not indecent, about her, but how could I say that and make it not sound vulgar—"but *God*, Miroux, you are . . . *different* from any other decent and civilized woman I know."

"I am half Assiniboin, raised alone by a French trapper. I never saw a town or had a dress of any material other than buckskin until I was almost thirteen. So, why are *you* different, Casey Wills?"

"Me?" I laughed. "There's nothing different about me, Miroux. You put me and ninety-nine other men in a box and shake it, and when you dump us out, you couldn't tell which of the hundred was me."

"You are wrong, Casey. You are different from the others. I see it in your eyes, and I feel it in your touch. It is here"—she placed a closed fist against her breast—"that you are different from the others. You have heart, Casey. You are only the second such man I have ever known with it—the first was my father. At times it has probably caused you great pain and you have cursed it because you feel things so strongly, so deeply. You have probably longed at times to be like the other ninety-nine men in the box, but you never will be, Casey . . . you never will be. Your body has settled along the Niobrara, but your *kukasa* has not settled anywhere—it is still restless, still wandering."

"My *ku—kukasa*?"

"Assiniboin for what some call the soul—the person who lives within."

I slowly nodded my head. It was strange that it should have been Miroux, but for the first time in my life I felt I was talking to someone who knew me, knew who I was inside. It was a strange feeling—frightening in a way.

"So much wisdom in such a small package," I said.

"I know little, but I *do* know about restless and wandering *kukasas* searching for whatever it is in this life they were meant to find and finding it always eludes them."

I stood up to put more wood on the fire and to pour more coffee into our cups.

Suddenly Miroux said, "I have plum stones, Casey. I forgot I had them . . . see!"

She opened up the leather pouch dangling from her waist and pulled out a handful of different-shaped small flat stones, some with different numbers of black dots painted on them and some with none.

"Let's play, Casey . . . I have not played in so long! I will teach you, *oui?*"

I shrugged and smiled. "Is this a civilized game you learned in the mission school?"

"No, it is Assiniboin—a game of savages."

"Good!" I said as I knelt in front of the log to smooth the sand with the palm of my hand. "I hate civilized games!"

So we played a game of savages on our hands and knees between the crackling fire and the log. It was a game of chance, similar to dice but with more rules and more ways to win and lose and a tally to be kept—a tally we kept in the sand with a short stick.

We played the game and laughed and drank coffee until darkness was suddenly upon the sand hills.

"I must go now," Miroux said as we finished the third game. She dropped the plum stones back into the leather pouch.

"Stay," I heard myself saying. "Stay the night, Miroux."

She looked up at me in silence—what I interpreted as a shocked silence. I was even shocked myself.

"Casey . . . I cannot," she said.

"It was a stupid thing to say," I admitted.

"I have been baptized into the Christian faith, Casey—and I have taken the Christian vows of marriage. I . . ."

"I meant I wanted you to share my *fire* tonight, Miroux, not my bed. But it was a stupid thing to say."

"It was not stupid, Casey. I would love to share your fire this night but . . ."

She stepped closer to me. "But . . ."

"But what?" I asked. "Is it because of DuPont? Of course it is . . . but he may not come back, Miroux. Seven months is a long—"

She turned and faced into the darkness, the light of the fire in her hair. "We cannot speak of this—"

"What, Miroux? Why won't you tell me about your husband?"

She breathed deeply before she spoke. "Because until two weeks ago, my fear was that DuPont would not come back."

"And now?"

Silence.

"And now . . . now I find myself fearing he *will* come back."

I had no words to say. I wanted to step close behind her and wrap my arms around her, but I knew I couldn't.

"I cannot share your fire this night, Casey—and I cannot come back. I should not have come this time. I thought I could be your friend. I thought friendship would be enough . . . but your *kukasa* has touched mine in such a way that friendship is no longer possible. I must go now, Casey."

"But how long will you wait?"

"The marriage vows I made before God said until death . . ."

"He may already be dead. How much longer will you wait? . . . Miroux!"

But she had slipped quickly and quietly into the darkness, leaving me alone beside the crackling fire.

15

Not once when I was drawing up the plans for my ranch, either in my mind or in the dirt, did I ever include a woman. Although I never considered myself an expert, I thought I knew more than most men about women. And I knew some about love, too. At least I knew enough about it to be sure that it equaled foolishness and trouble and should be avoided at all cost.

What I knew about women I had learned in whorehouses from Belle Fourche to Bandara, and what I knew about love I learned from Lillie Johnson while staying at Trujillo Camp on the XIT. I had thought I loved Lillie and couldn't live without her, and I'd even made plans to settle down with her, but when it came right down to it, the whole idea scared me so much I broke and ran for the rimrock. Looking back later, I knew that Lillie and I were both well served by that rimrock run.

Therefore, with all that worldly knowledge in my possession, I stared into the fire for two hours after Miroux left, then got up, kicked sand into the fire, and crawled into my bedroll on the floor of the barn, telling myself that I would forget all about her. I already had everything I needed *or* wanted to make me happy—a nice stake buried in a lard can in the northwest corner of the barn, four head of horses, and my own ranch built exactly where and how I wanted it. Miroux had been wrong—my *kukasa* was as settled along the Niobrara as my body, and I would prove it.

During the following days and weeks, I worked harder than ever on the cabin, if that was possible; determined to have the walls up and the tin roofs over the single-room affair and the dog run by Christmas.

I wasted not a minute of daylight on either end of the day—the ever-shortening days.

Luck was with me weather-wise, and for several weeks after that first light dusting of snow it could not have been a better fall for building log cabins on the edge of cedar thickets. The weather held and held and held—holding as steady as my progress on the cabin.

By the first of December I had begun to cut and plane one side of timbers to be used as rafters and started looking for timbers long and straight enough for one ridge timber and three brace timbers.

Then one day I felt a deep and sudden chill, and the sun, which had not yet failed to shine each day, though from an ever-sharper southern angle, slid one afternoon behind a heavy blanket of scudding clouds coming straight down from the Dakotas.

The temperature dropped as if it had no conscience, and by dark the Niobrara, which until then had sported only respectable morning skim-ice along its banks, was frozen over solid.

I was glad for the protection of the barn and I'm sure the horses, although they never mentioned it, were glad, too; those scuddling clouds from the Dakotas were riding point for the blizzard that was right behind them, bumping their hocks with ice and covering their tracks with snow.

There wasn't much to do but to move my fire inside the barn and wait for the blizzard to blow itself out, which it did in only twenty-four hours, but the fall was never the same. After that, it seemed that every living thing in the sand hills—the geese going south, the grouse hunting seeds in the draws, the coyotes putting on tallow and priming fur, everything—got more serious about survival, myself included.

The mild days of a long fall were gone. The weather that had been holding for so long broke at last, and no creature along the Niobrara needed to be warned it would stay broke for a long time.

Although much of the snow from that first storm would stay on the ground until spring—especially what was wind-whipped onto the north slopes—and although it became an everyday chore to chop a hole in the Niobrara to get water for myself and the horses, and although many days were miserable to work in, with the temperature at times hovering at zero or below, and although the rate of progress on the cabin slowed, my building did not stop. I was as driven to complete my little cabin as soon as possible, in spite of any and all hindrances, as the frequent snow squalls were driven across the sand hills by the arctic winds.

When Christmastime came—as near as I could figure it on the calendar hanging on the wall in the barn, because I had not marked each day as it passed but would forget a few days and then try to remember which ones to mark out—but when what I thought was Christmas came I had the brace timbers up and the ridge timber pegged to them and four of the eight rafters pegged to the ridge timber. Maybe it was not the right way to put up a roof, but it seemed stable enough on the barn and I had faith it would work for the cabin as well.

The Christmas before, Ab was fresh in his grave, and the Christmas before that Josh was fresh in his, both killed by horses and buried two hundred miles apart. Now, I was building my own ranch along the Niobrara, and Johnnie was whoring and drinking away his money, probably in Cheyenne.

Life in the Big Lonely was unpredictable—it could promise you less and give you more, and promise you more and give you less, than any place on earth; at least that was one of my firmer convictions.

The last piece of tin was nailed onto the cabin on the last day of 1889, and on the first day of 1890, I began plan-ing timbers to be worked into the sand and used as the floor. The last floor timber was put into place eleven days later.

With enough water thrown onto the floor and enough packing and sweeping, the sand set up nicely, and together the sand and the cedar timbers made a respectable floor, one not completely level or entirely without splinters, but one at least as good as the best a drifting cowboy had a right to hope for.

With the cabin now finished floor-to-roof and wall-to-wall, I saddled up and sat out once again for Chadron, riding into a bitterly cold wind and stinging pellets of snow. I needed grain for the horses and staples for myself. I was also anxious to see if the furnishings I had ordered some four months ago were waiting at Brewer's Mercantile.

Everything that I had ordered was there—the Monarch Wonder Stove, the bed frame and dresser, the felt mattress, the one-drawer oak table, the chairs, the kitchen cabinet, the lanterns—it was all there. Even the iron match safe with the fierce-looking bird with the needle beak was there.

This time I did what I should have done when I'd come to Chadron to get the tin—I hired a freight wagon and driver to haul my things to the Niobrara.

We had everything loaded but the mirror that went on the dresser and were tying it to the felt mattress so maybe it would make the trip in one piece when I casually said to Mr. Brewer, "Just curious, but have you seen my neighbors lately—the Seviers?"

"Haven't seen him, but there's Mrs. Sevier over there across the street right now, coming out of Gower's office . . . seen her go in there about half an hour ago."

Gower was Chadron's sheriff, and when I looked across the street I saw Miroux standing in the open doorway to his office. I couldn't hear her, but I knew she was saying something to someone inside. Then she backed out of the door and closed it, pulled the long coat she was wearing tighter around her, and adjusted the dark winter hood on her head.

Then she turned toward the street and looked in our direction. My hand started up and I was going to wave to her, but before I could, she turned and hurried down the boardwalk in the opposite direction, acting like she hadn't seen me at all.

"Now hand me that piece of rope, Nat," Mr. Brewer said, "and I'll run it over the mattress while Casey holds it in place."

I held the mattress and the mirror in place all right, but my mind was somewhere else—wondering why Miroux had been talking to Gower and why she acted like I didn't exist. The last time I had seen her, we ate and laughed together as we played with her plum stones; I asked her to share my fire all night and she said she couldn't because my *kukasa* had touched hers . . . and all of a sudden I ceased to even exist?

Had DuPont come back? Was that why she looked right through me? Or had Gower told her where he was?

She didn't matter to me, not in the least, and I couldn't have really cared less if her wandering husband *had* come home. Just the same, when Nat got to the fork in the road a mile south of town I stopped him and said, "Nat, just stay on the Pine Ridge Road. I got something else to do, but I'll catch up with you a long time before you need to turn off. See ya later."

I got off and used the side of my horse for a windbreak to roll a cigarette, and when I lit it and looked toward town there was already another wagon coming.

Miroux pulled her team to a stop and pushed on the brake when her wagon seat was even with me.

I reached a gloved hand up to my hat brim, pulled on it, and said, "Hello, Miroux."

Her eyes met mine for a second, then looked at the rumps of the team in harness.

"*Bonjour*, Casey," she said.

"How are you?" I asked.

"I am fine. . . . Was that your furniture I saw you loading on the wagon?"

"Yeah . . . I saw you coming out of the sheriff's office?"

"*Oui.*"

I expected her to tell me what she had been doing there, but the *oui* was all I got.

"You been makin' the winter okay?" I asked.

"*Oui*," again. "I have."

The longer we were there at the fork in the road, the more uncomfortable it became to be together. If our *kukasas* had touched before, they didn't seem to be touching now.

"Has DuPont come home, Miroux?"

She was silent for a moment. "No."

"I see," I said, but I really didn't see at all, didn't see why she was acting so cold. "I was just wondering. I thought about you the other day and wondered if he was home yet."

"Casey . . . I . . . need to go."

I was standing on the ground and had to look up to see her face, which I did, but I could read nothing in those black eyes—they seemed as cold as the toes inside my boots.

"Yeah, I gotta go too," I said, and even as I was saying it I was getting on my horse.

I looked down at Miroux. I thought she started to say something, but she held it back. Her horses jingled their harness, and mine squirmed because we were facing the cold wind and he wanted to turn his butt into it.

Then Miroux reached out and slapped her reins down with a pop against the horses' rumps and the wagon lurched forward and rattled on down what was called Sand Road. Of course, then it should have been called Snow Road.

"Damn," I said to myself with a weak laugh as I watched the wagon get smaller and smaller. "Who in the hell needs this?!"

Then I wheeled my horse around and hit a long trot down Pine Ridge Road, staying in the tracks cut through the snow by the freight wagon.

* * *

Nat and I got to the cabin way after dark, so we pulled the wagon into the barn for the night and carried the furnishings into the house early the next morning.

Nat could not get started back to town soon enough, saying, "You might not mind getting snowed in out here, Wills, but I think I'd sooner be in hell—hell ain't half as lonesome."

I smiled and nodded at him. "I can handle lonesome," I said. "Much obliged, Nat." Somehow I got the impression that Nat was not as impressed with my ranch as I was.

By noon I had the stovepipe in place through the roof, and an hour later the first cedar smoke from the first fire built in my cabin was curling toward the winter sky.

Just before dark, and for some reason I was not quite sure of, I walked across the river—*walked* because an iced-over river is dangerous to cross on a horse and was one ride I figured should be reserved for more important things than what I had in mind to do.

I walked across the river, climbed to the top of the ridge that looked down on the Niobrara from the south, and stood just before dark in the exact spot I had stood six and a half months earlier when I was looking for a place to build my ranch.

I was filled with pride. The little layout of a ranch below and across the frozen river, nestled like it was against a thick stand of tall cedars—the dark rails of the corrals standing out plain against the snow, the log barn and the log cabin with the two windows facing the river and all under the same long roof, and the gray smoke curling up from the cabin—all of it looked so much like what I had been dreaming of, what I had been drawing in the sand, and what I had imagined when I looked down from that spot for the first time, that I just stood there in the cold of the dying day for a while and admired it.

After I came down from the ridge and crossed the river again, I grained the horses and stepped inside the warm cabin, where I lit the table lantern and poured myself a cup of coffee.

I drank coffee and smoked Bull Durham while darkness fell on the first night I spent in my new home.

In a little while the beans I'd been cooking on the stove were soft enough to eat, so I dipped myself a big bowl of them. Afterward, I smoked another cigarette, looked out one of the windows into the cold night, looked at myself in the mirror on my new dresser, blew out the lantern, and crawled into my bedroll—no longer on the hard ground but now rolled out on top of the felt mattress in the bedframe made from the best selected hardwood.

The first night ever in my own cabin I dreamed Ab and Josh came splashing across the Niobrara with Johnnie, and all of them were laughing and happy and giving me hell.

And I dreamed that a slim, pretty woman with coal-black hair and eyes, and wearing a buckskin dress, waltzed with me to a beautiful sad tune played on a lone fiddle.

Time passed. Slowly. Suddenly, I was caught up, and I didn't have any reason to crawl out of my bedroll at the first crack of dawn. My ranch was built and the cows would have to wait till spring. I thought I would enjoy sleeping late or sitting in my warm cabin, drinking coffee, and napping or, on the rare days when the sun shone, sitting on the south side of the cabin in one of my forty-five-cent four-spindle, bow-backed, hardwood chairs. And at night I thought it would be the height of living to sit by the stove after supper and read *The Rubáiyát of Omar Khayyám* by the light of the table lantern, or to lean a chair up against the wall underneath the wall lamp and read by it.

Those were things I could do, all right, and I did them. The barn was there. The corrals were there. The dog run and the cabin were there. All of them mine.

So why did I feel so restless, so incomplete?

Why did I ride to Chadron again for no other reason than to buy whiskey when I had not touched a drop of liquor in months? And why did I begin drinking during the day so I would be drunk enough to sleep at night?

Why did these words from the *Rubáiyát*, read aloud in a

liquor-slurred tongue, cause me to slam the little book down on the table and walk away from it?

> *There was the Door to which I found no Key;*
> *There was the Veil through which I might not see:*
> *Some little Talk awhile of Me and Thee there was—*
> *And then no more of Thee and Me.*

The answer appeared one morning after I'd heated some water and shaved, but before I'd started the day's drinking.

I was chopping wood in a light mackinaw in the dog run, and it had just started snowing again, big flakes drifting slowly down from a leaden sky adding to the knee-deep fluff already on the ground.

It was the horses who told me. They stopped chewing their grain and all of them lifted their heads and perked their ears in the same direction. Whiskey snorted.

I laid the ax down and picked up the Winchester leaning against the barn and stepped out into the snow.

She was standing underneath the tall cedar in front of the cabin, wrapped in a hooded cocoon of marten and fisher fur, and for half a minute neither of us moved.

The snow that I'd had to wade knee-deep through, Miroux walked lightly on top of in snowshoes.

I remember no spoken words.

I only remember her suddenly being in my arms . . . How warm and soft, wet and sweet her lips were and how I couldn't kiss them enough . . . How I couldn't pull her body tightly enough against mine . . . How she kissed my face all over and how she kissed my throat . . . How the fur and the buckskin smelled . . . How her breasts felt through the buckskin as I put my hands inside the fur and caressed them . . . How I wanted to be inside the buckskin as well . . . How badly I wanted her, needed her . . . How I picked her up in my arms and how we fell in the snow together, laughing . . .

How there was no pretending when I carried her inside the cabin . . . How the fur cocoon slid to the floor as she reached up to unbutton my shirt . . . How breathtakingly beautiful and smooth her body was as I slipped the buckskin from it and let my eyes feast upon it from head to foot . . . How she took my awkward hand in hers and cupped it over her breast . . .

And how, when we lay on the bedroll on the felt mattress, my nakedness felt against hers. . . .

And what sweet peace and contentment my cabin and my *kukasa* knew as she lay in my arms afterward for a long time without speaking.

At last I started to say something, but Miroux's fingertip on my lips stopped whatever words were there. "Shh . . . ," she whispered. "Do not speak, Casey—not yet. I am afraid of it. Just let me sleep in your arms, and I will pretend I belong here."

16

Although I thought I knew myself and what I wanted, until Miroux came to me in the snow wrapped in marten and fisher fur I knew very little. The things I thought I wanted more than anything else in the world actually meant very little to me, and the thing I had been running from and telling myself I didn't need or want meant everything.

Everything.

Miroux stirred in me a passion and desire I thought were beyond me. But she also brought to me the sense of peace, contentment, and belonging I had been searching for all my life.

I rode through the deep snow to the Sevier homestead and brought her horses, her food, and her clothes back to my place. I also brought back the old fiddle belonging to Miroux's father, and many times after supper I would hand it to her and listen to her play. She played many different tunes, all of them beautiful, but none could compare to "The Waltz of the Pines" in either beauty of note or depth of passion—both the passion with which she drew the bow across the strings and the passion the tune drew out of this former drifter's heart. However much I loved it though, I also hated it, for it whispered things—about loss and about the uncertainty of life—things I did not want to think about, not after all the long years of drifting and searching without even knowing why I drifted or for what I searched.

I needed no one to tell me that at long last my soul—my *kukasa*—was at home. It was at home along the banks of the Niobrara, and there I wanted to spend the rest of my life, and I wanted Miroux to spend it with me. And when it was spent at last, however long or short a time God would grant me, I wanted the fingertips that gently closed my eyes for the last time to be Miroux's fingertips, and after she had closed them, I wanted to be buried along the Niobrara in sight of the cabin.

We lived a life of total isolation in the snow-covered sand hills. We neither needed nor wanted anything or anyone else. I turned all but two of the horses out on the open range where they could paw through the snow and nibble on the grass it covered. I never worried about them running completely away because I would keep a bite or two of oats out for them beside the corrals. Between the two of us, Miroux and I had enough human staples to last for months, and the cedar thickets and timber stands along the river were generous enough to supply whatever meat for the table we needed.

Miroux was an artist at tanning deer hides and fur pelts and making them into clothing. She made a buckskin shirt for me that was so beautiful I was afraid to wear it outside, but loved to slip it on after coming into the warm cabin from a cold day of hunting, or chopping wood. The pelts from a pair of wolves she caught in snares made from leather and placed in open trails leading to the river, she sewed together with sinew to make a blanket big enough for us to cuddle together under or make love on top of.

The days were mostly busy doing the things necessary to insure survival in a land known for its inhospitable temperament and brutal winters. But Miroux and I were both accustomed to such temperaments and winters and we not only survived, we did so with at least some degree of comfort. On the nights when Miroux did not play the fiddle, we played raucous games with her Assiniboin plum stones, read from the *Rubáiyát* to one another by the light of the

lanterns and talked about what it meant, or else we made
love on the bed or on the floor on the wolf robe in front of
the stove.

Whenever I thought Miroux looked the least bit uneasy
or only picked at her food I would ask if she thought she
was pregnant. Nothing would have pleased me more, and I
tried many times to talk about the child we might have
together, but for the most part it was a subject she sidled
away from.

Of course I no longer needed whiskey to sleep, only the
feel of Miroux's warm body next to mine. And I no longer
slammed the *Rubáiyát* down on the table and walked away
from it. Miroux had made my camp my home and I was
haunted by ghosts no longer . . . with but a single exception.

That single exception was the ghost of DuPont Sevier.

It was several days after Miroux came before she told
me what she had found out about her husband at the sheriff's office in Chadron.

"I found out the worst possible thing," she said. "And
that was nothing at all. Sheriff Gower sent letters to Cheyenne and Denver and Steamboat Springs and Leadville
and . . . nothing."

At times she seemed as happy and content as I was, but
at other times she was plagued with guilt. "What you must
think about a person as weak as me," she said one night as
she lay in my arms underneath the wolf robe. "One who is
ruled so easily by her passions and desires. As shameful as
it is to admit, I must, Casey—my desire to be kissed and
touched by you began the night you ate supper in my
house. That is when I began fearing DuPont would return.
That is when my sin began."

"How can it be a sin to love someone this much,
Miroux?"

"Adultery is always—"

"Then we'll be married, Miroux. We'll ride to Chadron
tomorrow—*tonight* if you want! If we hurry we can be man
and wife before sunup."

"I cannot marry again—if DuPont is alive."

"It has been nearly eleven months, Miroux . . ."

"Time means nothing to God."

"Maybe not to God, but to men it does, Miroux—and no man who could have you could stay away from you for eleven months—not if he was still alive!"

"But . . . we do not *know*, Casey! . . . I do not want to speak about it again."

"We *will* talk about it again, Miroux—but not now. You will see that I'm right. We will raise our babies here along the Niobrara, and when we go to town people will see us and say, 'There go Casey and Miroux Wills. Such a fine-looking man—makes you wonder how the homely widow Sevier ever trapped him!' "

"And," Miroux said, laughing, "they will also say, 'It is a good thing he built such a fine barn because I understand that is where he spends his nights!' "

And for a while again the ghost of DuPont Sevier was gone and the dream along the Niobrara was alive. But I knew it was only a matter of time until he would return and would have to be dealt with again. And again. And again.

A few nights later, as Miroux was snuggled in my arms asleep underneath the wolf-pelt robe, the answer to the question of how to put DuPont's ghost to rest forever came to me.

It came to me in a flash and I sat straight up in bed when it did so.

"What is it, Casey?" Miroux whispered in the dark. "What is wrong?"

"I'll find DuPont's grave for you!" I said.

"What?!"

"Once you know where he's buried you'll be able to bury his ghost too. I'll come back and get you and show you his grave. You can weep for him and put flowers on his grave if you need to. And we'll even put a marble head-stone on it if you want to. But you'll *know* what happened to him and you'll be released from your vows. And we can get married."

I thought she would be excited about the idea, but she said nothing for quite a while; when she finally did, there was little excitement in her voice. "*Oui* . . . I suppose you must. But how?"

"To start with, you'll have to tell me about him—which you have never really done. Tell me what kind of man he was and where he said he was going when he left. After that, it'll be up to me. It may not be easy, but there aren't many places where I haven't already laid tracks. I've got a friend named Johnnie Lester whom I'll bet I can find in Cheyenne, and I can get him to help me."

"When will you go?"

"I'll leave the first of April, and—"

"But that is only two weeks away."

"And I'll take the money for the cattle with me in case I run into some good young cows for sale while I'm lookin' for DuPont's grave."

"You talk about DuPont's death and grave so casually."

"I'm sorry, but I didn't know him."

"*Oui*, I know. It is hard to talk about him. It makes me feel unfaithful for not waiting longer."

"And how long would have been right, Miroux? Another year? Two years? Five? Ten? Until we were old and ready to die? Would that have been long enough to satisfy your conscience?"

"Casey . . ."

"Okay. But that's why I've *got* to find out!"

There was a long silence in the cabin, except for the usual night sounds, and I thought Miroux might have fallen asleep. But she wasn't asleep. She then said something softly, something that I knew she had put a lot of thought into, something I would never forget. "Casey . . . I can love you only as long as there is a chance it is *not* adultery. If DuPont is alive . . ."

She held her words—whatever they were.

"What?" I said.

"I cannot bear to think about it, much less talk about it."

"Finish it, Miroux."

A long silence.

"I cannot. . . . I cannot bear to think that I am the kind of woman who could allow even a small corner of her heart to wish her husband would never return, nor can I bear to think about what it will mean if he does."

"What *will* it mean, Miroux?"

The silence again.

"You don't love him—you and he never could have had what we have."

"No . . . I could never have loved anybody like I love you, Casey. As the spruce is to the northwoods, you are to me. . . . But DuPont is not—"

"*Was not*," I said.

"He was not a bad man and I loved him. Above all, Casey, I am a Christian woman, married in the Christian faith. I have spoken the Christian vows of marriage before God. In spite of the adultery I will have committed, and will have to live with if you find DuPont alive . . . *if* he is alive, he will still be my husband."

Now I was the one who was silent.

17

When I kissed Miroux good-bye in front of the cabin on the first day of April 1890, the ice on the Niobrara was ten days past breakup, and there were only small patches of snow left on the sand hills; the bluebells had just begun to bloom and the grouse were starting their strange courtship dances out on the meadows.

I crossed the Niobrara on the gray and stopped to look back when we reached the top of the ridge. Miroux was still standing in front of the cabin, watching me while cedar smoke slowly drifted skyward from the morning fire we had shared and that had warmed us together. I was in love with her beyond all reason and could not wait to top the ridge again, because when I did I would be coming back—*coming home*—with the knowledge Miroux needed to become Mrs. Casey Wills.

I waved to Miroux one last time and headed the gray down the off slope of the ridge.

I kept the gray in a jig of a trot all day and made camp that night just after crossing the North Platte River. The cold, hard ground I unrolled my few blankets on was a not-too-pleasant reminder of the long years I'd spent as a drifter—before I started sleeping on a felt mattress, and especially before I knew what it was like to feel Miroux's warm body snuggled next to mine underneath a wolf-pelt robe.

The second night I camped beside a lost spring and rode into Cheyenne at midday.

I had no trouble finding Johnnie Lester. I found him exactly how and where I thought I would—puss-gutted and pale in a back room of Rosemarie's Establishment.

I leaned on the door frame, looked at him, and said, "You could make a decent living traveling with the Ladies' Temperance Society as proof of the debilitating effects on the human body of whorehouse living and wholesale debauchery."

He looked up at me from the bed with red eyes for a few seconds, then wrinkled his brow and nose and said, "What?"

"Rosemarie said your money's almost gone, and it's a damn good thing it is. I'm not sure you could have survived us making one extra dime off those Banister horses."

"What?"

"Look at the difference in us—I'm lean and strong from the hard work of building my ranch and you're—"

"A contented and happy man—or was." Now he smiled at me and I think that was the first time it even dawned on him who I was. He rubbed his face and said, "Where's Ab?"

"Ab!?" I shook my head. "Your brain's in as bad shape as the rest of you. Ab was killed at the Rawhiders' camp in New Mexico when that horse fell over backward on him."

"That's right," Johnnie said. "The son of a bitch came over backward so quick Ab couldn't do nothin'—and I was the one who should've been on him."

"Get dressed, Johnnie. You gotta get out of here."

"I like it here. If I was a woman I'd be a whore."

"And I expect a damn fine one, too," I said.

"Where you been, Casey? Your money 'bout gone, too?"

I smiled. "No, I still have ninety percent of mine, plus I've filed a claim along the Niobrara River and built a ranch—barn, corrals, cabin, and all."

"Your life wouldn't have turned out so sour if Josh hadn't a got killed, Casey. To this day I still can't put a finger on exactly where you started goin' wrong, but I think you was *always* a little peculiar—did I ever tell you that?"

"Prob'ly," I said. "I used to spend quite a bit of time thinking about it myself, but hell, now I just accept the fact."

"I appreciate an honest man, Casey, and you always were honest—nobody can take that away from you. . . . Well, you got the money and Rosemarie's got the whores!"

"I reckon I'll pass, Johnnie," I said. "Get your clothes on—I need your help."

It was true that I needed Johnnie's help, but it was just as true that he needed to get away from the whiskey and the whores. I didn't like seeing him puss-gutted and pale and his brain floating in booze. Cowboys like Johnnie, who were the best hands in the roughest country and could handle the wildest cattle and rankest horses, tended to go to waste when they weren't out on the range. Everything worthwhile and wholesome they got out of life came from isolated cow camps and lonely canyon rims, and practically everything they got from town could be poured from a bottle or found in musty back rooms in saloons for two dollars.

I wouldn't have given a dime for Johnnie Lester in town or taken a million dollars for him out in the Big Lonely.

I finally got Johnnie dressed and out of the whorehouse. I'll leave it up to the preachers of the world to list the sins that Rosemarie would have to account for—and above all else some of them love listing sins—but she didn't pretend to be something she wasn't and she took care of Johnnie and his money where others would only have taken care of his money, and quick.

She said Johnnie had walked into her place, handed her the roll of money that was his share of the Banister horses, and told her to let him know when it was gone. He told her to give the hostler at the livery however much money he wanted whenever he wanted it for taking care of his horse and saddle. That had been the first of May, almost a year ago, and she acted embarrassed when she handed me the money Johnnie had left—eighty-seven dollars.

She shook her head. "I tried to get him to leave six months ago, Casey, because I didn't want to see him go through all his money at once . . . but the girls all liked him and he liked them and he said he wanted to stay—said he didn't have anywhere else to go and that it was against his principles to work as long as he had money. He said he couldn't be like you, and he talked a lot about this cowboy named Ab that got killed on a horse he said he should have been riding, and about Josh getting killed too. He said he wished all four of you were punching cows together on some good outfit. . . . And Casey, he said if he died here for me not to bury him in town, but on a hilltop outside of town. And he told me to show you where he was buried. He said he knew you'd come."

I couldn't look at Johnnie without laughing. "I never seen a son of a bitch let himself go to hell like you have!" I said as he was saddling his horse at the livery. "Your face is going to blister and peel like the hide slippin' off a dead cow. . . . Oh, in case you forgot, unless you want to get your saddle kicked to pieces, you fasten the front cinch first, and don't grab ahold of the damn cantle when you get on either—get a handful of mane in the left hand and take ahold of the saddle horn with your right and don't waller up like a farmer. And put your feet all the way in them stirrups and hold the reins in your left hand."

Johnnie grinned but didn't say a word, just kept on saddling his horse. I knew sometime or other I'd pay for it, but it wasn't often I had the upper hand on him and I thought at least one of us should reap some benefit from his dilapidated condition.

We made camp the first night not ten miles from Cheyenne—I figured ten miles of riding in a long trot was enough to sober up anyone who hadn't been on a horse in nearly a year. I boiled coffee over an open fire and gave Johnnie some pemmican to eat that Miroux had made.

Johnnie looked at the pemmican, then tasted a little piece of it and looked at me.

"Pemmican," I said.

"Indian food?"

"Depends on who's eating it, I guess—I figure when we eat it, it's gringo food. It's funny eatin' food out of your hand, huh, instead of out of a bottle?"

"It ain't as good as cheap whiskey, but it's not all that bad. . . . Did you say you filed a claim on a homestead?"

"Yeah—along the Niobrara River on the west edge of the Nebraska sand hills."

"And that's where you've been all this time?"

"I found the place about the first of July and started working on it the same day. Other than going to Chadron three times for supplies I hardly ever left the place."

"But . . . why?"

"Do you remember that time a couple of years ago when me and you and Ab were on our way to Kingston and we made camp at a little dry creek on the edge of the Guadalupes? I showed you and Ab something I'd been drawing in the sand. Remember?"

"Yeah . . . It was a picture of a river you said you'd never seen before and you had a barn and corrals and a house and all drawn along it."

"Well, I found that place a couple of months after we split up the Banister horse money in the Nations. . . . When I topped the ridge above the Niobrara River and saw it, it gave me the shivers. I marked a few trees that afternoon and was in Chadron by daylight the next morning to file a claim on it. . . . Now you ought to see it, Johnnie— it all looks so much like what I was drawing in the sand you wouldn't believe it. I got my own place, Johnnie. I've got a home. And . . . and . . ."

"And what?" Johnnie asked with a cocked eye.

"And I've got the prettiest and sweetest woman you ever saw, waiting there for me."

"Good gawd, Casey!" He laughed. "You've been telling me how hard you've been working and lordin' it over me for whorin' and drinkin' and blowing my money, while all the time you've been—"

"I haven't lorded anything over you, Johnnie—and I knew you would give me hell. You can say what you want about me, but you've got to understand that Miroux is the most decent woman I've ever known and I can't let you or anybody else say dishonorable things about her."

Johnnie looked at me again.

"God . . . You're in love again, aren't you?"

"Johnnie," I said, moving my hand back and forth between us, "let's get all of this over with as quick as we can. I'm going to say I'm in love beyond all reason, and you're going to laugh like hell again and say something smart about Lillie Johnson. Then I'm going to say that I'm not sure what that was with Lillie, but it was nothing at all like what me and Miroux have—*nothing*! I have a home for Miroux and plans for the future—and not just dreamer-plans either like cowboys on night guard always have, because I have the money and the want-to to make it work for us!"

"Damn! Damn! Damn!" Johnnie said.

"Now, to get this all over with at once, I'll lay all the cards on the table for you. Miroux had a husband—" Before Johnnie even had time to wrinkle his brow I put my hand up and said quickly, "But it's not at all what you think! I'm bettin' everything I've got that he's dead and buried. I want you to help me find his grave so Miroux can bury the past she had with him."

Johnnie shook his head and watched the coffee swirl around in his cup, but said nothing.

"Whatever you're thinking, you'd just as well say," I said.

Johnnie looked up at me with a wide grin. "I was just wondering which of us is the more pathetic."

As we lay in our bedrolls that night, listening to the coyotes howl and the hobbled horses munch on short spring grass, I said, "Have you decided which of us is the more pathetic yet?"

"When I do, I'll let you know," he said. "I've got some pretty strong clues right now, but I know it needs a little more study and I need a few more facts."

"Like what?"

"Well, you haven't given me one clue yet as to what this Miroux gal looks like. Has she got the customary number of arms and legs and eyes and breasts and—"

"She's part Assiniboin Indian and part French. She was raised a trapper's daughter and can run a trapline and skin a pelt. She's about five-three and weighs about a hundred and fifteen pounds, with soft tan skin and hair and eyes the color of midnight. She speaks French and speaks English better than either of us, and she plays the fiddle, too."

Johnnie whistled. "Is there anything this gal can't do?"

"If there is I haven't found it yet, and if I did, it wouldn't be important to me. You and me used to argue about the meaning and purpose of life, especially after Ab got killed—well, I've found mine in Miroux. For the first time in my life I know without a doubt not only what I want, but where it is and who I need to share it with to make it all mean what it needs to mean."

"Have you made love to her, Casey?"

I looked at him and thought quite a while before I answered. "Yes, I have."

"And what if we find her husband and he's *not* in his grave?"

"I don't think that could happen, Johnnie—but if it does, Miroux's the kind of woman who will honor her marriage vows . . . at all cost."

"Then I don't understand why you would risk messing everything up by finding her husband."

"I doubt I could explain it to you if I tried."

18

Early the next morning Johnnie and I rode south across the open prairie of Wyoming, bound for Denver.

"So, Casey . . . I guess this DuPont Sevier was a scoundrel and philanderer, a rogue and a knave, and a completely despicable human being much like many of our cowboy friends."

"I only wish he had been, Johnnie, but I think the truth is that his worst fault was that he was a dreamer, trying one business scheme after another. He got a letter from some banker in Denver he said he'd met one time. And, according to DuPont, the banker said he had learned of a mine of some kind that the right people could make a lot of quick money on. DuPont told Miroux he was going to check it out and would be back within three weeks. That was close to a year ago. Miroux said he wasn't selfish or mean and had never mistreated her in the twelve years they'd been married. They met at the mission school where Miroux went to live after her folks died. They moved a lot—following one scheme after another. The homestead they lived on in the sand hills was abandoned by someone else, and they'd moved in only a couple of weeks before Du-Pont left this last time. Miroux is the one who filed on the

homestead after a couple of months passed and DuPont
still hadn't come home—she had to stay there until Du-
Pont came back and was afraid somebody else might file
on the place."

We rode till noon and stopped to blow the horses and
make coffee to wash the pemmican down.

"I got it figured out," Johnnie said as we were throwing
our saddles on the horses' backs again.

"What?"

"Which of us is the more pathetic."

"I know I'm goin' to hear it whether I want to or not, so
go ahead."

"Well, right now I figure we're even—but if we find this
DuPont feller alive, Casey, *you're* going to be the most pathetic mother's son to ever ride a cow horse out of Texas."

The hardest thing about tracking anything, from a roguish,
old bunch-quitting cow to a missing French Canadian, is
cutting the first sign. And just like the hardest place to
pick up the trail of a roguish old cow would be where there
were a lot of other cows milling around, the hardest place
to pick up a human trail would be a place where there
were a lot of other humans milling around—and of all the
places I had ever been there were more humans milling
around Denver than any other place.

The first stop was the sheriff's office, in the Arapahoe
County Courthouse.

"And who are you?" the sheriff asked.

"A friend," I said.

"Goin' to a lot of trouble for a friend, ain't you?"

"He's a good friend," Johnnie said.

"Well, like I wrote and told Sheriff Gower, I couldn't
find any trace of anybody by the name of DuPont Sevier."

"Denver's a big place," I said, "must have a lot of
banks."

"Four—and I checked 'em all. Nobody knew anything
about your friend."

"Thanks, Sheriff," I said. "Sorry to bother you."

In the fourth bank we went in, the Merchant's State

Bank of Denver, we talked to the president, a Blair Stephens, and were told in a bankerlike way that the sheriff had already asked about this Mr. Sevier and the answer would be the same to us as it had been to him.

"And what would that be, Mister Stephens?" I asked.

"I know nothing about the man! Now, if you'll excuse me—"

"These other fellers in these offices," I said, "did you ask all of them—to a man—before telling the sheriff you'd never heard of DuPont Sevier?" I knew to ask this because in the other three banks we'd been in, the First State Bank of Denver, the Colorado National, and the Mountain States National, none of the bank presidents had asked any other employee anything.

"The question was put to me, not to my employees."

So, under the watchful and malevolent eye of Blair Stephens I asked the rest of the bank people if any of them knew a DuPont Sevier or anyone looking like the description I gave them.

None did.

As we were leaving the bank a thought struck me. I turned around and stepped into Blair Stephens's office again and said, "Is there anyone who was working here a year ago that's not here now?"

Stephens gave me a disgusted look. "No!"

"Have you had any employees die in the last year?" I asked.

"No! . . . Maybe Charles Farber—I'm not sure when he died."

"He have family?"

"Well . . . yes."

"In Denver?"

"Yes!"

"Where?"

"I don't know!"

"You keep records, don't you? I never heard of a bank that didn't keep records."

"Of course we keep records—all kinds of records!"

"Then go to the dead-employee records and find out where his family is—where he was living when he died."

Blair Stephens sat at his desk and held his head in both hands for a second, then yelled toward the door, "James, look up the last address we had for Charles Farber and give it to these . . . gentlemen."

The address was 112 Pueblo Street, and the door at that address was opened by a slim woman in a maid's uniform who looked at the two men standing at her door in cowboy garb and said, "Yes?"

"Ma'am," I said, tipping my hat, "I'd like to speak with Mrs. Charles Farber."

"Mrs. Farber is indisposed at the moment," she said and started to close the door.

"He won't give you a minute's peace, ma'am," Johnnie said, " 'less he gets to see her—not one blamed minute."

"Very well," she said. "Come with me . . . but wipe your feet first and don't sit on the furniture—your spurs might scratch it."

Mrs. Farber was in the backyard, drinking tea.

"I always wondered what a woman did when she was indisposed," Johnnie whispered.

Mrs. Farber, though, was a kind woman, an old woman, and we took off our hats when we talked to her.

"I'm sorry," she said. "I don't think I can help you— the name means nothing to me. It's possible Charles met him on one of his wild schemes though."

That struck a familiar chord. I raised an eyebrow.

"What kind of schemes?"

"All I know is that his last one probably would never have amounted to anything, just like all the rest—a gold mine of all things. Poor Charles, he was always looking for something and I never knew what. I don't think he even knew, for that matter."

"Where was this mine supposed to be?"

"I don't know, but Charles had mentioned something about needing to go to Leadville and meet someone and then they were going . . . somewhere." She held her hands up in the air.

"And he never got to go to Leadville?"

"No. He came down with the fever and died in a few days."

"And you never heard him mention a man named Du-Pont Sevier?"

"No . . . However there was a man at Charles's funeral whom I don't ever recall meeting before."

"Did you talk to him?"

"Yes . . . but it was a very trying time, Mister Wills, and I had so much to attend to and talked to so many people who offered their condolences that those few days are really all a blur to me. I do seem to recall that he spoke with some kind of foreign accent, though—if that is of any help to you."

By then I had been gone from Miroux and the Niobrara for ten days, Johnnie had been with me for a week, we had been in Denver three days . . . and the trail of DuPont Sevier had just been cut.

I sent her a letter:

> Dearest Miroux,
>
> I am writing from Denver. Johnnie Lester is with me. I have every reason to believe that we have just talked to the widow of the man DuPont came here to see. I think from here he went to Leadville, and within the hour Johnnie and I will saddle up and head there as well.
>
> I miss you and our little cabin along the Niobrara more than I can put into words.
> Love,
> Casey

The snow was still deep even in the middle of April on the Continental Divide, but the horses had little trouble as long as we stayed on the stage road.

Johnnie loved Leadville—thousands of people all crammed together at the top of the world for no other reason than to make money or spend money.

A man with the name DuPont and speaking with a French accent is a man set apart just enough to be remembered, at least for a few days, by those who came in contact with him, but the chances of remembering even somebody like him close to a year later is much smaller. However, after two days and nights we were reasonably certain that he had left Leadville with a man by the name of Red Walker, and the two of them were northbound for Meeker, at the foothills of the western slope of the Rockies, for reasons unknown.

Dearest Miroux,

I hope you got the letter I mailed in Denver. We are in Meeker, Colorado, now. It is certain DuPont was here with a Red Walker, looking for a place called Gibraltar. The land agent sent them to Rawlins, Wyoming. We will not know if they made it there until we get there. It is a very rough element that inhabits these mining towns. Robbery and murder are a way of life, but it seems DuPont at least survived Leadville and Meeker.

Must close. It is not a short distance to Rawlins and we will have to skirt around the mountains on top of that. Probably close to a hundred-and-fifty-mile ride. Will let you know what we learn in Rawlins.

Love,
Casey

Dear Miroux,

I am writing this letter on my saddle in front of the post office in Steamboat Springs, Colorado. We came here from Dixon, Wyoming, a rough little town along the Little Snake River, which is only a couple of miles north of the Colorado border and about fifty miles south of Rawlins. If my writing is any harder to read than usual it is because my horse won't stand still. It is the first day of May and the nose flies have enjoyed a good hatching and are driving the horses crazy.

I would like to tell you how much I miss you and long to hold you in my arms, but Johnnie are I are both anxious to get this over with and with what we learned over the past couple of days we both agree that after one month and perhaps eight hundred miles of travel behind us we are reaching the end. I know you are anxious for the news, so here it is—

The land agent in Rawlins remembered DuPont and Red Walker and knew enough about where Gibraltar was to send them here—Steamboat. He wasn't exactly sure where, but he said Gibraltar was a huge rock formation that was said to be sitting on a very rich vein of silver ore on the south side of the Little Snake River a few miles inside Colorado. The agent said DuPont and Walker showed him a title to it and wanted to know whether it was authentic.

The agent said the title looked official, but since the claim was located in Colorado, they would have to take it to the land office in Steamboat Springs, where the agent could look it up in his land books. Where the title—whether it was real or not—came from is a mystery.

From studying the map in the land office it looks like East Gibraltar, the name as it is on the map, is between Dixon, Wyoming and Steamboat Springs, although much closer to Dixon—maybe ten or fifteen miles from there and forty or fifty from Steamboat. We must have ridden only a few miles west of it on the way here, but there must have always been a mountain blocking our view.

Since Dixon is between Steamboat Springs and Rawlins, we stopped there to ask about DuPont and Walker, as well as Gibraltar. We learned that there has been a mine operating at Gibraltar for over two years—a fact the bartender also remembered telling two men who no doubt were DuPont and Walker—a bit of information that did not seem to set too well with the two men. We also were given this advice concerning Gibraltar—a man would be well advised to ride way around it—*way around it*.

And now guess what? The land agent here in Steamboat Springs said he is certain no one—no one—came into his office with a title to a claim at Gibraltar, wanting to know if it was authentic. He has no memory of anyone by the name of DuPont

Sevier or Red Walker. No one in town that we have talked to remembers them.

They never made it from Dixon to Steamboat Springs, and Steamboat is the only place they would have gone with a title to Gibraltar.

Whatever happened to them, happened between Dixon and Steamboat Springs. We're heading back out to Gibraltar.

I'm not sure how I feel right now, other than strange. I'm anxious for this to be over with, I am sure of that.

> All my love,
> Casey

19

We skirted around the foot of snow-covered Columbine Mountain to the east, and when we topped a ridge just north of the mountain we saw two rock formations rising up out of the lower and more level country to the northwest, about two miles away. They were huge and they cast long shadows from the late afternoon sun, East Gibraltar being the highest and casting the longest blue shadow. It had sloping sides of tallus about halfway up and from there on to its almost spire point it was solid rock. The other landmark rock was West Gibraltar.

The ridge we were on gave a man a good view of what lay north and west of Columbine Mountain. Below us, between our ridge and the two Gibraltars were about two miles of spruce and quakies, and beyond the Gibraltars was the Little Snake River cutting through a high sagebrush plateau, and beyond the Little Snake was the high desert of Wyoming, wild and blue with no end.

"A sight like this at sundown can make a man ponder, can't it, Casey," Johnnie said.

"Sure enough," I answered.

I spurred off the ridge into the shadow of the western mountains where the rim of sun no longer reached, and where the nine-thousand-foot air was suddenly and sharply cooler.

The next time we stopped was at the edge of a line of quakies on a small rise no more than a half mile south of East Gibraltar. The sun still shone on the spire of the rock, but dusk had already descended on the cluster of tin buildings and tents at its base. The yellow glow of lighted lanterns could be seen in at least a half-dozen windows.

We untied our coats from the backs of our saddles and put them on, then rode off the rise. About halfway from the rise to the buildings was a wooden sign that read:

WARNING! YOU ARE ENTERING GIBRALTAR, COLO. THIS IS A COMPANY TOWN. IF YOU DO NOT WORK FOR THE GIBRALTAR MINING COMPANY YOU ARE NOT WELCOME HERE! GIBRALTAR ORDINANCES STRICTLY ENFORCED BY DANIEL D. PARKE.

Johnnie pointed toward the rock towering over us to a rifleman perched on a ledge where the tallus stopped and solid rock began.

Three curs barked at us from the porch of one of the buildings, then came running out for a closer inspection only to find us unworthy of further attention.

We rode down the only street in town, a short and rocky street, past the Gibraltar Mercantile and the Gibraltar Bank, both of which were rickety tin buildings that looked empty. We continued past the tent that was the Gibraltar Bar; the lanterns were lit and voices drifted out. Finally we passed two long tin buildings that looked like barracks and stopped in front of the last one on the right; a sign read: Daniel D. Parke—Gibraltar Security.

A lantern was burning on the desk we could see through the window in the door. We tied our horses to the rail in front of the security building, opened the door, and stepped inside, seeing no one. Behind the desk, stacked three high and four deep, were wooden crates marked No. 2XX 50% Nitroglycerine Dynamite Cartridges.

On the dark end of the long building were two rows of four cells each, about six-feet square made of steel bars.

"Looks like nobody's home," Johnnie said.

Then we heard someone outside yell, "Hey, Dan! Whose horses are them?"

Then we heard someone hurrying through the rocks outside, and a square figure appeared in the doorway.

"Are you Mister Parke?" I asked.

"I'm Daniel D. Parke," a deep voice said. "What do you want?"

"First of all, Mister Parke, we're not troublemakers and we're not the law."

"What in the hell are you then?" Parke said as he stepped into the building, stood by his desk, and looked us over by the light of the coal oil lantern. He was a heavy-set man about my height, with narrow eyes, a broad nose, and a pocked complexion.

"We'd like to know what happened to a man we think came here with another man—and that's all. . . . We just want to know what happened to him. Like I said, we're not the law and we're not the man's kin. We just need to know."

"We don't take kindly to trespassers," Parke said.

"What do you do with 'em?" Johnnie asked.

"Ask 'em to leave."

"And if they don't?" I asked.

"We ask 'em again."

I'd stuffed a few hundred dollars into my pants pocket for just such an occasion as this, and now I pulled one out and laid it on top of the desk next to the lantern.

'All we want to know is what happened to a man named DuPont Sevier," I said. "Soon as we know, we ride out and you'll never hear from us again—except for this folding souvenir." Parke looked at the hundred awhile, then looked back at me and Johnnie. "And this one," I said as I laid another hundred on top of the first one by the lantern.

"Sevier, you said?"

"Yeah . . . DuPont Sevier. Spoke with a French accent and was with a man named Red Walker."

"No . . . I don't know."

I laid down a third hundred-dollar bill.

Parke looked at the money again without saying anything.

I reached down and picked the money up and stuffed it back into my pocket. "Let's rattle our hocks, Johnnie," I said. "I don't guess DuPont was ever here after all."

"Wait!" Daniel D. Parke said.

I pulled the three hundred dollars out and held it in my hand.

Parke dug into his ear with a fingertip and said, "And all you want to know is what happened to him, huh?"

"That's all."

"Okay. He was here, both 'em were. They were here and then they left."

I stuffed the money into my pocket again and started for the door.

"Wait! You find out and then you're gone? Right now? No matter what you find out?"

"No matter what," I said, holding my hands up. "All we want to know is what happened to DuPont Sevier."

"*S'il vous plait . . .*" A weak whisper came from the dark end of the building.

I looked at Parke and picked up the lantern off the desk and carried it toward the dark end of the building, not sure of what I had heard.

"HEY!" Parke yelled.

I looked in each cell quickly and each one I looked in was empty until I came to the fourth cell on the right. In that cell was a filthy, bearded man lying on the floor, clutching a blanket to his chin. His eyes were closed and his breathing was quick and shallow.

He spoke in a whisper, suddenly interrupted by a coughing bout that left him trembling.

I tried the cell door, but it was locked.

I set the lantern down on the floor and, reaching through the bars, flung the blanket he clutched away.

I pulled his dirty left trouser leg up to his knee and looked for the red, crescent-shaped birthmark on his left calf that Miroux had told me about.

By then Johnnie was standing over me, and I looked up at him.

In all my imaginings about DuPont Sevier the sight now
before me in the dim light of a smoky-globed lantern was
one that never entered my mind.

"Is it . . . is he . . . ?"

I nodded slowly.

"Well . . . I'll be damned," Johnnie drawled.

"Okay—so now you know," Parke said behind us.
"Gimme the money and get the hell out."

"Let him out," I said slowly.

Parke laughed. "In two goddamn weeks I will. That's
when his sentence is up!"

"What sentence?!"

"Trespassin' and stealin' ore."

"You can't—"

"Wanna bet?" Parke said. "You go to Steamboat Springs
and they'll tell you we take care of our own problems up
here. He was sentenced to a year at hard labor, and he's
got two more weeks to go."

"He won't live two *days*," I said. "Not in here. I'll take
him to a doctor."

Johnnie looked at me and raised his eyebrows. Then he
took my arm and dragged me to the side and asked in a
whisper, "I've missed somethin' somewhere, Casey. Let's
go back to Steamboat and talk to the law."

"He's damn near dead, Johnnie. We gotta get him out—
now!"

"Casey . . . *think about it!*"

I looked at Johnnie. "Are you saying I ought to—"

"I just said think about it, Casey—that's all."

I was still looking at Johnnie but I was remembering
something from thirty-five years ago—a barefoot boy holding a squawking, flapping chicken by the legs and talking
to a tall, slim woman with long hair and kind eyes as they
stood in front of a backwoods cabin along the banks of the
Little Kanawa River in West Virginia. "Yes, Ma," the boy
said sadly, "I know she belongs to Mister Griswald, but
he's got more'n he needs and we ain't got none. I
thought . . ." His mother walked over to him and put a
warm hand on his shoulder. "But right is right and wrong is
wrong, son, and no amount of wishin' or thinkin' will

change that. Now take the hen back to Mister Griswald, and go straight there right now, because the devil loves a dawdler, son. When you see the right thing, you've got to do it! Each moment you find some reason for not doing the right thing is just another moment the devil has to work his way under your skin."

"Parke!" I yelled. "I want you to let this man out right now! I've got to get him to a doctor!"

"You go to goddamn hell!" Parke said.

I walked up to stand face-to-face with Parke. "How much money to let him out—right now? How much?!"

"How much? . . . One thousand dollars!"

I ran outside to where the horses were tied and dug deep into my saddlebag until I felt the leather pouch containing the rest of my Banister horse money.

When I stepped inside the Gibraltar Constable's Office the lantern was back on the desk and I began counting hundred-dollar bills. When I'd counted seven, I reached into my pocket and pulled out the three hundreds I had in there and slammed all ten of them down on top of the desk hard. "THERE!" I said. "Now unlock his cell!"

"Casey," Johnnie said behind me, "are you crazy?"

"Two thousand!" Parke said.

I reached into the leather pouch again, pulled out the roll of bills, and started counting.

"Casey!" Johnnie yelled. "Don't—that's for your cattle!"

"Here come the prisoners back from the mine, Dan," a man said as he entered the jail. He stopped in the doorway. "What's going on here? Trouble?"

"Nothin' I can't handle, Mister Glover," Parke said as his left hand jerked the money pouch out of my hand and his right hand came up with his Colt. "These two fellers were trying to bribe me into letting Sevier out—only now they're going to be in jail themselves."

Johnnie came running from the dark end of the building and butted the man in the doorway with his head like a charging bull almost the same instant I pushed Parke's Colt down with my left hand and hit him on the chin with a right uppercut.

Hell was loose and things happened fast. . . . Johnnie knocked Glover back out the door and the two wrestled on the rocks. My uppercut landed Parke onto the top of the desk behind him, knocking the lantern off and breaking it.

For an instant it was all but pitch dark inside. Outside I could hear Glover cussing and grunting and the rocks rattling. Inside, Parke was cussing and trying to get to his feet and I was trying to see enough to decide what to do next when all of a sudden the building blazed into light—the coal oil that spread across the floor when the lantern broke burst into flame from the lighted wick.

Parke was almost to his feet when I hit him again. He was in enough of a daze for me to grab the Colt out of his hand.

"Casey! . . . Get out of there! Look!" Johnnie put his head inside the door and yelled, then was tackled from behind by Glover.

"Oh, my god!" Parke said the instant he rolled over on top of the desk and saw that the coal oil had run underneath the dynamite and set the wooden cases on fire.

I cocked his Colt and pointed it between his eyes. "Where's the key to Sevier's cell?" I asked.

"This goddamn place is gonna blow!" he said.

"The key!"

"You're crazy! Let me out of here!"

"The key—or you're gonna go with it!"

Parke's eyes were wide and glued to the burning dynamite cases as he fumbled for the keys to the cells in his pocket.

"Here, you crazy bastard!" he yelled as he tossed me a ring of keys and lunged out the door shouting, "Run! The dynamite's gonna blow!!"

"Casey!" It was Johnnie at the door again. Glover had run off with everyone else. "Get the hell out of there!"

"Get the horses ready!" I yelled. "I've gotta get Sevier!" I fumbled with the keys and ran toward DuPont's cell with the flames now licking at the top of the tin above the dynamite.

"Come on!"

The second key I tried opened the cell door. DuPont

couldn't have weighed any more than Miroux did, and I scooped him off the floor and carried him past the flames.

I didn't expect to make it to the door—but I did and suddenly I was outside.

"Here!" Johnnie said. "Throw 'im across the saddle in front of me and get your ass on that horse!"

Nobody tried to stop us because everybody was running like hell and bracing for the explosion that was bound to come.

We were halfway to the rise south of the mine when the dynamite went off. First there was a mild, muffled explosion followed almost instantaneously by a blast big enough to make the horses stumble and nearly knock us out of our saddles.

When the horses got their feet back underneath them they both were so scared they threw their heads up and ran out of control until we reached a rise where we were able to stop and look back.

"Ho . . . ly . . . catheron!" Johnnie said as he looked at Gibraltar. He held onto DuPont with one hand and pushed his hat back with the other.

I looked and shook my head. Close to half the tin buildings and tents that made up the town were down—blown over by the concussion from the blast just like they would have been from a hurricane. People were scurrying and running like ants in the firelight, and it looked like every horse and mule was loose. Men shouted, dogs barked, and mules brayed.

"Casey?"

"Yeah."

"Let's make it a point never to come back here."

"Okay."

"Casey . . . What about your money?"

"See that stuff fallin' from the sky over Gibraltar?" I asked. "Mixed in with all the dust?"

"Yeah . . ."

"Well, that's not mountain snow, Johnnie—that's my money. I didn't have time to get it."

"Good god, Casey!"

"Just shut up, Johnnie—it's hard enough watchin' them

miners down there scramblin' and jumpin' up in the air tryin' to catch my money before it hits the ground without having to listen to you, too."

I reined my horse around while Johnnie was still giggling and said without looking back at him, or Gibraltar either, "Let's rattle our hocks out of these goddamn mountains."

20

Blowing over most of the buildings in a town, even a company mining town, is a serious business and one we did not care to renegotiate. Nor did we care to stay long on the rise south of town and see if a company town would get a "posse" together and go in pursuit of those responsible for leveling it. The prospect of being overtaken by a posse led by Daniel D. Parke was not a particularly pleasant one and not likely to improve DuPont's chances of survival—not to mention mine and Johnnie's. We had enjoyed all of Colorado that we cared for and were craving nothing more than the lonesome flats of the plains and the prairies, where me and Johnnie both felt much more at home. That being the case, we had no trouble deciding which way to ride—north toward the Little Snake River and Wyoming.

"Does blowing up a company town make a feller an outlaw?" Johnnie asked after we'd ridden a couple of miles.

"How the hell should I know?" I asked. "I doubt if any of them hardheaded miners were hurt bad, and I'm sure they appreciated the money falling from the sky, too. But still, I expect if there's a post office in Gibraltar there will likely be dodgers with descriptions of two cowboys that some people might think have at least a passin' resemblance to the two of us decoratin' its walls—and for some time to come."

Johnnie started laughing again and said, "I guess we ain't got nothing to worry about then, Casey, because there ain't no post office in Gibraltar—not anymore anyway!"

DuPont slowed our departure from Colorado considerably. Before leaving the rise we put him astraddle in front of me and every few miles from then on we would pass him back and forth. Sometimes he was conscious enough to almost stay in the saddle by himself and sometimes he flopped around like a rag doll. I don't think he was ever conscious enough to know what was going on or what had gone on. We kept a coat on him all the time because he had a bad case of the chills to go along with the, at times, terrible, terrible cough.

We got to the Little Snake River just as the east was beginning to lose its nighttime luster and begin fading into dawn. Although we knew the Little Snake at that point was just inside Wyoming, a geographic fact that made us feel some better, we were also aware of another geographic fact that did not make us feel better, especially after having ridden all night—we were still no more than twelve or fifteen miles from Gibraltar, which Johnnie had started referring to as the "shortest town in the Rockies."

"How is he?" Johnnie asked as we let the horses drink from the icy waters of the Little Snake.

"Bad," I said. "Badder'n a by-god. We better stop in Dixon and see if there's a doctor there. I don't think he'll last till we get to Rawlins."

Dixon had one street and its sign boasted twenty-five people. The only sign of life we saw, though, was a scruffty coyote with big wads of shaggy winter fur on his sides, prowling for roosting urban chickens. I knocked on the door of the Dixon Hotel, and finally a man in a long night shirt opened the door.

"We got a sick man," I said, gesturing toward the horses with my head.

"You from Gibraltar?"

"Huh . . . Yeah."

"What happened out there last night? What was that explosion about dark?"

"I don't know. . . . We need a doctor."

"I don't want trouble," the man said. "Anyway, there's no doctor here." And he closed the door.

"Hey!" I said. "Open the damn door!"

"Casey . . . ," Johnnie said. "Across the street."

Across the street a lantern had just been lit and was in the hands of a woman standing in an open doorway.

I walked across the street and stepped up onto the boardwalk in front of the woman. "We've got a sick man here, ma'am," I said as Johnnie was crossing the street, leading my horse and holding DuPont in his saddle.

"Fever. Chills. Cough. Maybe pneumonia . . . I don't know."

"He been in the mine?" she asked.

"Yes, ma'am, he has."

"Miner's lung," she said. "What was that explosion out there last night?"

I didn't answer, not right away, and I guess I was still trying to think of an answer when she asked, "You boys have some trouble out there?"

"Yes, ma'am," I said. "We did."

"You're not miners, are you?"

"No, ma'am—I guess if you got me or Johnnie in a mine you'd have to tie us up and drag us in."

"You cowhands?" she asked.

"Yes, ma'am, we are."

"From Texas?"

"And about ever'where else too," I said. "We don't want to cause you any trouble, ma'am, but—"

"Hell!" she said. "I've had trouble all my life—and most of it from cowboys. So why do I still have a likeness for 'em? Me and the girls take the miners' money, but we all agree that a drunken cowboy is preferable to a drunken miner any day. I'm Maybelle Bogus—Bogus Belle some call me. Bring your friend in . . . Only thing is, I don't want to know what happened at Gibraltar."

Maybelle Bogus led the way with her lantern down a short hall and opened the second door on the left. "Put

him on the bed and I'll make a hot cabbage poultice for
him and soak it in vinegar, and I'll see if I can get some hot
broth down him. . . . There's coffee on the stove for you
boys. It'll take at least an hour to do the poultice right."

"An hour?" I said. "I don't know—"

"Oh, come on!" Maybelle said. "How much trouble
could you get into in Gibraltar, for gosh sakes? There's
hardly even a town there!"

"Yes, ma'am, that's a truth if I ever heard it," Johnnie
said.

"Well, you boys just as well relax—a cabbage and vinegar poultice can draw infection out of a miner's lungs, but
it has to have time to work."

"Would you have any grain for the horses, ma'am?"
Johnnie asked.

"In the shed out back—help yourselves."

"Thank you, ma'am, I will," Johnnie said. "I'll lead the
horses around to the shed and get 'em off the street."

"I'll keep an eye toward the river," I said, seeing that it
was now light enough outside to see.

I poured myself a cup of coffee and carried it outside to
sit on the boardwalk. I rolled two cigarettes in the cool
morning air and smoked them with the coffee. We had
been up twenty-four hours by then, and without my realiz-
ing it, my eyelids slowly reached a point where they would
not obey my brain and stay up.

I don't know if it was a sixth sense telling me something was wrong that opened my eyes or if it was the sound
of Daniel D. Parke's shotgun coming to full cock in his
hands.

When my eyes opened, Parke was towering over me on
a brown horse and both barrels of the shotgun were staring
down at me.

I don't remember thinking about it, but I knew the only
cover I had was the head and neck of the brown horse
Parke was on and I rolled off the boardwalk toward his
forelegs as I slipped the leather loop off the hammer of my
old Colt.

The brown snorted and boogered and one barrel of the
shotgun went off in my ear, at least it sounded like it did,

and my left side went numb. I didn't know how bad I was
hit, just that I was on my back and my eyes were full of
dirt and my left side was now on fire. But through that dirt
I saw the brown's hooves and eyes and nostrils—black
hooves, big eyes, flared nostrils.

And I heard Parke cussing the "brown son of a bitch!"
and somehow I still had the strength to bring the heavy
Colt up and thumb back the hammer. Then I remember
lying there in the Dixon dirt, thinking I was dying but just
waiting for the brown's head to clear out of the way, and
like everything was moving in molasses it slowly did move
enough so I could see Parke in the saddle.

I could see the muzzle of the shotgun falling toward me
again and I squeezed the trigger and the Colt jumped in
my hand.

The shotgun roared in my face again and for a second I
was both blind and deaf.

Then my ears started ringing and I saw the brown running south down the short street, but Parke wasn't on him
anymore.

Then I saw Parke. He was fifteen feet away, on his
back, twitching and staring up at the Wyoming morning
sky with blood soaking the front of his shirt and a little
stream of it coming from his mouth and running down his
cheek into the dirt.

Johnnie came running through the door, carrying a rifle,
and stopped on the boardwalk to look at me and then at
Parke.

"The son of a bitch," I said, but the burning along my
left side was too much. I dropped the Colt and laid down
on my back in the street.

"Casey!" Johnnie said and knelt beside me.

"What does it look like, Johnnie?" I managed to ask. "I
don't want to look."

By then Maybelle and three of her girls were in the
street, looking down at me.

Johnnie unbuttoned my shirt, pulled it open, and
looked at my side. Then he felt up and down my left leg
and left arm. I saw him look up at Maybelle, but he didn't
say anything.

"That bad?" I asked.

"I'm afraid it is, Casey," he said, shaking his head as he stood up. He dropped something on my chest. "I don't see how in the hell you'll ever wipe your nose again with your left hand."

I looked to see what had landed on my chest. . . . It was the tip of a thumb!

I held my left hand up in front of my face and saw where that particular thumb tip had come from.

"You can get up now, Casey," Johnnie said casually. "One of Parke's shotgun blasts must have been close enough so the shot ricocheted off the ground and hit you, but hell, it didn't even break the skin—'cept for that thumb! And we ought to get the bleedin' stopped."

Under the circumstances, the thumb I held in my hand as I sat up seemed like a miracle, and I couldn't have been more pleased to hold it.

Although my side still burned some—but nothing like it did when I thought it had been shredded to the back-bone—and the stump where the tip of my left thumb had been was throbbing and hurting some, when I looked at Johnnie and saw that look on his face I couldn't help laughing, and although it was a crazy time and place to do it, we both laughed until we cried and I had to lay back down in the street.

But we knew we had to get out of Dixon and get out quick. We were lucky, *damn* lucky, that Parke had come there alone, but there had to be others from Gibraltar looking for us as well.

"What about him?" I asked, looking at Parke.

Maybelle shook her head. "Don't worry about him. I'll put a blanket over him, and I'm sure somebody else from the mine will be here shortly. I don't know what you boys did out there, but it sure must have been something big, for Parke to come gunning for you."

"What about you, Maybelle? Will this get you in trouble?"

"Naw," she said. "No reason why it should—I'm not going to cover for you boys. I'll tell the truth to whoever. You came with a sick man needing help and I helped you all I could. Parke came at you with a shotgun and fired first—I know the difference in sound between a shotgun and a Colt. And I'll tell the law or anybody else that's what happened—*why* it happened I don't know and I'm glad I don't. Now you boys best get your friend and get on out of here. The boys from the mine can't get rough with us because we've got a corner on the market of what they can't get out of the ground and they know it.

"I don't know if your friend is going to survive the miner's lung or not. The poultice I put on him will help, and so will getting him down here in warmer and drier air, but I don't know—he could go either way. Here"—she handed a long-necked bottle up to Johnnie—"this is brandy with quinine in it. Try to get at least three swallows of it down him each day."

As we were riding out of Dixon, Johnnie stopped his horse and turned around to look down the street where Maybelle was spreading a blanket over Parke's body. "My God, Casey," he said. "Ridin' with you is like ridin' with Plague and Pestilence and I pity the next poor town we come across."

Maybelle's cabbage and vinegar poultice seemed to have helped DuPont, at least for the time being, which was a good thing because we were now completely soured on the idea of going to Rawlins or anywhere else within a hundred miles of Gibraltar to find a doctor. If anybody from Gibraltar came gunning for us again, they wouldn't find one of us lounging on the boardwalk of a whorehouse.

DuPont's chill was better and his coughing spells were at least further apart, if not less severe. The first night out from Dixon—which was actually only twenty-four hours after leaving Gibraltar—he was even conscious enough to ask, in a weak voice, where he was and where he was being taken but then immediately fell into such a fit of coughing that he was completely worn out by it, and when it finally passed he fell immediately into a deep sleep.

The next morning, with me holding his head and feeding him, he even ate a little pemmican and sipped a little coffee into which I had poured a little of the quinine brandy that Maybelle Bogus had given us.

Johnnie had been watching me, and when I laid Du-Pont's head down and walked over to where the horses were hobbled and threw the saddle on my horse's back he said, "I've done some strange things in my life, Casey, and I've seen even more strange things done—but I have never once seen or even heard of anything as strange as this thing here."

I looked at him, but I didn't want to talk to him. My left side was bruised and sore, and the end of my left thumb ached and throbbed . . . and my heart was in a state of confusion and despair.

"You've leveled a whole goddamn town and killed a man just to save the life of a man you wish was—"

"I killed Parke because he was trying to kill me!"

"But why were we in Gibraltar—because of DuPont Sevier? . . . You took a chance on getting yourself—and me—killed, just to save the life of a man you wish were already dead! Now go ahead and tell me just how logical that is, Casey."

"Yeah, I wish DuPont Sevier was dead," I said. "But for some goddamn reason that son of a bitch keeps drawing one breath after another, and as long as he does, I've got to do my best by him or lie to Miroux, and I could never do that. For some reason she thinks I'm a better person than I really am—so I have to *be* a better person than I really am . . . a better person than I *want* to be!"

We swung south of Rawlins and north of the highest mountains in the Medicine Bow Range, and for the next two days we made decent time and never saw another person. And for those two days DuPont stayed about the same, but then he started getting worse again. His chills came back, his breathing grew more shallow, his cough was still terrible, and he was unable to eat or drink.

"I figure we're half a day out of Medicine Bow," I said. "Tomorrow, I'm taking DuPont there and gettin' him a doctor. You're not obligated to go, Johnnie—you're not obligated to me for anything and I thank you for what you've done."

"Well, as long as I'm not obligated," he said, "I think I'll just tag along to see what kind of mayhem and destruction you bring to Medicine Bow . . . besides, now I'm curious as hell how this is all gonna turn out!"

In Medicine Bow we stopped underneath a sign hanging over the door of an unpainted frame building that said: JEREMY BLAKE, M.D.

I knocked on the door, and it was opened by a small man with gray hair and gray, bushy eyebrows, wearing eyeglasses and a white shirt with suspenders but no tie.

I pointed toward the horses, where Johnnie was holding DuPont in the saddle in front of him.

"What's wrong with him?" he asked.

"Chills, cough, and full of lung slime," I said.

"Who is he?"

"The damn fine husband of a friend of Casey's," Johnnie said.

"Bring him in and lay him on the bed and take his shirt off," Blake said.

Doctor Blake opened DuPont's eyes—by then DuPont could not open them by himself—and looked into them. Then he listened to his chest and rolled him on his side and listened to his back.

"How long has he been like this?" he asked.

"We don't know for sure," I said. "We found him like this a few days ago."

"From his emaciated condition, I'd say he's been ill for a long time. He's consumptive, has suffered severe and most likely chronic lung damage, and is on the threshold of death."

"What do we do?" I asked.

"You leave him here and I'll do what I can for him. We'll see which side of that threshold he and the Lord choose."

Johnnie and I made camp along the Medicine Bow River just outside of town. We seemed to have gotten far enough away from Gibraltar that what happened there was either unknown or uncared about, and for the first time in a while we were able to rest a little. But resting meant thinking, and thinking about what I had to think about meant there was no rest for me.

The next day I went to see about DuPont.

Doctor Blake was gruff as an old bear. "It's too soon to tell. When there is some significant change, I'll let you know. In the meantime I don't want you coming around here, making a nuisance of yourself!"

So the days began to pass as we camped along the Medicine Bow River and they were hell, those days. Idle time is most men's undoing, and so it was with me and Johnnie—mine was spent thinking of Miroux and reliving the time we'd had together and waiting. I tried to write Miroux, started a dozen letters—all of which wound up in the fire with only the words "My Dearest Miroux" on them.

Johnnie's idle time was spent in the time-honored fashion of most cowboys—going on drinking binges and coming back to camp drunk.

"It's been hell for you, ain't it, Casey?" he said one afternoon after we had been there ten days. "You just take life too goddamn serious. If DuPont beats the reaper it won't be the end of the world, you know. Hell's bells, I can show you at least two half-breed whores, if that's what you like. And you don't need to worry about Miroux none either—hell, ever'one knows a breed don't care who's between her legs, just so somebody is."

"Johnnie," I said, "if you wasn't drunk, I'd dot your goddamn eye for that."

"Well, if that's what you want to do, you shouldn't let me bein' drunk stop you," he said.

"For once in your life, you're right," I said, nodding my head. And then I hit him about as hard as I could with a short, right-cross on his left cheek bone that split the skin, brought the blood, and staggered him backward a couple of steps.

"You son of a bitch!" he said, looking at the blood on the back of his right hand where he'd touched it to his left cheek.

"There ain't no truth at all in what you said about Miroux."

Johnnie leaned over and let the blood run into the dirt. "That's what you said about Lillie Johnson too . . . but it turned out I was right, after all. Remember?" I thought the fight was over with, but knowing Johnnie as many years as I had, I should have known better—he straightened up and hit me in the left eye so hard I'd have swore he drove my eyeball out the back of my skull.

We were about to really get started when a stranger rode up.

We both looked at the shod hooves and the legs of a red roan horse, then I followed the legs on up and saw a man wearing a sheriff's badge, leaning on his saddlehorn and looking down at us.

"I don't mean to interfere with your fun, boys," he said with a stupid grin, "but are you the ones that's got a friend at Doc Blake's?"

"Yeah," I said, spitting blood and dirt out of my mouth, "we're the ones—why?"

"Blake says you'd better come get over to his office."

"What's happened?" I asked.

"He didn't say for sure—just something about some decision made by God and somebody else about something."

When we trotted around the corner where we could see Doctor Blake's office we saw him talking to a pale man in a dark suit underneath his sign.

Me and Johnnie looked at each other and he said, "An undertaker if I ever saw one."

The pale man in the dark suit and Doctor Blake finished their conversation as we stopped in front of the doctor's office.

"Hello, Doctor Blake," I said as I tossed the gray I was on some slack in the reins. "You sent for us?"

"Hello, gentlemen," Blake said as he looked up at us. "Yes, I *did* send for you—maybe you should get off and come into the office."

Me and Johnnie looked at each other again, then we got off and tied the horses to the railing while Doctor Blake waited for us just inside his open doorway.

"What is it, Doc?" Johnnie asked.

"Something best handled on the private side of the threshold," he said in a solemn voice.

We stepped through the door and saw that a curtain had been pulled in front of the bed where DuPont had been lying when we left him there.

Doctor Blake closed the door and pulled a bottle of Jim Beam off the top shelf of a medicine cabinet in the corner of the room and poured a little into each of three glasses, saying, "This is something that requires at least a modest imbibing of distilled spirits."

"Good lord, Doc," Johnnie said as he reached out and took his glass of Beam, "I never needed a man's dyin' as an excuse for a drink."

"We're not drinking to dying or to death, but to life," Blake said. "Not to mention a good bit of damn fine doctoring."

With that the doctor stepped to the curtain and pushed it to one side and we saw a pale, terribly thin, but clean and clean-shaven man sitting on the edge of the bed.

I studied him for a few seconds.

"DuPont . . . ?"

His eyes were sunk far back into his head and his voice was weak. *"Oui . . ."*

"Good gawd," Johnnie said.

"Surprised, gentlemen?" Blake asked with a satisfied grin.

DuPont covered his mouth, coughed twice, then asked in a raspy voice, "Are you the ones who brought me here? The ones Doctor Blake said were friends of my wife? Did Miroux send you? How is she?"

Johnnie whistled low, said, "Holy catheron," under his breath, and walked out the door.

"She's fine." In a few seconds I said to the doctor, "Can he ride?"

"In a few days."

I nodded and walked outside. When we were in our saddles again I looked down at Doctor Blake. "We'll get him a horse and saddle. What will we owe you?"

"I've figured it . . . thirteen and a half dollars."

I stood up in my stirrups, dug the money I had left out of my pocket, counted out thirteen and a half dollars, and handed it to him. "I'd like for you to write a letter for me—send it to Sheriff Gowers at Chadron, Nebraska."

"All right," Blake said, writing in his notebook. "And what do I tell this Sheriff Gowers?"

"Write this—Please inform Mrs. DuPont Sevier that her husband is alive and will be home soon."

"All right . . . and how do I sign it?"

"Your name," I said.

"And do I mention you?"

"No—you don't mention me at all. Just write what I said and mail it."

Johnnie went into town that night to get drunk again.

I stayed at camp and got drunk alone, trying to not think of anything—not the Niobrara and the home I'd built on it, not my dreams, not Miroux or the look that would come over her face when Sheriff Gowers told her about the letter he'd received from a Doctor Blake in Medicine Bow, Wyoming.

Maybe DuPont was a naturally quiet man. Maybe he was quiet because he was weak. Or maybe he was quiet because he just didn't like me or Johnnie. Whatever the reason, he said very little on the five-day ride from the Medicine Bow River in Wyoming to where the Niobrara sliced through the sand hills of Nebraska.

On a day in the first week of June, when the grass in the sand hills was green and the bluebells were blooming, late in the afternoon when the sun was disappearing in the far, far west and the air was beginning to cool and to smell damp, we topped a rise on the south side of the Niobrara at a place where it made a bend to the south and where across the river one could see a heavy stand of cedars and, at the edge of those cedars, a homestead with corrals and a barn and a cabin with a dog run in between, all underneath the same tin roof.

"Mister Sevier," I said, "your wife will probably be down there at that homestead—if not, she'll be at your place."

"Aren't you coming with me?" he asked.

"No," I said. "We have things to do and need to be about 'em."

"I . . . I don't know how to properly thank you," he said, and then coughed several times. "I know what all you have done . . ."

"No, Mister Sevier," Johnnie said seriously, "you ain't got a goddamn clue."

DuPont Sevier reached out and shook our hands and said, "I do not understand, but *merci*, Casey Wills and Johnnie Lester—*merci*."

We watched the Frenchman ride down the sandy slope toward the river.

"That's it, ain't it, Casey," Johnnie said. "That place down there is your place."

"Let's go," I said.

"What do you mean 'Let's go'?"

"I mean, by God, *let's go*! You understand plain English, don't you?"

"But . . . go where?"

"Since when did you give a damn?"

"But what about your place? What about that felt mattress and all that furniture you bought? . . . What about Miroux? . . . Aren't you . . . ?"

I reined the gray around. "Are you coming?"

"You're leavin'—just like *that*?"

"Just like that," I said.

"What about your other horses?"

"We can both see they're not in the corrals down there. Miroux took them with her, or else they're runnin' free somewhere."

"But that's the place you've been drawin' in the sand of a hundred creek beds on a hundred cow outfits. You built all that down there with your own hands. . . . Why would you just ride away from it? So we brought DuPont back alive—and so you lost all your money—that doesn't mean you have to leave your place!"

I knew Johnnie would never understand why I had to just leave it all behind—why there wasn't even a choice. Why it would be impossible for me to live there now, even without Miroux just only a few miles away—a distance not near great enough. Even without that, there were too many memories in and around that log cabin, too many memories in the murmuring waters of the Niobrara along whose banks my *kukasa* had been touched. Some things we do in this world are not of our choosing—to leave was no more a choice for me than it would be for the sweetness to leave the blades of grass on the sand hills when the killing frosts of fall settled on it.

A coyote on some hilltop a long ways away barked a few times and finished with a long, lonesome howl.

"Hear that?" I asked. "The Big Lonely's calling again and . . ."

By then DuPont had crossed the river and had just stepped off his horse in front of the cabin. I should have already been riding away instead of still sitting on top of the ridge, watching the cabin.

I shouldn't have seen Miroux come out of the door and stand underneath the edge of the dog run for a few seconds and then run into DuPont's arms as he stepped off his horse. Did she look up toward the ridge at me at all?

I shouldn't have seen them in each other's arms as man and wife.

Johnnie saw them, too. He looked down at them and then looked at me.

"Casey . . . ," he said.

"It don't matter," I said as I reined my horse around. "Let's drift."

22

I took the glasses off to clean them and to rub my sore ears for the fourteenth time that day. "I can't believe that all of a sudden I'm forty-six years old and wearin' glasses," I said. "But at least now I can tell those are cows down there in that draw instead of bushes."

"I'm just hopin' it'll make you a better hand," Johnnie said. "I am sick and tired of havin' to go behind you and gather stock—not to mention embarrassed as hell."

"The day *you* have to gather *anything* behind me, Johnnie, will be the day they freight ice out of hell!"

We were drifting across west Texas in the spring of '94. We had noticed that over the last couple of years work seemed to be getting harder to find—at least work that a self-respecting cowboy would tolerate—and we were on our way to south Texas. We knew of a few outfits where we had always been able to find work whenever we needed it—Ike Holt's Slash Seven outfit along the Hondo River west of San Antonio being one of those. Besides, we hadn't seen Ike since we sold the Banister horses in the Nations in April of '89, and we wouldn't feel right about being in his part of Texas and not stopping to say hello.

We heard a train whistle blow in the distance. "When'd

they put a damn train through here?" Johnnie asked. "Why, the last time we were here there wasn't a train within two hundred miles."

"It's called the march of civilization, Johnnie—and it's slowly puttin' men like us out of business. A steer or a cow can step in a boxcar in Goliad on Monday and be in Great Falls in time for Mass on Sunday."

"I've heard that, but even if it were true, it costs too damn much. And, let's say, one of them steers or cows jumps overboard and throws its head up and heads for the tules. What's that railroad gonna do then—blow its god-damn whistle and try to whistle it back?" He took his rope down, shook out a loop, then dropped the horn loop over the saddlehorn and pulled it snug. "No railroad can take the place of a good cowboy on a good horse, Casey. And just to demonstrate that principle to you I'll line one of them cows down there in the draw and choke her a little for you. You might want to clean them glasses again while I'm trottin' down there so your old eyes can take it all in, and if your senile old brain can remember back that far you might recall a time when you could handle a twine *nearly* as good as me." Johnnie was eleven months younger than me and he loved to remind me of that, and the older we got, the more he seemed to love it.

I watched Johnnie trot toward the cows in the draw for a few seconds before I jerked my rope down. When I passed him I was shaking out a loop of my own, and the race was on to see who could get to the cows and rope one first.

Drifting was not as easy as it had once been because of all the barbed-wire fences cutting up what once had been all open range, but sometimes even we took advantage of civi-lization's march. That night was one of those times—we camped beside a windmill and turned our horses loose in the water lot around it.

We were in our bedrolls not long after sundown, listen-ing to the windmill work slow and steady and the doves coo in the big cottonwood in the corner of the water lot.

"Your knees ever bother you, Casey?" Johnnie asked.

"Naw," I said. "Hell no! And neither does my shoulder."

"You ever think about Miroux much?"

"Who? Oh, her—aw . . . naw . . . hell no . . . not much," I said.

"You're a lyin' bastard, Casey—ever' now and then you still call out her name in your sleep. I wonder how that damn DuPont is?"

"Probably richer'n a foot up a bull's butt by now and living in some place like Kansas City or maybe even Montreal," I said.

"Yeah, probably—and just think, Miroux coulda had you and that one-room shanty along the Niobrara instead?"

"Yeah," I said and laughed, "just think."

We rode into Ike Holt's ranch headquarters a few days later, and asked some cowboys hanging around the bunkhouse where we might find Ike.

"He's up there at the big white house on the hill," said a tall, slim cowboy about our age, sitting on the edge of the first bunk. "I'm Pilot Judd, and I'm the cow boss, and I can tell you that if you're looking for work I do the hirin' and firin' and right now I ain't doing either—we're full up."

"We've known Ike for a while and just wanted to say hello."

"He's pretty busy," Judd said.

"Much obliged," I said. We stepped back outside and let the screen door slam behind us.

"Is it just me," I said as we started walking the short distance to the big white house on the hill, "or is there something about Pilot Judd that makes him as lovable as a ringtailed mare."

"I guess it's just you, Casey—he seems like a damn fine feller to me and one I'd love to punch cows for."

Then we heard someone behind us yell out our names and we stopped and turned around.

"Hell," Johnnie said as a cowboy stepped out of the bunkhouse, "ain't that the Mexican kid we called Help, who worked for us when we were gatherin' those Banister horses?"

"Yeah," I said, looking over the man coming toward us. "But he's not a kid anymore. He's taller than we are."

"Casey—Johnnie. You remember me?" he said when he reached us.

"Why hell, yes, we do," Johnnie said and we each shook his hand. "We were just talkin', though, that you've grown up since you helped us gather the Banister horses."

"Yes, sir," he said, "I'm twenty years old now."

"We just called you Help before," I said.

"It's Juan Corona."

"So you went ahead and made a cowboy, huh," Johnnie said. "I thought maybe you had the makin's when you were with us."

"Is that why you used to say, 'Hell, I've seen widder women who were more help!'?"

Me and Johnnie both laughed because we—and Ab, too—had chewed him out unmercifully at times.

"Well, I want you to know," Juan Corona said, "I learned a lot from all of you. You taught me good and got me started right. I've been on quite a few outfits in the last five years, and I learn something new about handlin' broncs and ringy cattle everywhere I go. And it makes me proud to be able to sit around the wagon at night and tell my own Casey Wills and Johnnie Lester stories—the story about Ab gettin' killed at that Rawhider Camp and then Johnnie killing Lon McDanials and us leavin' their camp with all them Banister horses has got to be sort of a legend, you know."

"You know, Juan," Johnnie said, "some history is best left in the gullet."

"I even heard a story not long ago that you even blew up a whole town a few years ago!"

"Hearing about something doesn't necessarily make it true. . . . How long you been working for Ike?"

"Just started a few days ago. When I told Mister Holt that I was with you all when you were gathering the Banister horses he told Pilot to find a place for me because anybody that Casey Wills and Johnnie Lester would think enough of to hire was the kind of cowboy he wanted on his payroll. I think it sort of galled Pilot, but he had to put me to work. And now you're here, too. We've been gathering steers to take north in a few days! Say—y'all ain't goin' too, are you?"

"Done been," I said, "and more than once. Besides Judd said he was full up."

"There's always room for good hands on this outfit!" a voice interrupted.

We turned around, and Ike Holt was almost already within hand-shaking distance. He was older and thinner, but grinning from ear to ear. "By God! It's good to see you two boys!" he said. "Come on up to the house and we'll have a drink—God, I haven't seen you boys since you paid me for the Banister horses you gathered and sold in the Nations. With the money you made on those high-steppin' little darlin's, I guess you've got your own outfit now."

"Well, not exactly," Johnnie said. "I invested mine in a whorehouse in Cheyenne and it was a wise and wonderful investment that paid unbelievable dividends for almost a year. Old Casey, though—hell, it was BANG! and his was gone, just like that."

Inside, after we'd passed the Old Crow around the first time, Ike looked at us and said, "Boys, if you haven't got anything pressing for a while, how about going up the trail to the Tongue River Reservation with my outfit?"

"Montana?" I said. "Damn—there's a hell of a lot of geography between the Hondo and the Tongue, Ike . . . and most of it we've done seen."

"Well, I wasn't offering it to you so as to further your geographic enrichment," Ike said with a smile. "It's damn important that my cattle reach the Tongue River Reservation by the first of September, and I need hands like you to help get them there on time."

"Why don't you ship 'em on a goddamn train?" Johnnie asked. "I hear they're the cat's meow in takin' cattle north now."

"I could—and I've thought about it. But the cattle market went to hell a few years ago and is just now starting to come back. I'm in deep debt to the bank in San Anton' and I need this government contract to keep them from foreclosing. The way I figure it, I can keep a trail outfit on the trail for five hundred dollars a month, which means I can drive my steers all the way to Montana for about a dollar a head and make a four-dollar-a-head profit. Or, I can ship 'em on the train and be sure of getting the contract, but it'll cost ten dollars a head to do that, which would mean I'd lose six dollars a head—and lose everything to the bank. If I can get the cattle up there by delivery date by trailin' them I'll get the contract *and* make money. And if I get the contract from the government the bank will extend my note.

"I wish I could offer to put either one of you in charge, but I already have Pilot Judd for that, so the best I can offer you is regular cowboy wages—thirty a month. I'd love to go with the herd myself, but I just can't."

"Hell, Ike," Johnnie said, "if you needed the help we'd help you for nothin', but we met Judd down in the bunkhouse and he said he was already full up."

Ike looked at us over the neck of the Old Crow bottle and said, "He may be full up with 'hands' but not with cowboys—and besides this is still my goddamn outfit!" Then Ike calmed down and said, "Pilot's not as important as he sometimes thinks he is, but he's a good hand—give him a little time to get used to you and you'll see. Will you go, boys? I really need you to. If we get the herd there on time, I'll even pay to bring all the hands and the best part of the remuda back to Texas on the train."

"Well, you've made it impossible for me to say no," Johnnie said. "I've been achin' to ride one of them clankity-clank sonsabitches for a long time, and I guess if I have to ride all the way to the Tongue River in Montana to get a free seat I will. . . . But now, Ike, old Casey here needs someone to take care of him while I'm gone. Is there an old folk's home in town that's got some old widow woman in it that's good at cleanin' glasses?"

What else could I do? I looked at Johnnie and Ike and smiled and took another pull on the Crow. I did not look upon a fifteen- or sixteen-hundred-mile trail drive with anywhere near the enthusiasm Juan Corona did, but it was work and Ike Holt was a good man to draw wages from, having the mind of a cowboy more than a cowman.

It was dark when we left Ike's house, so we unrolled our beds underneath the oak tree in front of the bunkhouse and slept there. The next morning when we stirred to life the only light we could see was coming from the cookhouse where a dried-up man with a white beard and white hair already had the coffee made.

Me and Johnnie walked in, introduced ourselves, and were greeted with a "Howdy, fellers, grab yourselves a cup of dip. I'm Billy Meeks. I've heard of you boys and I can tell by your looks this ain't gonna be your first trip up the boulevard," so for half an hour we talked to Billy Meeks about punchers we knew and drank black coffee and smoked Bull Durham before the other hands started coming into the cookhouse.

Juan came in with Bronc Kinkaid, a puncher of about thirty—a damn fine hand we'd worked with one time in the San Simón country of Arizona.

In another few minutes the other hands came in. Luther Atkins was in his mid-twenties and the possessor of a mouth full of crooked stained teeth; he would handle the remuda on the trail. Ramus Knight, almost a youngster, was no older than Juan. Lewis Anacho was part Apache and as quiet as Laredo Allen was talkative; Allen, in his early twenties and a flashy dresser, thought he wrote the book on women. Then there was Jim Napp, the drunk every outfit has to have but, like most of them, a good hand only until the neck oil worked its way to his brain.

Pilot Judd came in and filled his plate while we were eating, but didn't have much to say except "We kick 'em off the first bed ground at sunup in two days. Luther, when you bring the remuda in, catch these horses for the two new hands—they'll be the horses in their strings." He laid a slip of paper on the table by Luther's plate.

Luther looked at the names on the paper a few seconds, then glanced at our end of the table and smiled.

Being the last two men on the payroll and the last two to be assigned horses from the remuda it would only be natural to get something less than a top string of horses. Add to that the fact that we were hired by the owner himself after being told by the segundo that *he* did the hiring and the firing, it would also only be natural that the segundo would assign us the worst string of horses he could. . . . As a matter of fact, Johnnie and I concluded that had either of us been the cow boss and Ike hired somebody over our heads we would have rolled our beds and said adios. In fact, and under the circumstances, had it been anybody but Ike we would not have agreed at all to go up the trail with the outfit. It put Pilot Judd in an embarrassing position, and although he seemed to us to be an embarrassment to himself, neither could we exactly hold it against him for giving us the something less than the something less he gave us in the way of horseflesh.

The funny thing about it though was this: the worst of Ike Holt's horses were dreams compared to the best on a lot of the outfits where me and Johnnie had unrolled our beds. Of the ten head each we were given, there did not seem to be a single one who would go out of their way to kill either of us, though we each had two or three who would surely not pass up the opportunity should it present itself.

The cattle Ike had to get to the Tongue River Reservation were 2280 head of three- and four-year-old steers with at least half-longhorn blood in them. They looked like they were made for the trail—unlike a lot of the so-called "up-bred" cattle of Angus, Hereford, or Durham blood who had legs so short they could walk all day and not get out of the shade of a single, respectable south Texas oak. The looks of the cattle making up Ike's herd plus the fact that we were leaving the first of May, giving us four full months to cover roughly fifteen hundred miles plus a few extra, made me have no misgivings about Ike getting his government contract.

"Under ordinary circumstances I would agree with you," Johnnie said that last night in the bunkhouse as all the cowboys except Luther and Judd were intellectualizing about religion, politics, and women—the things they knew the most about.

"If that's the case," I said, "then I suppose we've never come upon an ordinary circumstance yet, because I fail to remember one time you've ever agreed with me."

"Well," he said, "I would for sure this time, except for this fact—I've put the pencil to it and the way I figure it is that the number of days divided by the number of miles in this saunter equals thirteen, and if that ain't a forebodin' omen then there ain't a whore in Helena."

"Speaking of whores," Laredo Allen said, "I don't care if there's nary a one in Helena and I don't worry about some old geezer dividin' this by that and comin' up with something else—what I want to know is how many whores there are between here and the Tongue River Reservation—hell, I'm a young virile man with wavels the size of grapefruit!"

"Well, young man," Bronc Kinkaid said, "I have news for you. They don't call a saddle a 'cod buster' for nothing, and by the time we get to Doan's Crossing those grapefruit will be the size of lemon . . . seeds!"

That was the ante for the next round of laughter and banter in the stuffy, coal-oil lighted, Bull Durham-smoked bunkhouse. I slipped out the door to go outside and smoke a cigarette underneath the oak tree and listen to a Texas coyote sing his lonesome nighttime melody to a million stars along the Hondo River. While that melody was still playing among the stars, a cool, fresh breeze touched my face in a way that suddenly reminded me of the smell and feel of soft black hair falling against the same cheek but from another time and place and along another river.

On the second of May, just as there was enough light to see a steer at a hundred yards but before the sun broke day, we rode to a fenced-in trap about a mile from headquarters. Our beds were in the chuck wagon, and Billy had gone on ahead to where we'd stop the herd at noon to change horses and eat.

Just before we scattered out in the trap to gather the steers and point them north along what had come to be called the Western Trail—Johnnie and I both were more than a little familiar with it—Pilot Judd pulled up and said, "Boys, me and Bronc will count 'em through the gate, and then I want Bronc and Jim ridin' point, Lewis, Laredo, Ramus, and Juan on swing, and Casey and Johnnie on the drag."

I looked at Johnnie and he winked and smiled. Bronc and Jim were the only other cowboys in the outfit who had been up the trail before, and neither of them had made half as many trips up it as me or Johnnie. Laredo, Ramus, and Juan were really still just kids, yet Judd had put me and Johnnie on the drag, the position always given to the least experienced hands, the bottom of the ladder on a trail outfit. I would be lying if I said it didn't sting, not because I thought I was too good to ride drag, but because it was as obvious as the dun ears on the dun horse underneath me that Judd was putting us in our places and making a point to do it in front of the whole crew, too.

I saw the other cowboys glancing at us, wondering if we were going to say anything, all of them as aware as we were what Judd had done. But we didn't say anything. It had always been my philosophy, and Johnnie's too, that if you didn't like something on whatever outfit or trail herd you were with you had the option to roll your bed or put up with it. Bellyaching and complaining were not an option. We had promised Ike we'd go north with his herd and do whatever we could to get them to the Tongue River Reservation by the first of September—and if we had to ride drag all the way to fulfill that promise, then we would.

Besides, riding drag on a herd of three- and four-year-old longhorn-cross steers would be easy except for being where the dust from about twelve thousand hooves would be the thickest. Steers of that age and breed, once they are trail broke, will get off the bed ground and string out and move like a snake through the grass. The only ones that have to be "driven" are the sore-foots and occasional cripples—just keep them pointed in the right direction, keep the flanks from widening out too much, and let them walk. So, other than hurting our sensitive pride a little, the come-uppance Judd had given us didn't amount to much. "Besides," I told Juan as we were waiting for the steers to make their way through the gate out of the trap and onto the trail, "maybe it'll make Pilot quit ringin' his tail and make him easier to get along with."

I had had some understanding of Pilot Judd's feelings about the way Johnnie and I were put in his crew, but I thought his feathers were just ruffled and things would work themselves out in a short time. Ike had said he would be okay, and I had faith not only in Ike's judgment of his personality but also of his cow sense. That was why I couldn't believe it when after two hours of hard riding back and forth and we'd finally gotten the herd to start stringing out on the trail, he loped back to the tail end and waved Johnnie and me to him and said, "I want the drags pushed up more! Don't let them mess along and get lazy on you. We need to push them hard for the first few days so they'll be tired and ready to rest when we bed 'em down at night. Keep the drags pushed up into the rest of the herd. The closer we get to the bed grounds each day the more important it is to push, push, push, so they'll be so tired they won't even consider running."

Me and Johnnie just looked at each other for a few seconds after Judd rode off, then Johnnie pulled the makings out of his vest pocket, began rolling a smoke, and said, "Where in the hell . . . ? Why in the hell . . . ? What'n in the hell did Ike do—save up his Arbuckle's coupons and get 'im a trail boss? You don't push the goddamn drags up on a herd like this as long as they're keeping up—if you do, you'll just cause the tail end to fan out and then you *really* have hell! And hell and by God, can you imagine what's gonna happen if he don't give 'em time to fill up with grass and water before we push 'em onto the bed grounds?"

"Yeah, Johnnie," I said, "and if it don't happen tonight, it'll sure as hell happen by the third night."

I was wrong.

It didn't happen until the fourth night—although how those steers put it off that long has always been a mystery to me. Not only did Judd insist on putting them on the bed ground tired and with empty stomachs, he was also prone to picking the bottom of a wide draw to bed them on—not the high ground that would catch the cool summer night breezes and where the longhorns instinctively would feel more secure from things that go sneaking through the dark of night.

The first night, though, was not without incident, one of which would plague us for some time. Luther Atkins brought the remuda in late in the afternoon so we could catch our night horses. After we had done so, but while the remuda was still behind the rope corral, Bronc Kinkaid said to Judd, "I guess you want to hobble the remuda."

"No," Judd said, "Luther can handle the horses."

"They'll be hard to handle tonight," Bronc said. "The smell of their just-left home is still in the air, and if they do get away, they'll head for it like a Baptist to a bottle."

"The point is," Judd extolled, "if they're goin' to run, then it's better they do it now and get it out of their systems. Like you say, at least if they run from here, we'll *know* where to find them come daylight."

The real point, of course, was not to let them run at all. As Bronc and nearly everyone else in the outfit with the possible exception of Ramus Knight and Laredo Allen knew, you always hobbled the whole remuda with short ropes until they were trail broke and several days from home—it took some extra time in the evenings to hobble a hundred and fifteen or twenty head of horses, but it was time well spent.

What boogered the horses that night was anybody's guess. And whether it was a real danger or one only concocted inside a horsehide covered skull from a low-growing shinnery bush did not matter one bit, because after that first horse boogered and snorted and started to run, every horse in the remuda suddenly started to.

We moved the herd only about three miles north that day after riding all the way back to the ranch on our night horses and getting the remuda. But much more important than that was the fact that once horses have been spooked as badly as they were, for whatever reason, they don't get over it quickly; they're much more on edge at night, constantly on the lookout for the monster they barely got away from before.

"And," volunteered Jim Napp on one of the rare occasions he volunteered an opinion on anything, "when you have somebody jinglin' horses who don't savvy any more about them than Luther does, then you got trouble aplenty and for a long time."

And trouble aplenty was what we had with the horses, until Pilot finally decided we'd better hobble them at night for a while, but even after that they were spooky at night and ready to scatter—and did three more times—for the next two weeks.

The run the steers had on the fourth night out wasn't bad and was caused by Lewis Anacho's night horse stepping in a gopher hole and falling while Lewis was walking him around the herd. In fact, it was a pitiful excuse of a run, especially for a herd that had every right to be on edge, and it seemed that most of the steers were just waiting for some cowboy to get in front of them and bend them into a mill. But still, by morning they were scattered over several miles and we lost a day getting them thrown together again.

"You fellers are so damn good at this," Billy Meeks said as we were eating supper on that fourth afternoon, "that you ought to consider takin' it up professionally. Why here it is, only the fourth day on the trail, and we must be—aw, hell—we must already be twenty miles from the ranch!"

"Well, I warned you," Johnnie said as he wiped his mouth on his sleeve and dropped his tin plate into the washtub filled with hot water. "Y'all remember what I said about them whores in Helena?"

"Yeah," Laredo Allen snapped, "didn't you say that since there was only thirteen of them it would be unlucky for me to woo them all in one night?"

A few days later, at a place called Indian Lakes—seven rocky-bottomed lakes filled with crystal clear water and about a mile from one to the next—we lost six days and seventeen steers. The trail from the lakes went almost due north, there was no doubt or question about that, just like there was no doubt or question that for some reason two herds on the trail ahead of us that spring had veered off the trail toward the northwest. We did not veer to the northwest, just like we did not make an effort to find out why the others had. Of course, most of us had a pretty good idea why and had discussed it among ourselves even after Judd made the decision to stay with the trail—water. The trail north of Indian Lakes was drier than seven kinds of hell and the scattered watering holes that were usually there were not even decent bogs. One after another of them, dry—dry, dry, dry.

About midday of the second day out from the lakes Judd finally decided he ought to ride ahead and find water and told Bronc to keep the herd moving north at all cost. But Bronc and the rest of us—and another twenty besides, if we'd had them—couldn't stop the cattle from doing what they finally did, turning back. They didn't do it all at once and we fought them for at least two hours, but finally they more or less all turned south across a mile-wide front that had no real leaders in it; you could slap an old steer across the face with a doubled lariat and he would barely blink. They had no turn left in them—it had dried up.

We quickly had a little parley on a hilltop overlooking the now abandoned, disorganized herd. The younger hands were big-eyed and quiet—all even Laredo Allen could say was, "Damn—we lost the whole shiterie!"

"What do you think?" Bronc Kinkaid asked.

"Judd left you in charge," I said.

"But I'm askin' your opinion—what do you think a feller should do?"

"Well, we're not gonna turn 'em, that's for damn sure," I said. "I think we can all agree on that. They're goin' back to the last place they had a drink and that's Indian Lake. I think most of 'em will make it, too, but when they do they're gonna be scattered out to beat hell. If I was segundo I'd leave a couple of men here to push the stragglers on to the lake and cut the ears off any that die on the way, and then I'd take everyone else back to the lakes and string 'em out on the lower side for about five miles and stop the herd there—keep 'em from drifting south after they've watered." I shrugged and said, "I don't know what 'n the hell else a man can do."

Bronc thought for a few seconds and slowly nodded. "I agree. Juan, why don't you and Ramus stay behind 'em and the rest of us will stop 'em at the lakes. We'll tell Luther—whenever we find the wandering boy—that you'll each need another horse, then we'll have him take the remuda back to the lakes, too."

"What'll we tell Pilot when he comes back?" Juan asked.

"Tell him how much we enjoyed his absence," Johnnie said.

"And then ask him what in the hell he knows on Ike Holt," Bronc Kinkaid said with a laugh.

It worked well enough and brought us out of a jam. We only had seventeen steers die—twelve before they got to water and five more afterward. When Pilot came in while

Juan and Ramus were pushing the tail end to the lakes a full day after the rest of us got there, he didn't have much to say and didn't even act all that upset over the lost days and dead steers. Johnnie said he guessed he was so tickled he finally got to see somebody pushing the drags up that nothing else mattered.

By the time we drove the herd away from Indian Lakes the second time—this time veering to the northwest—we had been gone two weeks and were yet barely a hundred miles up the Western Trail from San Antonio. By then we were thoroughly convinced that Pilot Judd had never taken a herd up *any* trail before, in spite of the fact that he talked like he'd been born on the trail and raised as a dogie on dust and stolen milk. It was nothing but a sheer mystery how Ike Holt, of all the cowmen in the entire Lone Star State, had ever come to hire him as his segundo. But our hope was that the two weeks of hell and headache—caused mostly by Judd's lack of cow sense and his bullheadedness—had taught him at least some things to avoid and some other things to do on the trail. If that happened, then those two weeks of hell and headache and lost time and steers would not be entirely for naught.

Of course, then we had no idea of the hell and headache—and the heartache too—coming down out of the Bighorn Mountains.

24

The steers finally became more or less trail broke, or, as Lewis Anacho analyzed it, "Them sonsabitches finally broke themselves in spite of everything five gringos, one Mexican, and one heathen Apache 'breed could do to keep 'em from it."

We crossed the Colorado without incident, the cattle only having to swim twenty feet or so to reach the north bank.

Any river crossed without incident is a cause for thanks from those who have been on the trail before, but for the young, the brash, and the bold in our ranks who had not seen the elephant, it was a bitter disappointment.

"So I guess I'm a veteran drover now, huh?" Laredo said in a mocking tone as we were eating supper shortly after bedding the herd on the north side of the Colorado. "I've crossed my first swollen, rampaging river. I can't wait till I can lord it over some greenhorn, like you old hooters do."

"Laredo," Jim Napp drawled, "if you was any greener we'd have to trim the shinnery outa your ears. You ain't *seen* a river yet. And when you do, you'll want to run the

other way so hard we pro'bly couldn't hold you to a snub-
bin' post with a three-quarter rope."

Everybody laughed but Pilot Judd and Luther Atkins.
They were sitting together on the ground away from the
rest of us, eating their supper and talking low. It was not
the first time I'd seen them do it—in fact, Luther was
about the only one in the crew Judd talked to at all, other
than to give an order. I glanced at Johnnie and saw that he
was watching them, too. Then about the same time we
both smiled and held up our hands and shrugged our
shoulders.

Bronc Kinkaid had been observing the same thing.
"Looks like our wandering horse rustler and our trail boss
may be joined at the hip," he said.

"Now that would be a hell of a pair to draw to, wouldn't
it?" Billy Meeks said with a chuckle.

A few minutes later, Pilot walked to the end of the
wagon, dropped his plate into the washtub, and said,
"Men, things have lined out so good now that when we get
near Abilene in a few days I'll go in with Billy to get supplies and bring back a case of Old Crow for you."

After Pilot walked away, Bronc said with a big grin,
"What a damn fine fellow."

"A prince of a man!" Jim Napp chimed in.

"You know," Johnnie said, laughing, "recently I've
been starting to see Pilot in a whole new light, myself."

"Just how recent was this revelation," Billy Meeks
asked.

"Started about a minute ago," Johnnie said, "and I'm
pretty sure will last at least as long as the Old Crow does."

The crew, taken as a whole, got drunk near Abilene.

Just like most any crew of cowhands would do after
they'd been on the trail for three weeks, two of them full
of hell and headaches, and the boss gave them a case of
Old Crow whiskey and disappeared.

Ramus, Laredo, Juan, Billy, and Jim got damn drunk
and either passed out or slept so hard they were the same
as passed out, while Lewis Anacho took to the warpath,

performed some kind of whirling-dervish dance, and disappeared into the hills in search of scalps.

I cannot say that Johnnie, Bronc, and myself were entirely without blemish or sin in the affair, but I can say that within the first two hours of the onset of the celebration we realized that shortly there would be no one to day-herd, night-herd—or any other kind of herd—the cattle *or* the remuda. Where Luther and Pilot disappeared to we didn't know.

"I ain't saying a little whiskey along the trail ain't a nice gesture," Johnnie said as he rocked on his hunkers and took another drink. "But can you imagine a trail boss droppin' off a whole case as a reward and then just disappearing without warning us that night guard goes on the same as before and that the herd'll be kicked off the bed ground at sunup? And all this before the drive's even got to the Red?"

"All I know," said Bronc Kinkaid, tightly clutching the long, brown neck of his whiskey bottle, "is that what could have been a nice sippin'-slow drunk for all of us has been spoiled by greed and gluttony—the scourge of the human race."

"Good God!" Johnnie exclaimed. "When you get to drinkin' a little you're as foulmouthed as Casey is. . . . Whatdaya call the way he's talkin', Casey."

"Waxing eloquent," I said.

"Yeah . . . waxin' eloquent. Well, let's bring in the remuda and hobble the ones that want to wander off, and then we can rotate the night guard on the herd—two on and one off."

While we were hobbling the horses, Luther and Pilot came trotting back to the wagon. It was just before sundown and they had been gone several hours.

"What 'n the hell are you doing, hobbling those horses?" Judd asked.

"You know"—Johnnie looked up from between the forelegs of a little sorrel—"I would have thought you'd have said, 'Why in the hell are these men drunk?' or 'Why isn't there anybody beddin' the goddamn steers down?' But instead you ride up to the only men on the job and

say, 'What'n the hell are you doing hobblin' those horses?'!
Well, I'll tell you why we're hobblin' these horses—because that sorry excuse of a horse wrangler there beside
you wasn't here to do it!"

"You can't talk to me that way!" Luther Atkins said
from atop his horse.

"I'll tell you one goddamn thing, Luther—you wouldn't
make a sweat bump on a horse rustler's butt! If you could
drive a stud to a horsin' mare it would surprise the hell out
of me!"

"I'll whip your ass, old man!" Luther said as he swung a
leg over the cantle of his saddle and stepped to the ground,
where Johnnie greeted him with a hard right to his nose
followed immediately by a left to his chin that snapped his
neck back and dropped him in his tracks.

It was all so predictable I couldn't help but grin. Johnnie did not back up—*never*—and although Luther was as
big as Johnnie and twenty years younger, there was no way
in hell Luther Atkins could have even tied his pants on
Johnnie. The fight was already over before Luther knew it
had even begun.

Pilot Judd said loudly, "That's enough! I won't put up
with fighting and insubordination! Bronc, are you throwin'
in with these two?"

Bronc was calm. "I don't throw in with nobody, Pilot,
but what Johnnie said is true."

"I should never have let Ike talk me into putting you
two on," Pilot said, looking at me. "You've been much
more trouble than you've been help. I don't do things on
the trail the way you're used to doing them, and you think
your way is the only way . . . but for now, I'd like to let
the matter rest. . . . Agreed?"

"Pilot," I said, "most of the trouble we've had you've
brought on yourself. The last thing we want is a bunch of
trouble on this drive—hell, it's far enough to Montana
when everything goes smooth. We came as a favor to Ike—
to help him get the herd to Montana by the first day of
September, and we're stayin' for the same reason. We
know you didn't appreciate the way we were hired, and I

can't say I blame you for that, but we've made no trouble and want none."

By then Luther was getting to his feet and blinking his eyes like a cow that's just getting her air back after being choked. "You son of a bitch," he said, "I wasn't ready!"

"Shut up, Luther," Pilot said. "And take care of your horses."

By then we had lost another full day, and we grazed the steers the next morning until ten o'clock before Lewis came off the warpath and down from the hills and the rest of the sorry-looking crew could set a horse—except for Jim Napp, who would stay drunk and ride on the top of the bedrolls in the wagon until we reached the clear fork of the Brazos.

"I wish Ike could see this mess," Johnnie said.

"Yeah . . . if I didn't know better, I'd swear Pilot was doing everything he could to be sure we *don't* get to Montana by the first of September."

"That's being too kind to him, Casey—I just think he's too dumb to know any better. If Ike wasn't as good a friend as he is, I'd leave this outfit for a goddamn tomato factory."

I laughed. I could see Johnnie working in a tomato factory—stovepipe boots and big-rowled spurs jingling, sunburned, rawhide skin, bowed legs, tall-crowned hat and neckerchief, and him cussing a blue streak.

"Yeah, Johnnie," I said as I wiped the tears out of my eyes, "you should try a tomato factory sometime."

Pilot Judd had had little to say to me or Johnnie before, but now he had nothing at all to say. He ignored us completely, and now he also ignored Bronc and said nothing to him. When he left the herd for any reason, he put Lewis Anacho or Laredo Allen in charge.

"That's what you get for associating with folks like us," I told Bronc, who laughed.

Luther Atkins became even more of a coyote than before, slinking around the wagon but hardly talking to anyone other than Pilot Judd. He for sure sidled away from Johnnie.

* * *

Things went smooth enough for a few days, but there was rain up the trail and when we reached the Brazos we found it on the rise and too high to cross for three days.

When we finally did get across, we noticed that Laredo Allen had little to say this time in any sort of mocking tone, or any other tone for that matter, about crossing "swollen" and "rampaging" rivers. A river like the Brazos, when it is angry and on the rise, is nothing to trifle with and is usually a sure cure for the swaggers.

The Wichita was on the rise, too, and scary as a goblin, especially since there was a fresh grave on the south side, the eternal home of a cowboy with no more rivers to cross.

With the condition of the Brazos and the Wichita it came as no surprise to us when, a day's drive from Doan's Crossing on the Red River, we encountered a rider traveling south on the trail who told us the Red was in such a "helluva sorry state" that it was unfordable.

When we got within three miles of the river the next day the herd was stopped and Laredo sent on ahead to find out what was happening. He was back in two hours with the news that the river was still uncrossable and that two other herds were waiting ahead of us. About the only surprise in that information was that only two herds were waiting ahead of us. Only a few years earlier there would have been eight or ten herds waiting to cross this time of the year.

We should have held our herd at least a mile off the trail, not within a few hundred yards of it, while we waited for the river to fall. There was plenty of grass along the trail, but it was asking for trouble and the trouble you ask for with a herd of twenty-eight hundred longhorn steers you are usually given. Me and Johnnie knew that, Bronc knew it, Jim Napp and Lewis Anacho knew it, but none of us had Judd's ear enough to convince him of it. So we grazed the herd close to the trail and held our breath that none of the steers in front of us had a run, because if they did, the cattle from those herds would spill right back down the trail that was familiar to them—and into our herd.

We heard the rumbling as we were catching our night horses two days later, and in less than a minute, without waiting for an order from our segundo, we were mounted and trying to move our herd farther to the west—but we didn't get it done before a moving wall of cattle covering a mile-wide front came over the hill and swept our herd along with them like tidewater sweeping a piece of driftwood along the beach.

By sunup there were twenty-five cowboys drifting close to six thousand head of cattle onto a level roundup ground so we could start separating the two herds.

Counting the days we'd waited along the trail before the two herds mixed and the time it took to separate them afterward—during most of which time the Red was fordable—we lost another four days off our march to the Tongue.

Things lined out pretty decent for a while again after crossing the Red River—at least decent compared to what most of the drive had been. The whole outfit, horses, cattle, and cowboys, never had once come together in the rhythm that has to be found on the trail for things to really go like they should. With this outfit there was always something out of sync. If the herd was settled and content at night and moving up the trail like they should during the day, the crew was drunk, or if the crew was sober, the herd was restless. And almost without fail, it seemed like just when everything else began to go smoothly, Luther would have trouble with the remuda again. Twice as we were crossing what had once been wild Indian Territory but was now the Territory of Oklahoma, with a farm or homestead every few miles, the remuda ran off during the night and we spent most of the next day finding them, and more times than most of us could count we would have to wait for Luther to bring the remuda in so we could change horses, which we did four times a day. Sometimes the wait would only be for a few minutes, but several times it was for half an hour or more, during which time we would cuss Luther. If Judd ever said anything to Luther about the way he was handling the remuda it was done during the times they would get their heads together and talk low during supper.

And then Ike Holt, coming from the north and riding alone on a rented horse he got in Dodge City after riding the train there from San Antonio, intercepted us on the prairie between the North Canadian and the Cimarron Rivers a few miles south of Kansas.

Pilot Judd rode out to meet him, and they had a long parley on a hilltop while we put the steers on the bed ground. For once, Luther had the remuda at the wagon when we rode in, so we were able to catch our night horses before supper. While we were doing that, Ike and Pilot stood in the shade of a nearby cottonwood and continued their parley, a parley which, it was not hard to see, did not employ all the rules of parliamentary procedure and one that continued until Billy hollered "this larrupin' kaseen is done" and they came to the wagon.

There were four of us sitting together cross-legged on the ground with our tin plates in our laps—me, Johnnie, Bronc, and Juan. In a way, it was comical to watch as Ike and Pilot Judd filled their plates and looked around for a place to sit. Of course they had the whole world to sit on, or at least to the four horizons, and on that stretch of prairie the horizons seemed as big as the whole world and then some. But we could tell Ike wanted to come over to where we were, and Pilot was pointing, first to where Lopin' Luther was sulking by himself and then to the same cottonwood where they had been talking earlier.

"Ol' Pilot's in a pickle," said Bronc Kinkaid. "He don't want Ike more'n an arm's length away, but he sure as hell don't want to eat over here with us."

"But if I know Ike Holt," I said, "he won't let Pilot Judd, or anybody else, lead him around."

"But then you're forgettin' that somehow, some way, he got Ike to let him be his segundo," Johnnie said.

"That is an undeniable truth I'll have to agree with," I said, "and one that I have yet to fathom how it could have come about. Pilot Judd must be the world's most convincing speaker."

"Maybe," Bronc said, "but he's yet to convince me of a damn thing."

Then we saw Ike look at Pilot and shake his head, gesture toward us, and start our way with Pilot stepping in his tracks.

The telling moments of our lives usually pass unnoticed and it is only in looking back that we recognize them. So it was with the moment Ike made up his mind to join the four of us sitting cross-legged on the Oklahoma prairie.

25

"Pull up a piece of terra firma," Johnnie said as Ike and Pilot stood in front of us, holding their plates in their hands.

They sat down, facing us, with about six feet of Oklahoma in between.

"How are you boys?" Ike asked. He did not look good, and it was easy to tell he was bothered by something—a something that was easy enough to guess: by then we should have been a hundred and fifty to two hundred miles farther up the trail than we were.

"We're fine, Ike," Johnnie said. "We got good weather, good food, and good Holt horses to ride ever'day."

"Pilot said you have had considerable hell in the past, though," Ike said.

"We've had that," Johnnie agreed.

Then it grew quiet except for the doves cooing in the cottonwood and a couple of hobbled horses nickering to each other in the remuda a quarter mile away.

"The herd is two weeks behind where it should be," Ike said.

I looked at Pilot. He was scratching in the dirt with a short cottonwood twig.

"Everything I've got is riding on the outcome of this drive," Ike said. "I would like your opinion as to why you're two weeks behind where you should be."

The silence again.

Then Ike looked straight at Johnnie and said, "I'm askin' *you*, Johnnie."

Johnnie's plate was in his lap and he had been looking down at it, but now he lifted his head and looked at Ike. "If you had not asked me directly, Ike, I would not have said anything—I've never believed in whinin' to the big boss about the way a wagon boss or a trail boss is runnin' his outfit. But since you have asked my opinion directly, I can't lie." Now Johnnie looked at Pilot and said, "I'm glad you're here to hear what I have to say, Pilot, because I wouldn't want you getting it secondhand and not getting it right. . . .

"Ike, the Red and the Brazos were on the rise and waitin' for them to fall some should have cost us four days, and those are the only days we should have lost."

Pilot's face was turning red.

"Then what about the other days—why did you lose them, Johnnie?"

"In my opinion, we lost them because Pilot savvies cattle about like a gopher savvies the gospel."

Pilot stood up, so mad he was shaking. "The truth is, Ike—and I didn't say it before because I knew they were friends of yours—but the truth is Johnnie and Casey both have been the main source of most of the trouble we've had ever since we left the ranch. They've been jealous because I was in charge and have done everything they could to turn the rest of the hands against me. . . . I should have put my foot down before we ever left the ranch, and now I will. I cannot work with men I did not hire and cannot fire! They're nothing but a couple of drifting malcontents. Johnnie has already been in a fight with Luther, and if it wasn't for me we would be without a horse wrangler right now. Any outfit would be better off without them. They not only refuse to follow orders, but for the years of experience they're supposed to've had they know very little about handling cattle or horses. If you want me—"

"The truth is, Pilot," Ike said calmly, "I don't want you . . . and never did. You know I hired you at the bank's insistence. Davis had me over a barrel, said he would do what he could to keep the board of directors off my back until after the first of September, but he strongly urged me—that's the way he said it—to hire you to get these steers to the reservation in time to secure the government contract. Now I'm beginning to wonder if I haven't been set up. You see, if this herd *doesn't* get to the reservation on time, Davis just got himself a ranch dropped in his lap that I've been puttin' together for over twenty years.

"Roll your bed, Pilot," Ike said, "and in case you don't savvy what that means, it means you're fired!"

"Goddamn you, Johnnie Lester!" Pilot Judd said. "You backbitin' son-of-a-bitchin' bastard!"

Ike was on his feet in a flash. "That's enough, Pilot! I'll give you a damn horse just to get rid of you! Take whichever one you want and throw your wood on him and leave—now!"

"You old bastard, you can't fire me! I work for James Davis!"

"So—" Ike laughed with some degree of satisfaction— "I was right." Then wheeling toward Johnnie, he said, "Johnnie—will you take charge of the herd and do what you can to get it to the reservation on time?"

"Hell, Ike . . . ," Johnnie said, "I ain't . . ."

"I'm askin' you as a favor, Johnnie . . . please. I'd take charge myself, but I don't think my health could take it, and besides, I've got too many other business matters that have to be attended to, to stay with the herd all the way through. Hell, you'll have Casey here—and maybe Bronc and Juan and some of the others—to help you. If you don't get there by September first—well, at least I'll know I had one of the best goddamn cowboys there was, tryin' his best, and he had one of the best crews helping him. What do you say? Will you help me save my outfit?"

"Hell . . . Ike," Johnnie moaned, "I ain't never craved to be top screw—"

"But will you be—for me?"

"Aw hell . . . Ike . . ."

"Just till you get to the Tongue River Reservation?"

"Hell . . . okay—but *just* till we get the cattle delivered."

"That'll be long enough," Ike said with a grin as he extended his hand to Johnnie.

"You can't do this!" Pilot Judd almost shouted.

"It's done," Ike said.

I saw Pilot's hand start for the .45 riding in the holster high on his right hip.

"Look out, Johnnie!" I yelled.

Johnnie lunged at Pilot just as the Colt went off, the bullet kicking up the dirt twenty feet away and whining off into the distance as they locked horns.

Pilot was a strong and active man, but at last Johnnie wore him down, as he almost always did, because there was no quit and no fear in him. He left Pilot lying in the dirt with only Luther to help him lick his wounds.

With all the commotion, the entire crew was assembled long before the fight was finished. But when it was finished at last, Johnnie took a few minutes to get his breath and a drink of water and to pour one last dipper from the water barrel on the side of the wagon over his face, washing the blood, sweat, and dirt into his shirt collar. Then Johnnie, still breathing hard, wiped his face with his shirt sleeve and said, "Boys, y'all pretty well know how this has come about. I didn't ask to be the segundo, but fate being what it is, it looks like I will be until we deliver the herd. . . ." He paused to catch his breath again and to spit a little blood into the dirt.

Luther was taking Pilot toward the cottonwood tree, but Johnnie's next words caught them before they reached the shade. "Luther, in case you were plannin' otherwise, you'll be leaving with Pilot—not because we had a fight or because you are a poor excuse of a horse wrangler, which goes without saying, but because, unless I miss my guess, some of the foolish things you've done have not been entirely out of ignorance. Ike will give you your wages and I'm sure he'll give you a horse just like he did Pilot to get you away from the outfit. I want you both gone in an hour, and I don't want to see either of you within a mile of this herd again."

Then Johnnie looked at the rest of the cowboys gathered to the side of the wagon and said, "If any of you boys think I'm too much to stomach until we get to the Tongue, Ike will pay you off right here and then I'll shake your hand to show you there are no hard feelings and next time we see each other we'll have a drink. If you'll stay with me, I don't promise anything other than your wages, my appreciation, and some long and hard days with your feet hangin' down. We still have at least eight hundred miles of trail ahead of us, and we have some time to make up— time that won't be made up lounging in our hot rolls or leanin' against the wagon, fightin' flies. On top of that, we'll be a little shorthanded. But after we get to the reservation we *will* kill the fatted calf, and in a way it hasn't been disposed of in recent history. Ike has promised he'll pay the freight to haul us all back to Texas on the train, and I'll try to finagle some way to pay the fare for each of you to have the company of a tender trollop on the return trip."

Not a man lined up in front of Ike to get his pay, but they did shake Johnnie's hand, and Johnnie told each of them how glad he was they were staying with the outfit. He said we would rotate positions on the drive, from point to swing to drag and back to point and he turned the remuda over to Ramus Knight. There was now a *cowboy* in charge, and the whole outfit seemed to have already taken on a new and fresh air.

Even the trail gods seemed pleased with the change of leadership over the Slash Seven herd, and as we made our way across western Kansas the weather held steady. There was enough rain to keep the grass along the trail washed and fresh and enough to keep sufficient water in the creeks and the rivers and the bottoms of the draws to water the herd, but not so much that fording was any more than a pleasant diversion.

It was June, and June days in western Kansas are long, sixteen to eighteen hours, and we were that many hours in the saddle. But nothing was forced. The steers seemed to naturally come off the bed ground at daylight to graze without us driving them off, and by the time the sun was full up they had already grazed two or three miles ahead with only two riders there to drift them north in their grazing. By not "driving" them and surely not by "pushing the drags" but just by seeing to it that each step they took was in the direction of the Tongue River in Montana, most bed grounds were twenty miles up trail from the one of the evening before. Under Johnnie's leadership the outfit soon fell into the rhythm it had been searching for since leaving the Hondo.

Across the Arkansas River, White Woman and Ladder Creeks, Smoky Hill River, Hackberry Creek, and the plains and draws in between, our herd moved ever northward without incident or happening, like a mile-long snake.

But western Kansas had changed and was still changing. Once considered the great American desert and uninhabitable by civilized persons, it now was touted as the most fertile, tillable soil west of the Mississippi and a farmer's dream come true; not a day passed on the trail when we didn't see plowed fields and fences where once there had been nothing but open range. And hardly a day passed when we did not see at least one farmer standing on the edge of his field and holding a shotgun—ready to do battle with 2863 Longhorn steers just to save a few rows of corn. It was a mystery to us, but also a steady source of amusement.

The only thing resembling an "incident" anywhere in Kansas occurred when we were kept from entering Thomas County by a group of ten farmers, all armed, who called themselves "grange deputies," and said they would have no more of Texas herds destroying their crops. But a few miles is hardly worth a fight with ten grange deputies, so we threw off the trail, skirted the county, and threw back on the trail north of it.

* * *

The first day Johnnie took over the herd we crossed the Cimarron River and knew we were in Kansas. Eighteen days later, making it the first week in July, we crossed the Republican River into Nebraska.

A week after that, we reached Ogallala and the Platte, and there the trail gods frowned on us and brought rain. When the sun disappeared, so did the easy dispositions and good will of the crew. The Platte was on the rise and unfordable. The honeymoon was over.

Johnnie had talked the boys out of a trip to Dodge City, but then Johnnie had been new to the job, the weather was good, and the men were fresh from loafing along at Judd's slow pace. But now the weather was miserable, the men had nearly a straight month of sixteen- to eighteen-hour days behind them, and Johnnie was no longer new. He allowed them a night in Ogallala, which resulted in Lewis Anacho and Laredo Allen in jail for disturbing the peace and Jim Napp in a drunken stupor for two days—the same amount of time it took Johnnie to get Lewis and Laredo out of jail.

The Western Trail branched at Ogallala: the north and most heavily used branch crossed the Platte and then went on to the Dakotas, and the west branch followed the Platte valley into Wyoming and crossed near Fort Laramie before going to Montana.

The Platte was still on a tear and a steady drizzle had set in, but with his crew all at the wagon again, Johnnie was not about to keep them near Ogallala another night. So we set out parallel to the Platte at a slow and miserable pace.

Every creek that fed into the mighty Platte from the south and west was running, most of them full, and we had to cross each and every one. Some days we were lucky to make five miles. The drizzle broke after two days, only to be replaced by afternoon downpours and thunderboomers. The herd was restless and didn't want to bed in the mud and the wet grass, and the guard had to be doubled—each man pulling a four-hour shift after dark.

One night I overheard Laredo saying to Ramus, "I wouldn't have thought it, but the son of a bitch has let his authority go to his head just like all bosses do. He's impressed with himself now and don't give a hang about us."

I stepped into their sight and said, "Laredo, you don't know squat, and you sure as hell don't know Johnnie Lester. He's pulled more guards than anybody and is up before anybody. Hell, how many times has he helped you bring the remuda in before daylight, Ramus? I know Johnnie hates being boss just as much as some men love it—but if I had my own outfit and there was any way I could, I'd want Johnnie Lester in charge of it. Neither one of you will ever work under a better cowboy if you go up the trail another hundred goddamn times!"

Pumpkin Creek was a river itself, higher in the middle than on either bank, and cottonwood trees floated along that had been washed out further upstream. Johnnie looked at the Pumpkin for a few seconds from the hilltop we were sitting together on, without comment. Then he said in an even voice, "All things considered, Casey, I'd rather be in Cheyenne with a whore and a bottle."

Rather than wait for the Pumpkin to fall we drove the herd parallel to it for three days, skirted around its mouth, then pointed the leaders northwest again.

The weather finally dried out, and for two days we made good time. Then we reached Horse Creek just before crossing into Wyoming, and, for a change, found water running only in the normal channels—but since the creek had been up for several days previous, the sand in the creek bed was waterlogged till hell wouldn't have it.

"You know what you get for being boss?" Johnnie said, when we held the herd up after crossing Horse Creek and saw the creek bed behind us littered with struggling, bogged-down steers. "Wormwood and gall . . . That's the reward you get for bein' in charge of a trail herd. Wormwood and gall!"

Forty-one steers had to be prodded, poked, pulled, and dug to get them out—forty of them survived our efforts to save them. But we lost yet another day.

Coming into Wyoming, though, seemed to swing our

luck back toward the good, and by the time we reached
the crossing on the Platte, at a place called Forty Islands,
just below old Fort Laramie, the weather was hot and dry
and the Platte gentle. But the time we made up in Kansas,
we had lost in Nebraska. When we crossed the Platte and
pointed the leaders toward the north and west again for the
last stretch of the drive, it was the thirteenth of August and
there was roughly two hundred and fifty miles of Wyoming
plus a few in Montana between us and the Tongue River
Reservation.

Again we—2862 long-legged Texas steers, 136 head of remuda horses, and nine cowboys—fell into the rhythm of
the trail in an easy but continuous march northwestward
across the high, dry sagebrush country of Wyoming.

We were not able to achieve the twenty-mile-between-
bed-grounds average that we'd had in Kansas because the
Wyoming prairie is more broken up by more creeks and
rivers and washes than the Kansas prairie, but we were
able to maintain the pace necessary to get us to our destination by the prescribed time, or so every man of us figured—and every man of us *did* figure it.

The farther we got across Wyoming, the more important
a topic it became, and bets were wagered and rewagered
almost nightly about how far we would get the next day or
when we would cross the Belle Fourche or Powder Rivers
or when, to the exact hour of the day, we would first see
the Tongue River itself.

"I don't give a hank about seein' the Tongue River,"
Laredo said after supper one night, "but I am rather
lookin' forward to seein' a Tongue River Crow squaw."

"Your wavels comin' down on you again, Laredo?" Jim
Napp asked.

"Considerable," Laredo said, "and now even *bigger* than
grapefruit. I've been dreamin' ever' night about red nip-
ples on tan skin and smellin' the smoky aroma of a buckskin dress."

"Humph," grunted Billy Meeks, "it ain't no squaw that
I been dreamin' of!"

"And what makes you think there's a Crow squaw low-class enough to bed you?" Jim Napp asked.

"Hell, any squaw—Crow, Sioux, Cheyenne, it don't matter—is just like a bullin' cow; and she don't care who's between her legs just so somebody is and I figure—"

Before I even fully realized it, I had Laredo's shirtfront in both my hands and had pulled him to his feet. I was close enough to his face to bite his nose. *"You vulgar-mouthed little bastard,"* I growled.

"I . . . hell, Casey . . . ," Laredo said in a stunned voice. "What are you doin'?"

I looked him in the eye for another few seconds before I opened my hands, let him drop, and walked away from the wagon into the moonlight.

"You're not ever gonna get over her, are you, Casey?" I looked around and Johnnie was behind me, rolling a cigarette. "I bet the prettiest little virgin in Wyoming Territory could offer herself to you and you'd turn her down. Right? It would be like castin' pearls before swine. . . . And you still won't talk about it either, will you? Well, hell and by God, I just wished I could have seen her! That way I coulda judged for myself if she was worth all the misery you've enjoyed because of her. . . . Oh, one more thing—don't be jerkin' my cowhands around like that until we get to the Tongue."

26

The hell of it was, it was dry on us all the way to Powder River. And less than fifty miles beyond the Powder lay the Tongue. Dry—with just enough water in the springs and the bigger creeks to water the herd.

Dry all the way across the sagebrush, from Walker Creek, to Box Creek, across the Dry Fork of Cheyenne River, on to Sand Creek, across the headwaters of the Wind River, east of the Pumpkin Buttes, across the sandy little creeks and sagebrush hills that make up the headwaters of the Belle Fourche and even across Wild Horse Creek—dry.

For two weeks beyond the Platte—dry . . .

But Powder River was anything but dry.

The older hands on the crew—me, Johnnie, Billy, Bronc, and Jim—had had an uneasy feeling for several days before reaching it that it would not be, as was often said, "a mile wide and an inch deep."

The Bighorn Mountains, far to the west and a day's ride on a long-winded horse even beyond Powder River . . . the Bighorn Mountains, out of which came Willow, Middle

Fork, North Fork, and Crazy Woman Creeks, creeks that spilled into Powder River above the point we would cross . . . the Bighorn Mountains that by day were no more than a blue ghost on the far side of a sagebrush world . . . the Bighorn Mountains, that by night were invisible—became silhouetted, for three nights running, by second- and third-guard display of flashing lightning coming from them in eerie silence but for an occasional far-off and dim rumble of thunder.

"Goddammit to hell!" Johnnie said on the afternoon of the twenty-sixth of August when we saw Powder River for the first time.

Bronc whistled low. "Look at that son of a bitch roll!"

Powder River was churning with runoff from the Bighorns—a brown soup of water, foam, and trash. It was a half mile wide and higher in the center than on either bank. It had deep swirls and high swells, and you didn't need to be told it had little regard for any life other than its own.

"Well . . . there hasn't been any lightning in the west for the past two nights," Johnnie said, "so it oughta be goin' down . . . We've got a couple of days to spare, so after we let 'em water we'll pull back a mile or so and loose-herd 'em and wait."

It was quiet in the sagebrush that evening and night. We'd been on the trail a few days short of four months and had covered close to fifteen hundred miles, the last eight hundred of those at a not-so-leisurely pace, and I guess we were all—cowboys, cattle, and horses—tired. The steers had full bellies of water and, after awhile, of grass and they bedded down before dark to chew their cuds.

"*I'm ridin' Old Paint, I'm leadin' Old Dan, goin' to Montana to throw the hoolihan. They feed in the coulees and they water in the draw—their tails are all matted, their backs are all raw . . .*" Bronc was leaning against his bedroll, looking toward the west where the sun had just sunk out of sight behind the Bighorns, spinning a spur rowel and singing low in a deep, smooth voice. "*. . . Good-bye Old Paint, I'm*

leavin' Cheyenne—Good-bye Old Paint, I'm leavin' Cheyenne—
I'm goin' to Montana, good-bye Old Paint, I'm leavin' Chey-
enne."

Bronc was a good hand—a good man—with no afflic-
tions or character flaws other than those gathered during
eighteen years of trail dust and saddle leather. He kept
mostly to himself, but could always be depended on to be
in the right place at the right time. He seemed a little
melancholy that night—but then the rest of us were too.
". . . Well, when I die, take my saddle from the wall; strap it on
my pony an' lead 'im out of his stall. Throw my bones on his
back, turn our faces toward the west, we'll ride the prairies that
we love the best. Good-bye Old Paint, I'm leavin' Cheyenne—
good-bye Old Paint, I'm leavin' Cheyenne . . . Goin' to Mon-
tana, good-bye Old Paint, I'm leavin' Cheyenne."

The next morning, when we rode to the river before
sunup, it was five feet from the tracks the cattle and horses
had made the afternoon before to the edge of the water.

Johnnie smiled. We all smiled. The water was falling.

Johnnie lived on the east bank of Powder River that
day, sticking sagebrush sticks in the sand at the water's
edge every hour or so to measure its progress.

By noon the water had fallen twenty feet. By sundown
it had fallen another thirty, and the deep swirls and high
swells that had been in the center the day before were
gone and the river was flat.

"It's still a booger," Johnnie said. "It's still swimmin'-
deep for three hundred yards, but there's no more foam or
trash on it and at the rate it's falling we should be able to
cross tomorrow afternoon. Then we'll have three days to go
the fifty-or-so miles to the Tongue, where Ike's supposed
to meet us with the Indian agent and a band of Crow to
take over the herd."

"Have I ever told you how well you wear responsibility?" I asked Johnnie later.

"No, you ain't, and I don't want to hear it now. I just
want to get these sonsabitches delivered."

"Well, I can't help it," I said. "I've got to say that

you're the best trail boss we've had since we left the Hondo."

"Damnin' with faint praise, huh? Well, you see, Casey, I've got skin as thick as a brush bull's hide, so whatever you say rolls off me like this water's rollin' to the Yellowstone. Pilot called us a couple of drifting malcontents, but he was wrong, at least he was about me—I was a *contented* drifter. I never became *mal*contented until I let Ike talk me into being responsible for all these cattle, horses, and men. But I'll *be* a contented drifter again, and in only four more days, God and Powder River willing."

When the last guard came in at daybreak the next morning we sat around the wagon, drinking coffee and waiting for Billy to get breakfast cooked. The steers were coming off the bed ground and grazing, but we knew they weren't going anywhere so we just let them spread and graze. Ramus brought the remuda in, and we threw them in the rope corral, caught our horses for the morning, and turned the rest out to graze the morning away, too. Johnnie had said we'd cross the river in the afternoon, which meant a lazy morning in which we were more than willing participants.

"Come and git it before the flies do. Where's Johnnie?" Billy said.

"I sky-lighted 'im trotting down toward the river when we were comin' off last guard," Laredo said. "Yonder he comes now."

"Why in the hell do you reckon he's in a high-lope?" Bronc said.

"In all likelihood," Billy said with a straight face as he put a little more salt in the coffeepot, "it's on account of my cookin'."

"In all likelihood," Jim Napp countered, "anybody high-lopin' on account of your cookin' would be high-lopin' the other way."

Johnnie came trotting straight to the wagon without hobbling his horse. "Boys—the goddamn Powder's frothin' again."

Foam on a river usually always meant a shortly-coming rise in the water.

"There was lightning up in the Bighorns again last night, but that's not what's comin' now—that won't be here for another day or so. I didn't want to cross till this afternoon, but I don't think we can wait. I'm goin' to cross it now and check it out while y'all eat your baits, roll your beds, and put your guns or anything else you want to in the wagon. I'll be back in an hour or so. Ramus, bring the remuda in so ever'body can catch his best river horse, and then y'all throw the herd together and wait till I get back. . . . If there's any way in hell to get across now we'd better do it, because it's been said that time and tide wait for no man and I sure as hell think that goes double for Powder River."

In twenty minutes the remuda was back in the rope corral and I was catching the horses that the boys called out the names of, usually the strongest horse in each man's string but for sure the best swimmers and the most reliable ones in water.

By the time we had the herd thrown together and Billy had the wagon loaded and ready to go, Johnnie came back over the rise from the river and waved us together. His clothes were wet from the neck down, as was his saddle and the sorrel he was riding.

"Boys, it's already on the rise, but I've been to the other bank and back. I'm satisfied we can ford it, just like I'm satisfied it would be better if we could wait, but we can't. There's going to be some bog on this side just before they hit the water, and I can't find a damn place where there's not, but I don't think we'll have much trouble there until maybe along toward the tail end when it gets really worked up and soupy, but we'll just have to do the best we can.

"Once you get in the water, the bottom's solid enough, but when they have to start swimming the current's strong enough to carry 'em downriver about two hundred yards before they can walk out on the other side. The other bank will be a pretty steep slope that leads up to some tamaracks, but it's not a long slope and its solid and it's sandy enough so it shouldn't get too slick.

"I don't think they'll want to take it, so we'll take the

remuda in front and chop off about two hundred steers to crowd in behind 'em. Once that first bunch starts following the horses into the water we'll push the rest of the herd in behind them. Casey, I'd like for you to help me point 'em, and Bronc, if you and Jim don't mind, I'd like for you to flank us up."

Then Johnnie looked at his crew of cowboys a few seconds in silence and then he said, "There ain't a man-Jack of you that I'd trade for the whole goddamn herd and I know Ike feels the same. If I wasn't satisfied we could make it I wouldn't even ask you to try, but you have my word that we *will* make it . . . and then we'll only be three days from that fatted calf and those tender trollops in Sheridan. . . . So, hell, gentlemen, let's gird up our loins, kick these long-legged darlin's across Powder River, and take 'em to Montana."

Johnnie knew how to get cattle across a treacherous river—hell, if he didn't know, nobody knew.

The horses smelled the water, got a drink, snorted a few times, then followed a little sorrel that was in Johnnie's string into the soup. We pushed the little jag of steers we'd cut off from the herd into the tail end of the remuda, and just as the last horse took the water so did the first steer.

Johnnie was on the downriver point and I was on the upriver. Bronc was flanking Johnnie, and Jim was flanking me.

A river looks one way sitting on a horse on the bank and looking down and across it, and it looks another way when you get down in it, especially if your horse is a low swimmer and swims with nothing but his head out of the water and there's waves in front of you that you sometimes can't see over to see the other bank. If a man isn't a little boogered of a river running like Powder River was that day, it's only because he's either a fool or has never been out of his own backyard before.

The water got deep quicker than I thought it would, and the current was stronger than I thought it would be.

"Damn! Damn! Damn!" I muttered under my breath as the cold water struck us and swept us downstream.

Ahead of me, bobbing up and down in the water, were

123 horse heads and alongside of me were the horned heads of the lead steers in the little bunch we'd kicked into the river just behind the remuda.

Behind me, I could hear the other boys whooping and yelling as they cut off a bigger bunch of steers—about five or six hundred—and tried to get them across the boggy stretch and into the water before the last steer of the first bunch was swimming.

When I saw the lead horse come up out of the water and shake and then start up the short slope on the west bank, I looked back and saw that the steers were taking the water on the south bank and I felt good about the crossing.

By the time the last horse in the remuda stepped out of the water, half of the steers were already in the river and swimming. Here they were three or four abreast, and there they were fifteen or more, but they were taking the water and swimming so smoothly and with no gaps in their ranks that they looked like a single giant serpent snaking its way gracefully across Powder River.

When the head of the snake neared the opposite bank and began rising out of the water it suddenly balked and began folding back upon itself. It happened so quickly and was so unexpected and was done with such grace—in those first few seconds at least—that it took a few seconds to understand what was *really* happening.

At first, I thought what I was seeing across the water couldn't be true.

I said out loud to myself, *"That can't be a goddamn horsebacker!"* At the top of the short slope? Just as the last of the remuda disappeared over it and the first of the steers were starting up it?

It couldn't be. No way in hell.

But it was.

"Who is that son of a bitch? . . . Holy shit, that's Pilot Judd! The son of a bitch better have sense enough to get out of the goddamn way!"

And then something even more unbelievable happened—he waved something. *"Is that a goddamn slicker he's wavin'? If he turns those lead steers back . . . My God! The worthless son-of-a-bitchin' dirty bastard is turnin' 'em back on purpose!"*

Hell for a cowboy could be an eternity of feeling the fear and panic and helplessness that comes over him when he's crossing a dangerous river with a herd of cattle and sees the leaders turned back just as they reach the opposite shore.

For a short while, steers kept taking the river from the east bank—bailing into the water one after another, two to ten abreast, with horned heads held high, unsure of themselves but willing to follow those in front of them nonetheless.

But even while steers were still bailing into the river from the east bank, those that Pilot Judd had boogered with his slicker on the west bank were panicked and headed back toward the east shore.

Somewhere near the center of Powder River, the snake of cattle folded on itself completely and stopped.

Then the herd began moving again, this time back toward the east bank, some fifteen hundred head of Texas Longhorns in a panicked rush for the safety of dry ground in a river hungry for hide and horns—and saddles and souls.

I felt my own panicked rush for the safety of dry ground and turned my horse around and made him swim against the current and away from the cattle.

I made it. In fact, *most* made it back across to the east bank, and, once there, *most* made it across the bog. But still, a lot of cattle were lost to Powder River that day—and that wasn't even near the worst of it.

"It was that goddamn Pilot Judd over there, wavin' his slicker, wasn't it, Johnnie?" Jim Napp asked when we met again on the east bank with the cattle scattering to hell in the sage behind us—at least those that hadn't drowned in the river or bogged down in the sand. "I saw the bastard, but couldn't believe it!"

"Where's Bronc and Laredo?" Johnnie asked. "Anybody seen 'em?"

Lewis Anacho stood up in stirrups and pointed toward the river. "Looky yonder, where all them steers are bogged down—what's that reflectin' the sun?"

We rode down to the edge of the bog for a look, but even before we pulled up, we could tell it was the shank of a bit reflecting the sun.

The shank was part of the bit that was in Laredo Allen's horse's mouth. It was the only part of the horse that wasn't covered in wet sand. The horse was dead, trampled to death in the bog along with so many steers, some dead and some still alive, in such a small area that it wasn't possible to tell how many there were.

"SHIT!" Jim Napp said and pointed to something ten feet to the right of the dead horse—a boot barely visible between two steers.

We slid off our horses and walked on top of dead and bogged steers to the boot.

Laredo was dead. You never know for sure how those things happen, but somehow he had let his horse come out of the river in the wrong spot and the horse had bogged down. The mad rush of panicked Texas steers did the rest.

After we got Laredo out of the sand and onto the bank, Johnnie stood up and said solemnly as he looked across the river, "Billy, will you stay here with 'im? Fellers . . . we better find Bronc."

Juan found Bronc's horse in ten minutes. He was drowned and floating on his side with three dead steers who had all hung up in a little rocky cove a half mile downriver.

We put three ropes on the horse's hind feet and pulled him out of the water. An hour later and another three miles downriver, hung up in some brush along with a lot of trash, something caught my eye.

"Gawdamighty, Bronc," I said when I saw him facedown in the water, bobbing up and down like a fishing cork. "If I know you, you swam your horse right into 'em and tried to keep 'em from turning back."

27

All men are humbled by death, and all the more so when it is sudden and unexpected.

Wrecks can happen crossing dangerous rivers, and Powder River that day was a dangerous river. Dangerous rivers and the wrecks that can and do occur on them were a natural fact of cowboy life that all of us accepted without question. There was hardly a major river on any cow trail that did not have a wooden cross at its banks marking the grave of a cowboy who lost his life in the water. Some rivers— the Platte, the Red, the Brazos, the Yellowstone—had more than one such wooden cross on their banks. Rivers are natural forces that man has no control over; their rising and their falling are natural, and death on them is natural too, just as the fear of them is natural in horses, cattle, and cowboys.

But what occurred on Powder River on that twenty-eighth day of August 1894 was not natural. Johnnie knew what he was doing, and to a man, we all had faith in his cowboy skills and his trail sense. Under his leadership we had attacked the dangerous Powder with as flawless a plan as can be devised against so powerful and unpredictable a foe, and that plan was being carried out with such cowboy skill that I couldn't help the bolt of pride that I'd felt when I saw from the back of my swimming horse the lead steers rising out of the water ahead of me and the long, graceful line faithfully following them to the safety of that short slope on the other side.

By rights we had conquered Powder River. Yet, only three hours after the first remuda horse took to the water we were all back on the east bank, hats in hand, sitting in shocked silence on our horses or standing on the ground, holding the reins in front of us. The bloody, unrecognizable body of Laredo Allen and the ghastly water-logged body of Bronc Kinkaid, his brown eyes and mouth still wide with the disbelief he must have felt as he and his horse were pushed underneath the surface by an unstoppable wall of panicked Longhorns, were stretched out in the wet sand before us.

But the dead at our feet, the dead—and the hundred or so still struggling—in the bog, and the dead in the water were not dead by the whim of nature.

They were dead by the whim of man.

None of us had ever seen or even heard of anything like it happening before. We could hardly fathom it.

Although cowboys might dislike and even fight each other out of the saddle, once in the saddle they help each other, depend on each other, lay their lives on the line for each other. It was an unwritten code and one that was seldom if ever talked about, and yet it was the code which the breed lived—and at times died—by. And by God, it was a code you did not break.

"It was Pilot," Johnnie said in a hushed tone, his eyes riveted to the bodies of Bronc and Laredo. "I guess you all know that, but I'm tellin' you anyway. Luther was there too, but he stayed back in the brush and probably didn't have enough sense to know what Pilot was doin'. It wasn't no accident either, we all know that. Maybe Pilot didn't intend for anybody to die, but Bronc and Laredo died and Pilot will have to be held accountable. It's up to me to do that holdin' and I just want you to know that I will.

"Now boys," Johnnie said quietly, "let's carry 'em back

up on the grass. . . . Billy, will you cut some sheets from the wagon tarp to wrap 'em in?"

That done, the bodies wrapped in the wagon tarp and lying in the grass a quarter mile from the river, Johnnie looked up and said, "I'd better get across the river and bring the remuda back before the river rises any more."

"I'll go with you," I said.

"No, Casey—I don't want you to go, but if you don't mind, would you take Juan and Ramus and start pullin' the steers out of the bog that are still alive. If the river rises more they'll all drown. Billy, I'd like you to saddle one of the horses you've got under harness and help Jim and Lewis try to get around the lead steers that're headed back down the trail toward Texas. They're spooked and they're gonna scatter all to hell, but maybe y'all can get in front of 'em and turn 'em into a mill till we get some help out to you."

All hope, of course, of meeting Ike at the Tongue River by the first of September was gone. It would take two or three days to get all the different little bunches of steers together again that were scattered in the sage. But even with that done, there was no way the steers were going into Powder River water again, not spooked like they were. A hundred men wouldn't be able to push them across until the river fell at least half the level it was, and even then we'd have to take them to a different crossing, for steers have memories too.

When we laid Bronc and Laredo in the ground that day at sundown, we stood over their covered graves with hats in hand and sang "We Won't Have to Cross Jordan Alone." It was the one and only time I ever saw tears in Johnnie's eyes.

After burying Bronc and Laredo, we went back to pulling the live steers out of the bog and continued working by lantern light throughout the night.

In the end, we pulled twenty-six steers free, leaving sixty-three dead in the bog, including the five we shot just before the rising water reached their nostrils.

We worked all that day with no sleep, but by evening we had 2346 head of steers on the bedground, only some 500 short.

The next morning Johnnie came to me before we caught horses and said, "Casey, I'm goin' to turn the herd over to you and go after Pilot."

"Hell, Johnnie," I said. "Wait till we deliver the herd and we'll go together."

"I can't wait," he said. "I thought I could, but I can't. Ike asked me to take the herd and I did it as a favor, and now I'm asking the same favor of you. Ike's contract is lost, that's for sure, so there's no need to hurry or to take another risk crossing the Powder before it falls. Will you have enough hands if I leave?"

"We'll get 'em to the Tongue, Johnnie," I said. I knew it wasn't any use to argue. Had the tables been turned, I would probably have been asking the same thing. And we would deliver the herd. Hell, we were almost there anyway.

"Be careful and keep a tight cinch, amigo," I said as I reached out and shook his hand. "You know Pilot's the only one bearin' any guilt over what happened here, don't you?"

He gave me a noncommital shrug and said, "Give my apologies to Ike—tell 'im if he knows where Laredo's and Bronc's families are to split my wages between 'em."

We finally crossed the Powder River six days later, in another spot. By mine and Jim Napp's count we were seventy-one head short of what we should have had once we subtracted the sixty-three lost in the bog. There might have been a few of that seventy-one we just didn't find in the sage, but for sure most of them drowned in Powder River.

A day out from Powder River, on September 5, we met Ike coming to see about us. By then he knew he was not going to get the government contract and had had time to deal with that in his mind, but the news of the deaths of Bronc and Laredo and how they died hit him like a jolt.

"I wanted to save my goddamn ranch so bad I lost sight of everything else!" he said. "I knew Pilot wasn't any goddamn cowboy the first time I talked to him, but still I consented to lettin' him be my segundo. Can you figure that?"

"I think you and Johnnie are both losing sight of the fact that no one on God's green earth would have dreamed Pilot Judd would do what he did. The only one responsible for what happened is Pilot Judd."

Two days later we arrived at the Tongue River and met the Indian agent from the Tongue River Reservation and his band of Crow cowboys.

We strung the steers between us and counted them and turned them over to the Crow, and I was glad of it. The joy that should have been there at the delivery of a herd brought so far, over so many obstacles, was not there, and we were silent in our day's ride from the Tongue River in Montana back across the Wyoming border to Sheridan. In Sheridan Ike paid us off, paid our fares back to Texas on the Burlington and Missouri as he had promised, and shook each of our hands.

Lewis, Jim, Juan, Ramus, and Billy all left on the train the next morning, with Ike there to see them off.

"You're not getting on the train?" Ike asked.

"No," I said, "I figure I better go see if I can find Johnnie."

Ike nodded. "Let's walk back to the stock pens where the remuda is."

When we got there we leaned on the wooden fence and looked at the horses.

"These will all go to the goddamn bank too," he said.

"Is it really that bad, Ike?"

He looked at me and grinned. "Yeah . . . but what the hell." And then he looked at the horses again and said, "Do you know how long it took me to breed a remuda like this?"

"It's the best remuda I've ever seen, Ike. You can't put your bridle on one you can't make a hand on. . . . I know how it must hurt to lose 'em."

The silence stretched out for a few seconds as we watched the horses nibbling the loose hay on the ground or playing. "Casey . . . I want you to pick out any two head you want for yourself and pick out another one for Johnnie and tell him he can have the one he left the herd on, too. . . . Do this for me, Casey—God, I want to know that there's still at least four head of good Holt horses pulled up between the knees of good cowboys somewhere."

"Hell, Ike . . ." I thought for a few moments, then looked at Ike and said, "I'd like to have that slim chestnut sorrel with the slit left ear that I call Chip and that good-headed bay over there on the other side of that cowhocked dun—old Deuce. He's a little cold-backed, but he's a cowin' son of a bitch, Ike. And I know Johnnie would like a little horse he called Flax, a little sorrel with a rough head but a big heart—he was the first one to take the water that day on Powder River."

"They're yours," Ike said. "Let's get 'em out and put 'em in a separate pen right now."

"Say, Ike," I said. "Why don't you come with me. Let's go find Johnnie together . . . and then let's all three of us find Pilot together."

Ike grinned. "It's temptin', Casey, but I've got to go on back to Texas and face the music."

"So the crooked banker wins?"

"No, Casey . . . Hell no, that crooked son of bitch doesn't win. You see, he gained a ranch but lost his integrity. So I figure he really lost more than I did. I don't think that banker intended for Judd to go the length he did to keep us from getting to the Tongue River on time, so I'm just going to give him a damn good thrashing instead of a good killing."

Just then the depot agent came out to the stock pens, holding a slip of paper up in his hands and said, "This is addressed to Casey Wills, Ike Holt, or any person with the Holt outfit."

"Well," Ike said, "you're looking at all that's left of the Slash Seven—what's it say?"

The agent adjusted his glasses and read: "*Am in Bluff*

City, Kansas, jail stop Might should come quick stop Signed Johnnie stop."

I smiled. "It's nice to know some things in life never change. Mister agent, figure some way to get me and three head of horses to Bluff City, Kansas, as quick as you can."

28

Bluff City, Kansas, was a few miles north of Oklahoma Territory and a few miles west of Caldwell and the Chisholm Trail, the first trail I'd ever taken cattle up. The last time I had been to Bluff City, though, was when we drove the Banister horses out of New Mexico to the Oklahoma land rush six years ago. Then there had been no train going into Bluff City. Then Abilene and Ellsworth were the closest railheads for cattle coming out of Texas, but that had been in '88—by '94 railroads were not hard to locate.

The train started slowing down a mile east of Bluff Creek. I had forgotten how many trees that part of Kansas had, and how ungodly hot and humid it could be in early September.

"Where's Bill Long?" I said when I stepped into the sheriff's office.

The man sitting behind the desk, a man of about thirty, wearing shoes, gray trousers with a matching gray vest, and a white shirt, looked up and looked me over for a few seconds and then said, "I'm J. M. Calder, sheriff of Bluff City. Bill Long is gone"—Calder stopped to look me over again—"just like Bluff City's tolerance for Texas cowboys who have no regard for law and order. Didn't you see the sign just outside of town explaining the no-firearms ordinance—or did you choose just to ignore it?"

"I just got here on the train," I explained.

"There's a sign at the depot too."

"I didn't see it," I told him.

"You can't wear that pistol on your person, and you sure as hell can't walk around town, carrying a rifle—those days are gone!"

"I'll be getting a room at the hotel—I'll leave them in it."

"See that you do—and see that it's the *next* thing you do. Do you have business in town or are you just—"

"My name is Casey Wills and—"

"Casey Wills, huh?" He opened the top desk drawer and pulled out a slip of paper and looked at it. "Uh huh . . . You're one of the ones Lester sent the telegraph to in Sheridan, Wyoming, with the—let's see here—the Holt outfit. Just what does that mean, Wills?"

"What does what mean?"

"The Holt outfit?"

I pushed my hat back off my forehead a little and said, "It was a trail outfit—we took a herd of steers from San Antonio to the Tongue River Reservation in Montana for Ike Holt. . . . Where's Johnnie?"

"Where in the hell do you think he is? He's back there in the cell block, locked up."

"What's the charge against him?"

"Where do you want to start? . . . Carrying a firearm inside the city limits, discharging a firearm inside the city limits, disturbing the peace, assault with a deadly weapon, manslaughter, attempted murder . . . and murder in the first degree if Judd dies."

I shook my head and raised my eyebrows. "What happened? Judd still alive? What about Atkins?"

"So you know everyone involved in this blood feud, huh?"

"I wouldn't call it a blood feud. . . . I wouldn't call it a feud at all."

"Well . . . then what in the hell would you call it,

Wills? I understand it started in Texas, was carried all the way to Wyoming, and finally here to Bluff City for its bloody culmination!"

Calder dropped the paper back into the desk drawer, closed the drawer with some authority, let out a long breath, shook his head, and said, "A shoot-out in the middle of the street in broad daylight, for God's sake—a shootout that cost Clois Newman his life!"

"Clois . . . who?"

"Clois Newman—owner of Newman's Dry Goods—was killed by a stray bullet while he was setting up a display in his store window. It's over, Wills. . . . The Texas reign of Bluff City is stopping right now. We don't care what happened in Texas or in some place in Wyoming called Powder River for God's sake!"

"Well, two damn good men by the names of Laredo Allen and Bronc Kinkaid care what happened in Wyoming at a place called Powder River, I can tell you that much— and if you'd been there you'd care too!"

"Well," sighed Calder, calmer now, "I wasn't there . . . and neither was Clois Newman. He was home with his wife and family on Peach Street. Now he's in the cemetery."

"I'm sorry for him and his family—I really am," I said. "Johnnie would not have had that happen for anything in the world. Can I see him now?"

Calder opened the desk drawer again and pulled out a set of keys and with one of them opened the heavy door leading to the cells. Just before he swung the door open for me he said, "The grand jury is waiting to see if Judd lives or dies. I've charged Judd and Lester both with manslaughter in the death of Clois Newman, but that won't mean anything more than a ten-year sentence. But if Judd dies"—Calder opened his eyes wider and nodded his head—"I can charge Lester with murder and ask for the death sentence, and get it. This thing should *not* have been brought to Bluff City."

* * *

Johnnie was standing with his back to me, looking out the barred window of his cell. "Sheriff Calder spoke real highly of you," I said.

Johnnie turned around. "Casey! Damn . . ." He let out a sigh of relief and stretched his mustache into the first grin it had been stretched into since Bronc and Laredo died that day on Powder River.

"I should have had better sense than to let you come without me."

"You get the herd delivered?"

I nodded. "Six days ago."

"How'd you get here so quick?"

"The clankity-clank train you wanted to ride brought me."

"How's Ike?"

"Heartbroke over Bronc and Laredo dying in Powder River. He wanted nothing more than to find Judd himself. He said he was sorry he put you in the position he did. He said he's going to lose the ranch for sure and the only thing he can do about it is to kick his banker's ass all over San Antonio. I just hope like hell that if he decides to go to war with him instead of just kicking his ass that he's a little more strategic in his battle planning than you were. And he gave us two head of horses each—said you could keep the one you left the herd on and I picked old Flax for your other one."

"The hell! . . . That little Flax is a good horse!"

"See if you can keep from ruining him, then," I said with a grin.

"You have any more trouble on Powder River?"

"No . . . we waited five days for the water to fall and moved upriver about a mile to cross, but then we snaked 'em across Powder like pattin' for a dance. Looks like you're the one who ran into trouble."

"What . . . This?! Hell, this ain't no trouble, Casey!"

"It'll do till trouble comes," I said.

"Just because one of Judd's bullets killed a man on the street—"

"Calder's charged *both* of you with manslaughter."

"I shot twice and hit Judd both times. He emptied his

revolver, and I was the safest one in town because he was *aimin'* at me."

"Why right in the middle of town, Johnnie? And especially why in the middle of a Kansas town that suddenly doesn't have any more use for cowboys than a banker does scruples?"

"Wasn't my choosin', Casey. I picked up their trail in Sidney, but was always about a day or two behind. I figured I was still behind when I followed them here, and I guess they thought I was, too. Anyway, I tied my horse up and was going to the hotel to see if they'd been here and met them just as they were coming out. Atkins dove behind a water trough and never even anted up. Judd opened with a shot that I think went off before he even cleared leather. I had to call, Casey. . . . I came to kill Pilot, we both know that, but I never meant to do it in the middle of a town. I wanted to take him back to Powder River and hang him right there at the crossing where the last thing he would see would be Laredo's and Bronc's graves."

"Where'd you hit him?"

"Once in the leg and once in the stomach."

"What about Luther?"

Johnnie shrugged. "I never fired a shot at him. After Judd went down, I ran over to the trough and Luther was behind it, cowering like a rabbit and beggin' me not to kill him. Hell, I never had planned on killin' him, because he wasn't the one who turned the herd back that day."

"You know that Calder's not only got you charged with manslaughter, but he says that if Judd dies he'll charge you with murder and ask for the death sentence. You know that don't you, Johnnie?"

Johnnie nodded. "Yeah, I know—but I *couldn't* have been the one who killed Newman and anyone who seen it knows the same thing. And how could any jury, grand or otherwise, blame me for comin' after Judd after what he did? And besides, Casey, he was the one who fired first. There must be some witnesses."

I held my hands up. "Johnnie, I don't know any more about witnesses than I do about why in hell you let it happen in the middle of town, but in case you haven't noticed, this isn't the high, dry, and lonesome sagebrush country of Powder River, it's the low and humid farming country of southern Kansas. The people here aren't exactly cowboys—they're shop keepers and paper publishers and schoolteachers and preachers, and the ones who aren't are farmers who might drive the milk cow into the barn on old Dobbin but they've never taken three thousand longhorns up fifteen hundred miles of trail, called a roundup wagon home, stood night guard in a freezin' rain, or nighthawked a remuda of horses."

"Casey . . . you ain't trying to scare me, are you? I know this isn't Wyoming, but it is just a few miles off the Chisholm—and have you forgotten the times we got good and drunk here and dipped our wicks in the soiled doves of the Bluff City Recreation Parlor?"

"And I guess you've noticed that where the Bluff City Recreation Parlor used to be there is now a Methodist Church and that Bill Long has been replaced by J. M. Calder."

"Casey . . . What has happened has happened. We can't undo the past and I can't see any future in worrying about it. What has happened has been terrible, the worst thing I've been through in my life—Laredo and Bronc are dead, just like Clois Newman is, and all because of something Pilot Judd chose to do. But if there's any justice in this world, what began on Powder River ended when I shot Judd—that is, *if* Judd has the decency to give up the ghost. He owes Bronc and Laredo a dyin'. You and every cowboy who was there that day know that, and it was my duty to see that Judd's debt was paid. It wasn't a duty I asked for—it was a duty demanded of me because Bronc and Laredo were *my* responsibility."

I couldn't argue against anything Johnnie said, but as Bluff City mourned Clois Newman and waited to see if Pilot Judd would live or die I sensed something that was indeed worth worrying about. The story of the string of tragedies beginning on Powder River on the twenty-eighth of August and continuing on to their fair town on the seventh of

September was told a hundred times, a thousand times, and each time it was told, the storyteller, instead of showing compassion for the dead on the banks of Powder River, seemed only to be incited by them, like they had perished for no other reason than to ultimately spill the blood of the innocent on the streets of Bluff City, Kansas. What I sensed was that the people of Bluff City cared nothing for the fact that duty and honor required Johnnie to see that Pilot Judd's debt not go unpaid. They had no sense for justice, at least not the kind of justice meted out where Johnnie had lived his life.

And, even if Bluff City had a sense of what was right, that said Johnnie was justified in what he had done, they cared a lot less for it than they did for what I had heard called the "hammer of justice."

On the eighth day after I got to town Pilot Judd died. Johnnie looked thoughtful and slowly nodded his head when I gave him the news.

On the ninth day the grand jury indicted Johnnie for first-degree murder, and he was shocked. And he was even more shocked when I told him who the star witness for the prosecution would be—Luther Atkins.

"Who?" Johnnie said. "Hell, he dove behind the goddamn water trough and covered up his head before the first cordite was lit! How could he have seen what happened?"

The trial was scheduled to begin on Thursay, the twenty-fourth of September.

The *Bluff City Mirror* was usually only published on Saturdays but had a special Monday edition on the twenty-first which, other than a short article about an upcoming ice-cream social at the Methodist Church and the marriage announcement of Julie Ann Smyer to Roger Smith, was devoted to stories about the upcoming trial, the defendant, and the victims.

The editor of the *Mirror* said in an editorial on page two:

> *Perhaps it is up to the people of Bluff City to step forward and send a message to all drifters, drunkards, and ne'er-do-wells with the dusty Texas hats and shotgunned boots,*

*the noisy spurs, and the penchant for loose women, hard
drink, and violence that they would do well to avoid us
from here on and ever more!*

I could tell the good people of Bluff City had the collective need to "hammer" someone who fit that description
with their justice and that nothing less would pour oil on
their troubled waters.

I carried that edition of the *Mirror* to the jail and handed it
through the bars to Johnnie and said, "I could not have
described you better myself. The man who wrote that is a
damn fine writer."

After Johnnie had had time to read the editorial, I said,
"I don't think the 'message' he's talking about has anything to do with converting you to Methodism. I think it
has more to do with sending your soul right on to the Lord
in the sorry state it's in right now, with your penchant for
loose women, hard liquor, and violence still intact. And
that being the case, I'm going to start keeping our good
Holt-bred horses saddled and our cinches tight, as I think
when the opportunity presents itself we should roll our
beds and go back to the high, lonesome sagebrush. I think
our time would be better spent sniffing under rocks and
chasing rabbits than in trying to convince anyone here that
you did not kill Clois Newman and that the killing of Pilot
Judd is probably the only honorable thing you've ever
done in your entire misspent and ill-planned life. . . .
When the time comes, which horse do you want to be in
the middle of?"

"You talkin' about a *jail break*, Casey? You think this
deal is gettin' that serious?"

I rolled my eyes and threw my hands up. "You've been
indicted for first-degree murder in a town that's looking for
some way to extract its pound of flesh—or in this case, a
hundred and seventy pounds of flesh, specifically yours."

Johnnie was silent for a moment, then he said, "You're
serious, aren't you, Casey? You'd break me out of jail?"

"Well, I sure as hell wouldn't expect less from you if the tables were turned."

"Throw my wood on old Flax, then," Johnnie said, "and get the kink out his back. . . . Are the horses soft?"

I grinned. "Not as soft as you."

29

The same day I told Johnnie I was going to start keeping our cinches tight so we could go when the opportunity presented itself, I was handed a telegram by Sheriff Calder.

"I took the liberty to read it," he said. "I've sent a telegram to the governor, requesting army troops. If it's war you want, Wills, I will goddamn sure as hell oblige you!"

I took the telegram from Calder and read it: To Casey Wills stop Just got the word in Texas about the trial stop Am on the way with Billy, Jim, Ramus, Lewis, and Juan stop Signed Ike.

"I'm giving you fair warning right now, Wills," Calder said. "If they come up here thinking they can just get Lester out of jail and take him back to Texas, it *will* be a war—but one of the shortest and most one-sided in the history of Kansas. You cowboys will be licking your wounds all the way back to the Lone Star State—those of you who are able to lick at all, that is!"

Damn, Ike, I thought. I know you mean well but all you're doin' is causing Calder to bring in the troops. The whole damn affair had gotten plumb out of hand and was unraveling like a broken rope. I knew me and Johnnie had to be gone before the troops and the cowboys got to town.

"There won't be a war," I said. Of course there would be if Johnnie was still in jail when Ike and the cowboys got there, but I didn't tell Calder that. "At least if there is," I went on, "I won't be a part of it. I'm leavin' now. Whatever happens, you can't blame me."

Calder looked at me again the way he did the first time I walked into his office, only this time he said, "A cowboy with sense? Remarkable, Wills! At least you'll be alive to read about the asses your cowboy friends make of themselves."

"A *cowboy with sense*, huh? Well, I'll show you some sense, all right," I said to myself as I saddled two of our horses—Johnnie's Big Track and my Chip—about noon and led the other two out of the livery to hit a long trot out of town toward the west, being sure as many people saw me leaving as was possible.

Once out of town, I kept trotting west and did so for four hours, only stopping to water the horses now and then.

Then I found a good thicket of brush around a little seep hole and unsaddled and hobbled Chip and Big Track out of sight, rubbed them down with grass, patted them on the butts, and headed back toward Bluff City with the other two.

I spent that night in some trees along Bluff Creek about three miles east of town.

Caldwell was about twelve or fifteen miles east of Bluff City, and the next morning I rode Deuce into it bareback with no spurs or chaps or hat and stopped in front of the Caldwell Mercantile, where I pretended to be a farmer needing a little dynamite to blow out some stumps in my field.

I wasn't an expert on explosives, but I'd had a little experience with them.

"How much will ten sticks of that number-three cost?" I asked.

"Thirteen cents each—a dollar thirty total."

I counted my money. Train fare and hotel rooms and meals in cafés and livery bills had about used up the money Ike paid me in Sheridan. "Make that nine sticks," I said.

"It's best to use a two-inch wood auger to drill a hole in the stumps to put the dynamite in," the store clerk said. "Will you be needing one of those?"

"No," I said. "I don't use augers for my stumps. Can you put that dynamite in a bag?"

I had no great scheme for getting Johnnie out of jail—just blow a hole in the side of the jail, get Johnnie, and ride like hell. About thirty miles west of town we would switch to the other good Holt horses, fresh and hobbled and waiting in the brush. By daylight the next morning I expected to be sixty or seventy miles from Bluff City.

By chance, this was the night of the ice-cream social at the Methodist Church I'd read about in the *Bluff City Mirror*. This was good news to me because most of the town would be there and surely anyone with a stomach full of Methodist ice cream would not be eager for a hard nighttime ride with a posse.

About an hour after the gaslights had been lit along Main Street I came into town, riding Deuce and leading Flax. The ice-cream social was working wonders: I didn't see a soul on the street. There was a slight nip to the night air, a hint of fall. The air smelled of damp leaves and town. I hoped that soon me and Johnnie would be smelling sage and feeling the fall breeze blowing across a dry lake bed or lonesome flat in some place where he would have been looked down upon only if he had *not* killed Judd and where I would be only if I had *not* broken him out of jail.

I rode up the alley behind the jail and waited and listened in the dark for any sounds coming from inside the jail or from anybody on the street. I heard none and finally said to Johnnie in a whisper, "If I were you, I would get on the far corner of that cell and pull that sorry excuse of a bed on top of me." Then I dug a little hole in the ground underneath the rock wall below the window, twisted the fuses of five sticks of dynamite together, struck a match and lit the fuses, then quickly pulled two more sticks of dynamite out of the sack and put those on top of the other five. I ran as hard as I could around the corner of Able's Drug Store, where the horses were hobbled.

I learned later that I should have gotten number-one dynamite because it was 60 percent nitroglycerine and recommended for the "very hard rock" of which that jailhouse was constructed.

The result of those seven sticks of number-three dynamite planted underneath the edge of the jail was the interrupting of the ice-cream social at the Methodist Church and the awakening of every dog in town—but no appreciable damage to the jail itself.

A young jailer by the name of Matt Taylor was on duty that night, and when I saw the dynamite had not even cracked the rock wall I ran around to the front of the jail and met Taylor as he was running out.

"What in the hell was *that?*" he asked with eyes wide.

I pulled out my old Colt, cocked it underneath his chin, and said, "Goddammit, that was me. Unlock that door to the cells and let Johnnie out!"

"I . . . I can't," he stuttered. "J. M. don't leave the key with me at night!"

I reached into the bag, pulled out another stick of dynamite, lit the fuse, and tossed it against the door. "If I were you, I would run like hell, Taylor!" And he did.

That stick of number-three blew the door open and rearranged a portion of Calder's office.

I rushed through the dust and the smoke into the cell block. "If we ever do this again," I said hurriedly to Johnnie as I put the last stick of dynamite underneath the edge of the door to his cell, "remind me not use number-three dynamite on rock walls."

"You gonna light that son of a bitch right here?" Johnnie asked.

I struck the match, and while it sputtered to flame I looked at him and said, "Unless you can figure out some other way of getting this goddamn door open."

Johnnie rushed to the bunk he had dragged next to the bars and hurriedly pulled it back to the rock wall, leaned it on edge, and crawled behind it as I touched the match to the last fuse.

The blast sprung the door just enough so that Johnnie and I both working on it finally popped it open.

"Thank God!" I said. "Let's go before that Methodist bunch gets here!"

By the time we got to the horses we could hear men running and shouting, but we raced the horses down the alley and headed west and soon had left Bluff City and its barking dogs and shouting men behind.

We gave the horses their heads and let them stretch out and run for five miles in the moonlight, only taking hold of them when we needed to skirt around a farmhouse so as not to set the dogs to barking. It was my hope that Calder would think we would head south and cross the border into Oklahoma Territory as soon as we could, and I didn't want any barking farm dogs giving away the fact that we were going west instead.

I looked at Johnnie, and from the moonlit smile on his face I could tell how good it felt to have a horse between his knees again.

Two hours later we rode into the brush patch where Big Track and Chip were hobbled and waiting. Flax and Deuce were used up and stood with heads down and sides heaving while we jerked the saddles off them. They had given us all they had and we had seen no sign of a soul after us. When I slipped the bridle off Deuce I patted him on the butt and said, "Rest awhile and then tank up on grass and water and then you and Flax had better get the hell out of Kansas before they make farm horses out of you."

With the moon high overhead we put Big Track and Chip into a long trot and by daylight had gotten all the way to Mule Creek, at least seventy miles west of Bluff City.

When we reached Mule Creek we bushed up in some tamaracks and pulled the saddles off the horses to let them cool down. It was hot and humid and we didn't want to gall their backs.

"Damn Kansas heat!" Johnnie said. "And damn these Kansas varmits!" he said as he slapped his neck. Then he started laughing. "Can you believe we're bushin' up like a couple of old wrinkle-horned bunch quitters and runnin' from the law?"

I lay back in the grass and started laughing, too. "Can you imagine how mad J. M. Calder is?"

"We're goin' to make it, ain't we, Casey? By god, we're goin' to make it!"

"You never really thought a bunch of Kansas farmers could keep a couple of bunch quitters like us out of the tules, did you?" I said.

Then Johnnie laughed again, gave a loud yee-haw and said, "I don't give a damn what anyone says about you, Casey—I never did think you were plumb crazy . . . a little different than everybody else, maybe, but not plumb crazy."

I laughed.

"I've wanted to be like you, Casey."

I sat up and looked at him. "What—? Hell, you've been making fun of me for fifteen years at least, Johnnie, for bein' like I am—and you've never had a care in the world."

"Is that right?" Johnnie said.

"Yeah, you know it is. You've always been like a coyote—all you ever needed to be happy was the sunny side of a creek bank and every now and then a little tawny-haired trollop to chase down it."

Johnnie laughed a little again, but this time it was not a particularly happy laugh. "I never thought of it exactly like that, but I guess you're right, but, you know, Casey . . . ?"

"What . . . ?"

"I guess I've never really had a care in the world, but then I've never had a dream either."

"You're damn lucky for it, too . . . You ready to rattle the hocks of these Holt horses on out of this state?"

Now Johnnie laughed again and stood up. "If there are

any horses that can get us out of the state we're in, then it's gotta be Holt-bred horses. I'm ready!"

We were trotting along somewhere between Mule Creek and the head of Salt Fork Creek. The country was more broken here, with red washes and small cedars. We were keeping to the bushes and the low places as best we could when we spotted several riders cresting a hill about a mile to the northwest.

We jerked the horses around and back into some cedars.

"What do you think?" Johnnie asked. "Is that a posse?"

"I don't know. I don't think a posse could have gotten in front of us, but then I'd just as soon never know one way or the other. I would like for that to be one of the mysteries of life I die in old age never knowing. What do you say we ride south and cross the border into Oklahoma?"

"You know," Johnnie said, "that's where I had my heart set on going all along—and we'll have these nice hot bushes full of bloodsuckin' varmits to follow all the way there."

We rode in the Kansas heat, sticking to the brush and washes whenever we could, for another couple of hours. By then we were thinking that the riders we had seen were not members of a posse after all. We began to feel good again.

And then the shots in the distance—three of them.

We immediately pulled up again.

"What do you think?" I asked.

"I don't know," Johnnie said. "Maybe a hunter."

"Yeah . . . maybe," I said as we put the lathered horses into a trot again. "Let's get down in that draw and work our way down it for a while."

We watered the horses and drank our fill from a shallow pool of warm slime at the head of the draw, and a mile later came onto a grassy flat in the heat of the day where the Oklahoma horizon was only a couple of miles away, writhing and dancing under the shadowless sun.

And out of that writhing and dancing Oklahoma horizon we saw riders writhing and dancing toward us.

We wheeled the horses and headed back north in a hard run, hoping to get back to the draw in that direction, hoping the riders coming from the south had not seen us.

But suddenly, out of nowhere it seemed, there were other riders, many of them, in a long lope with rifles already out, coming out of the head of the same draw we were racing toward for cover.

Again we slid the horses to a stop in the middle of the grassy flat and spun them on their hocks a few times, looking now at the riders coming out of the draw from the north and now at those coming out of the dancing Oklahoma horizon to the south.

"No way around it, Casey," Johnnie said. "I don't know where they came from, but those are both posses and they're ridin' like hell after me and you! I'll bet right now you're thinkin' that you should have left my ass in jail."

"No—right now I'm thinkin' that I'd like to be on the sorriest cow outfit I've ever drawn wages from, bitchin' about the remuda or how stupid the wagon boss is. But I guess we have to play the hand dealt us."

Johnnie laughed. "Hell, this hand won't even beat openers, Casey."

"One thing's for sure—there's no going north or south, Johnnie, and I sure as hell don't want to go back east."

"What about eternity?"

I looked at Johnnie. "What in the hell do you mean?" I asked.

"Do you believe in it?"

"I've heard quite a little talk about it, and I can't say I haven't given it some thought of my own—but for all that, I've yet to meet anyone who's actually been there and come back. Why? You planning on going there yourself?"

Johnnie looked at me and grinned. "Yeah . . . and I think we can get there right through there." He extended his right arm toward the line of broken hills to the west and seemed to be sighting down it. "I think we can squirt

right through there, Casey—right between both posses—
and reach those hills in front of 'em. And if we can, then
we should be able to reach the brush along Salt Fork
Creek . . . and hell, if we do that, then we can sneak out
in the dark and drift all the way to eternity—*if* it really
exists."

Johnnie looked to the north and then to the south, at
the two posses closing in on us, then he looked at me for a
few short seconds in silence before saying, "Keep a tight
cinch, amigo."

"You too, Johnnie," I said. "See you in the brush along
the creek, huh?"

"Yeah, Casey—see you in the brush . . . or maybe on
the rim beyond. . . . Wherever we meet, it's been a hell
of a ride for a long time, ain't it?"

Then Johnnie leaned over and extended his hand
toward me.

Our hands were hot and sweaty, but the handshake we
shared was solid as a rock. "It *has* been one hell of a ride,
Johnnie. . . . Thanks . . . thanks for all of it!"

It seemed like ther was more that should be said, but
maybe the solid handshake and the few seconds of silence
as we held it said it better than awkward cowboy tongues
could have ever managed. Besides, there was no more time
for talking.

We pointed Big Track and Chip west, touched our spurs
to their bellies, gave them their heads, and leaned over on
them.

They were running wide open in nothing flat, neck and
neck, ears laid back and heads stretched out. Then Chip
gained a little and Big Track's head fell back to my stirrup.

I heard shots ring out from the posse coming from the
south and instinctively ducked a little as the horses
jumped small bushes and deep trails.

I glanced back at Johnnie as he reached back and
tapped Big Track's butt with the ends of his bridle reins
and smiled.

More shots.

Johnnie pulled his hat down and yelled, "Powder River
be damned!"

Then Big Track went down. As quick as that. His front feet went out from under him like he'd been forefooted and the other end of the rope was anchored to the bottom of a stout post. He went down in dead run and rolled with his head between his knees and when I looked back his heavy butt had already come over and was just whipcracking the ground. Both of Johnnie's feet were still in the stirrups and his neck was bent at a sickening angle underneath Big Track's butt.

I slid Chip to a stop and wheeled him around on his right hock to go back to see about Johnnie. But just as I started back a searing pain struck my left side, and I watched helplessly as the Kansas sod came up to slap me in the face.

When I came to again it was almost dark and I was laying on a couple of blankets in the bed of a wagon and my mouth was so dry I couldn't work up enough spit to swallow any of the grit in my mouth. The blankets gave very little padding and the jarring from the rough wagon caused almost more pain in my left shoulder than I could stand. Almost as soon as I could focus my eyes well enough to see the individual leaves of the trees hanging over the road we were traveling down I felt my stomach coming up and forced myself to roll to the right and hang my head over the side.

"Hold it!" someone yelled. "Wills is conscious but he's sick as a dog!"

After I threw up I eased myself back down on the blankets, thankful that the wagon wasn't moving and hoping that it wouldn't until I died.

"Goddammit, Wills . . ."

I opened my eyes and saw J. M. Calder leaning over the wagon.

"How . . . oh damn . . . how's . . . Johnnie?" I asked as I closed my eyes.

"Let's go, Doug!" Calder yelled. "But keep 'em in a walk till we get out of these rocks."

I managed to force my hand high enough to hook my

fingers over the top of the side board and pull myself up enough to look over it. I saw Calder riding away.

"Calder!" I yelled.

He stopped and turned in the saddle and for a few seconds just looked at me. Then he said, "Lester is dead, Wills."

I looked at Calder, unable to say anything while his words tried to work their way into my brain. *Johnnie dead?* My shoulder hurt too much and my brain was too fuzzy. *Johnnie dead?* Why hell, just a second ago we were leaning over on good Holt horses and it was even kind of fun thinking we could outrun two posses and get back to the sage—of course, in our hearts we knew we couldn't and we both knew where the "rim beyond" lay.

I started to lie back down on the blankets, but then pulled myself back up and yelled at Calder who was riding away again. *"How?"*

Calder stopped and twisted in his saddle and looked at me again. Suddenly this was very important, and I asked it slowly, forgetting a moment about the pain and sickness. *"How'd Johnnie die?"*

Calder pulled off his hat and wiped the sweat from his face with a sleeve and put his hat back on and pulled it down before he answered. "Broken neck . . . when his horse fell. That ground was rotten with gopher holes—his horse must have fell through one with both feet. You were shot in the shoulder when you stopped and came back for him—but you'll make it."

There was no more to say. As I eased myself back down on the blankets there were tears in my eyes but there was also something that—in spite of everything—felt right in my soul. "By God . . . a fittin' way for you to die, Johnnie," I muttered to myself, and I pictured him, and always would, the way he looked just before Big Track fell on him—astraddle a good horse and smiling with his hat brim pushed up against the crown by the wind.

"What'd you say, Wills?" the man on the wagon seat said as he twisted around to look down at me.

I didn't answer.

"Pro'bly talkin' outa his goddamn head, Doug," someone I couldn't see said.

"I reckon so," the driver said as he turned back around on the seat and slapped the team's rumps with his lines. The harness creaked and the wagon rattled and started rolling again. "J. M. said he was a crazy bastard anyway. Said they both was."

30

When the sun came up the next morning, less than thirty-six hours after I had blown open Johnnie's jail cell, I was back in that same jail, lying on a cot in a cell right next to the one with the barred door hanging by one twisted hinge like a broken wing.

Outside the jail I could hear birds chirping, a dog barking, and the rumble of a wagon down Main Street. My glasses were gone, my shirt was lying at the foot of the cot, and my left shoulder was bandaged but still ached like the dickens, just not as bad as I remembered—what little I *could* remember—from that wagon ride from hell of the night before.

I saw Calder step around the sprung door that separated his office from the cells and walk toward my cell with a cup of coffee in one hand and my glasses and a newspaper in the other.

"You're awake, huh?" he said, stopping at my cell and looking through the bars. "Doctor Newsome dug the bullet out of your shoulder after we got here last night. You lost quite a bit of blood, but the bullet had lost a lot of velocity by the time it hit you and it only cracked your shoulder bone. Doctor Newsome said it would heal okay.

The men who fired on you did so without authorization, but it was a tense time and the men in the posse were mostly farmers and were nervous and excited. . . . You want these glasses and this cup of coffee?"

"Where're our horses?"

"Over at the livery—the two you were riding yesterday *and* the two you turned loose along the way—a farmer found them. That was another way we knew which direction you were headed."

"Where's Johnnie?" I asked.

"Don't you remember?"

"Yeah, I remember . . . but where is his body?"

"It's over at Maxwell's Funeral Home."

"When Ike Holt and the boys get here, they'll want to take him back to Texas. No offense, Calder, but the last thing Johnnie would want would be to be buried in the Bluff City cemetery."

"When Ike Holt and the boys get here," Calder said, "there better not be any more trouble. Captain Berryman is camped right outside of town with a squadron of troopers."

"You can tell Captain Berryman to give 'em 'at ease,' " I said. "There won't be any more trouble, but you better be at that train when it stops and bring Ike and those cowboys straight over here to this cell before somebody tells 'em Johnnie's dead and I been shot." Then I managed to get up and step gingerly across the small cell with my spurs faintly jingling. I reached through the bars to take my glasses and the tin cup of coffee from him.

"Thanks," I said after I put my glasses on and had taken a sip of coffee.

"This is a special edition of the *Mirror*," Calder said as he unfolded it and held it up so I could see the front page and the inch-high headline DESPERATE ATTEMPT TO THWART JUSTICE FOILED! Right underneath that was a subheadline that said: POSSES FROM KANSAS, OKLAHOMA COMBINE TO DO IN CRIMINALS—ONE DEAD, ONE WOUNDED AND CAPTURED.

"Do you want to read it?" Calder asked.

"No," I said. "I don't need to read it—just make damn sure you bring Ike here before *he* reads it!"

Calder folded the paper up and started to walk out.

"How'd you get posses out in front of us?" I asked.

"How? Hell, Wills, with telegraphs and trains, that's how! Thirty minutes after you blew open that cell door I'd already telegraphed the sheriffs in Ashland and Dodge City to be on the lookout for you, and the sheriff in Medicine Lodge was already getting a posse together to cut you off if you went west. I knew Marshal Heck Thomas wasn't far across the Kansas-Oklahoma border in Pond Creek, so I wired him and he got a posse together down there and spread some men out along the border to be on the lookout for you down there.

"I got a posse together here and got the train to make a special midnight run to carry us and our horses to the breaks of Mule Creek a few miles northeast of Coldwater. We're the ones you saw earlier in the afternoon when you started going south. I sent a man back to Coldwater to wire Pond Creek and let Thomas down in Oklahoma know where you were and that you were headed in his direction. . . . You know the rest."

I nodded once.

Calder started to leave but stopped again and said, "I answered your question, Wills—now you answer one for me."

I took a sip of coffee and looked at him. Calder could look a man right in the eye and not blink or duck his head. I always admired that in a man, whether I liked the man or not.

"I don't think you're a criminal, Wills, so why in the hell did you do what you did?"

"Because Johnnie was no more a criminal than I am, and for some other reasons you probably could never understand."

"But he *had* been indicted on some pretty serious criminal charges—manslaughter and first-degree murder. You and he both said from the begining that he shot Judd. Maybe he *wasn't* the one who fired the bullet that killed

Clois Newman, but hell . . . I just want you to make me understand why. . . ."

"Where were you raised, Calder?" I asked. "How were you raised?"

"I was born in Newburgh, New York, and my father was a fabric merchant. We moved out here after he bought a business in Kansas City."

"You've come from a different world from me and Johnnie, Calder. I don't think you could ever understand how all of this started, how honor and loyalty and duty were involved in what me and Johnnie both did. In places like Powder River, Wyoming, where there's thousands of square miles of lonesome on all sides, the only law is the law of right—and it's enforced by guts and determination. I don't think you could understand what it means to be responsible for a crew of cowboys who would follow you off hell's rimrock if you asked them to and to be responsible for getting twenty-five hundred head of Texas Longhorn steers to a designated place at a designated time, not for the money but because you respect the man who hired you and because everything you are—and everything you stand for—is in what you do.

"But try to picture the Powder River on a dangerous rampage. It's the only thing standing between you, your cowboys, and all those steers getting to your destination safely, and hopefully on time. Those men trust you when you tell them that if they help you get that herd of steers across that dangerous river, you promise to get them all across safely . . . and then you see it all working just like you promised them it would—working because of your cowboy skills and because of their faith in *you*. And then, because of something *one* man does, not accidentally, but on purpose, the whole damned thing goes to hell. You not only lose a lot of cattle and any chance of getting to your designated place on time, you also lose two of those punchers who believed in you and who against their better judgment tackled a river they ordinarily would have camped beside and watched. You drag their bodies out of the bog and the water and wrap them in a piece of wagon tarp and bury them in a place so lonesome that even God forgot where He put it. Can you imagine the debt you would feel to those men—a debt of honor—that the man responsible be held accountable? Well, that was the position Johnnie was in, and he did what he had to do. The trouble was, Calder, this thing got carried to a different country than where it started."

"And maybe to a different time, too. Hell, Wills, there're laws—"

"I'm not saying that what Johnnie did was *right*, Calder, but even though he used poor judgment in letting it happen in a place where an innocent man like Clois Newman could get killed by one of Judd's stray bullets, what he did *was* honorable. It was not only honorable, it was demanded by those events on Powder River I told you about and by the code Johnnie Lester lived—and died—by."

"Why didn't you tell me this before?"

"You heard it. The story was all over town about the things that happened on Powder River that day, but it didn't make any difference then. Clois Newman was dead, people were outraged and seeking their pound of flesh— nothing else mattered."

"I guess maybe I did hear it, but I never heard it like you just told it," Calder said.

"That's because you weren't willing to listen then."

Calder let out a sigh and said, "You know it's still not over, don't you? You'll have to—"

"I have a debt to pay to the State of Kansas, Calder, and I've yet to have a debt I didn't pay. You don't need to worry about another jailbreak."

"Not even when Ike and the boys get here?"

"No."

Calder looked me in the eye without flinching or ducking away again. "Word of honor?"

I looked back into his eye the same as he was looking into mine. "Word of honor," I said.

When I woke up that afternoon and heard the ruckus outside I would have bet it was Ike and the boys—and I would have won.

The ruckus moved right into the jail, with Calder threatening to bring in Captain Berryman and his troopers if there was a hint of trouble and promising immediate jail time for anyone who didn't immediately comply with the no-firearms ordinance by leaving their guns with him. While Calder was talking loud and making promises, Ike and the boys were cussing—Jim Napp and Billy Meeks were the loudest—and demanding to see Johnnie and wanting to know where I was.

Finally, I heard Calder's voice yell over the other voices: "Matt, go tell Captain Berryman to bring in his troops!" Then Calder led the way back to the cells, in front of the cowboys who were all still armed and who, when they saw me locked up and bandaged, immediately started asking questions faster than I could possibly answer them.

"Wills," Calder said, "the troops are on their way—I just hope you can calm this bunch down before they get here!"

"Unlock my cell door," I said.

"You're crazy as hell, too! If you think you can intimidate me—"

"I'm not trying to intimidate anybody, Calder, but . . . dammit, just unlock that door and let 'em in here so we can sit around and talk! Hell, the U. S. Army will be here in ten minutes—and besides, you've got my word of honor there won't be any trouble—but you've *got* to treat these men with respect and not like a bunch of criminals! Just open the door and get out of the way and keep those soldiers out in the street. And get us a bottle of whiskey in here, too."

Calder's face turned red. "Wills, you want me to unlock your cell door, let these men keep their weapons, *and* not only furnish them with liquor but let them drink it in my jail?"

"Yeah," I said, "that's right—and then just get the hell out of the way. You have my word of honor, remember?"

"You have no idea how little that means to me right now, Wills," Calder said.

"Then be hardheaded and go strictly by the book and let those troopers come busting in here and see what happens. Maybe nothing. Or maybe some good men on both sides die and Bluff City becomes a hundred times more famous than me and Johnnie could ever make it."

Calder thought for a few seconds, rubbed his chin with his hand, then walked to the door, unlocked it, and stepped back into his office.

Ike pulled the door open and they all moved inside the little cell. Everyone who had been at Powder River that day, and was still alive, except for Luther Atkins—and he never counted for a thing anyway—was there. Jim Napp. Billy Meeks. Juan Corona. Ramus Knight. Lewis Anacho.

"Talk, Casey," Ike said.

"Calder!" I yelled. *"Where's that whiskey?"*

Calder stepped inside the cell block again with a nearly full bottle of Jack Daniel's in his hand and a scowl on his face. Juan stepped into the hallway between the cells and caught the bottle when Calder tossed it. Then Calder stood at the end of the hallway with his arms folded.

"Take the lid off and pass it around, Juan," I said.

After the bottle had been around once, I said, "Johnnie's dead. Big Track fell on him late yesterday and broke his neck. His body is over at the funeral home. I would like for you to take him back to Texas and bury him there."

"Good God," Ike said and the cell got quiet. Then after a few moments Ike said softly, "We heard he was in jail for shootin' Judd."

"What happened to you, Casey?" Juan asked.

"Keep that bottle going around and I'll tell you all of it."

And I did. But before I was finished I looked at each of them and said, "Now, Ike, before you and the boys start talking about taking me with you when you leave here and about finding Luther Atkins and hanging him for volunteering to be the state's key witness against Johnnie, I want to tell you that Powder River has claimed enough men. If you do anything to Luther, Calder will have to come after you and some of you will probably die, too. That would only make Johnnie's dyin' seem to have been in vain, and I don't want that. Johnnie did what he *had* to do, every man here knows that. It's just a shame that Clois Newman had to die and the whole thing get so out of hand, but that's what happened and Johnnie never whined about it and he got to die on a good horse, headin' for a far rimrock with a clear conscience and a smile on his face. The rest of us should be so damned lucky. Now I've got a debt to settle with the State of Kansas and I'm not going to whine, either. Whatever that debt turns out to be, I'll see it through—but it's gotta stop *right here*.

"Now there's about one drink apiece left in that bottle, so let's pass it around one more time and lift it to the memories of Bronc and Laredo and Johnnie Lester—good cowboys who didn't shirk their duty and who've made it to the rim and beyond. Let's drink to 'em and then let 'em rest in peace. The Powder River affair is finished."

And so they all swore it would be. J. M. Calder looked at me and nodded.

Since I was obviously guilty as sin of the charge of "breaking a lawfully incarcerated individual out of a duly constituted correctional facility and doing physical damage to said facility" and certainly desiring no trial before twelve good men of Bluff City, Kansas, all that was left to do was to appear before the Honorable William Isaac Sawyers for sentencing, which occurred on the fifth of October 1894.

Ike stayed and appeared before the judge on my behalf, going on so much about so many of my admirable qualities that it was embarrassing and until I thought surely Judge Sawyers would nominate me for the priesthood instead of sending me to prison. J. M. Calder even stood before the judge and said he thought I was an honorable man living by an archaic code of justice. He took into account that I was careful not to hurt anyone in the jailbreak and said he could see no benefit to society by imposing the maximum sentence of five to ten years on me.

Then it was my turn to stand before the Honorable William Isaac Sawyers.

"What do you have to say for yourself, Mister Wills?"

"Guilty, Your Honor," I said.

I was hoping for three to five years in the state prison, but was prepared for more. The sentence, though, rocked me back on my heels.

Judge Sawyers said to me, "Casey Wills, you have pled guilty to the charges brought against you, and as a result it is the judgment of this court that you spend one year in confinement. And at the request of Sheriff J. M. Calder it is further ordered that your confinement be spent in the jail here in Bluff City so you can help repair the damage you caused to the facility. Mister Calder, take charge of the prisoner. This court is adjourned."

In a million years, I would never have dreamed I could be so happy at the prospect of spending a year in the Bluff City, Kansas, jail.

Ike was shaking my hand and telling me he would take care of my horses and that they would be on the train one year from that day. Next October! For a stove-up cowboy still healing from a bullet wound and facing a year in jail, I felt unbelievably good. I don't think I could have felt any better. I almost felt reborn. I wanted to clap my hands together and dance and make my spurs jingle and say, "Yes! Yes! Yes!"

I guess for drifting men, little victories mean a lot and happiness comes in strange ways.

31

I cannot say that I would necessarily recommend a year in the Bluff City jail under J. M. Calder to anyone—especially to anyone used to being able to roll up his bed and change his scenery on the merest of whims. And I cannot say the year passed quickly and pleasantly. But I can say that J. M. Calder turned out to be, as I had suspected even before the day of my sentencing, a fine man. And I can also say that the year *did* pass and that the State of Kansas was not shorted by a single day of it as I marked each and every one of them off, one at a time, on a calendar hanging on the wall of my cell.

My shoulder was competely healed by the first of December, and Calder put me to work reshingling the roof of the jail house, which I was more than glad to do because I had all of the sitting in my cell and staring at the walls I wanted. Besides, I was never afraid of manual labor the way Johnnie was.

After I was finished with the reshingling, Calder put me to work ripping out the boards on the floor that my weak-kneed number-three dynamite had damaged and replacing them with new ones. After that, there was scraping and painting to do, and before the year was up I was even shoeing his horses for him.

With Johnnie's death the mood of Bluff City noticeably changed. The town's collective desire to extract its pound of flesh from a drifter and ne'er-do-well with a big Texas hat and noisy spurs had been satisfied. The affair that had engaged every mind and tongue in town for days and days on end was suddenly forgotten and I became no more than a curiosity to them.

Although the days were pretty busy, at least after my shoulder healed from the bullet, my nights were spent almost entirely alone in my small cell. I had plenty of time for thinking and wondering what my life would be like after I finished my sentence. I would be forty-seven years old. Not exactly a kid. I still loved the cowboy life and always would—the horses, the cattle, the men, and the country they called home—but there was not much romance left in endless nights on the ground around a wagon or staying in a bunkhouse with a bunch of kids or drifting again—and especially drifting without Johnnie. Johnnie had made the drifting tolerable when it was bad and a delight when it was good. But Johnnie was gone.

I naturally spent a lot of time thinking about the most dramatic and telling event of my life—a life which, upon reflection, was not an unexciting one. But of all the things I had done and seen and of all the places I had been, the telling event was my falling in love with Miroux. Time works wonders, and I could not think of her and the short time we had shared together with more pleasure than pain. But, God, I did think about her and wonder what her life had been like over the years. Were she and DuPont still at their homestead just back from the Niobrara or had they moved? Did Miroux still dress in buckskins most of the time? Did she play the fiddle? What was DuPont doing for a living? Was he still chasing dreams? Or had he found his?

And I thought about the home I'd built among the cedars on the north bank of the Niobrara and wondered what had become of it. Did anybody file on the homestead I left behind? If so, who was it? And were *they* still there?

I had plenty of time to write during the long nights, so I

could have written a letter to Mr. Brewer at the mercantile in Chadron or I could have written to Sheriff Gowers—assuming they were both still alive and in Chadron. But if I wrote them asking about the Seviers there was a chance they might mention my letter to Miroux or DuPont if they were still there and I didn't want that. If I wrote and asked my questions and asked them not to mention my letter to anyone, they might think that unusual and mention it anyway.

But I thought of a way to find out if Miroux and Du-Pont were still there, and just after the first of February I told Calder I had been wondering about a friend and his wife who had been living along the Niobrara River, south of Chadron, Nebraska, and asked him if he could wire the sheriff there and find out.

The next day, while I was working on the floor of the jailhouse on my hands and knees, Calder stepped inside the door and said, "Casey, I got a wire from Sheriff Gowers in Chadron today and he said your friends have been gone for almost three years. He said they moved back east but he didn't know where."

"The Seviers?"

"Yeah," he shrugged. "Sorry?"

That night I caught myself planning again, the first time I'd done so since taking DuPont back to Miroux. I wrote Mister Brewer at the mercantile in Chadron and asked him if he knew who was living on my old homestead.

Three weeks later, Matt Taylor came into the jail house and said, "I've got a letter here for you, Casey."

I opened it and read:

Dear Mister Wills,

I must say it was a surprise to hear from you after all this time. It was almost as much of a surprise as when I learned you had abandoned your homestead, especially after being so particular about how you built it and what you furnished it with. Anyway, I trust you are well.

About your inquiry—although there have been two or three different people to live in your place off and on over the years, to the best of my knowledge there is no one there at present and certainly no one has lived there long enough to get a title to it. I have no idea what kind of shape the place is in—however, I suspect it is somewhat in a state of disrepair.

Yours truly,
Glen Brewer

"J. M.," I said, "I need a favor."

Calder looked at me and smiled. "Let me guess—you want me to let you out early so you can get back to cow country before branding."

"Will you?"

"Not unless the governor himself tells me to."

"Then will you use whatever influence you have with the sheriff in Chadron to use whatever influence he has with the agent at the land office there to hold a homestead open for me until I can get back there this fall and file on it? It's the same one I filed on in eighty-nine—the sheriff will know where it is."

"Why should I do that?" Calder asked.

"So I'll have a place to go to after my year is up here."

"Why should I care if you have a place to go to or not?"

"Because if I don't," I said with a shrug and a smile, "I'll just hang around town and invite a bunch of my drunken cowboy friends to hang around with me and you'll have drunks shooting out your new electric streetlights every night and you'll have your clean jail full of them wondering what's for supper."

"Say no more!" Calder said with his own smile. "Say no more!"

"Will you let me know?"

"Yeah."

A few days later Calder said, "Gower remembered you and said he would talk the land agent into holding it until the twentieth of October."

I was going back to the cabin among the cedars beside the Niobrara! I would have no cattle and no money buried in a lard can to buy any with, but the Niobrara was in cow country and I knew how to survive in cow country.

* * *

The first of May I wrote a letter to Ike:

> Dear Ike,
> The days seem to drag by but then before I know it another week has been marked off my calendar. October, though still invisible beyond the rim, is at least beginning to cast its pale light on the horizon.
> You owe me nothing, so for you to try to give me anything more would be an insult. But I do have a business proposition for you. If you by chance were able to salvage any young studs from your remuda I would like to trade Chip and Deuce to you for one. I am going to be able to get the homestead back where I built the house and barn and corrals that I was telling you about, and I would like to have a stud of the same bloodline as those good cow horses you raised so I can raise some of my own.
> If the trade is satisfactory to you just send the stud on the train in October instead of Chip and Deuce, and I will get a saddle horse somewhere to ride to the Niobrara.
> > Thanks,
> > Casey

With those simple plans laid and at least some of them seeming to be taking shape, I began to look more toward the future and my life after Bluff City and the Powder River affair, and the wait for October became harder and harder to bear.

Finally, October 5 arrived, and with a handshake from J. M. Calder and Matt Taylor, I buckled on my spurs and walked out the door a free man. My debt to the State of Kansas was paid in full.

When the train arrived, I told the conductor who I was and asked if Ike Holt had sent a horse for me.

"I don't know—why don't you ask him yourself."

"You mean Ike Holt himself is on the train?"

"That's right, Casey," I heard Ike say behind me and turned around to find his hand outstretched to me.

"You didn't need to come up here, Ike," I said as I shook his hand.

"Good to see you, Casey—damn good! I brought your horses."

"What do you mean horses? Didn't you get my letter about wanting to trade you Chip and Deuce for a young stud if you had one?"

"I got it, and I brought the stud for you—a two-year-old red dun by the same stud as old Chip. I also brought Chip and Deuce to you."

"Ike, dammit, I told you you weren't going to give me anything else."

"Not plannin' on it, Casey—but if you accept the offer I have for you you'll need a couple of good horses."

"What are you talking about?"

"This. I was able to salvage a little out of the ranch—not much, but a little. And I've been able to get a little more backing and a chance to start building again. I don't have much time—I have to be on this train when it pulls out again. But I wanted to come up and look you in the eye when I offer this deal to you so we'll both know where we stand.

"You say you're going back to that homestead you had one time and that you'll have access to some free range to graze cattle on?"

"Yeah, but I don't have any money to buy any cattle right now."

Ike pointed a finger at me. "I know," he said, "and I've got a little money, but no grass. How about us being partners on say a hundred head of bred heifers due to start calving in the spring—I'll furnish the heifers and you furnish the care and grass. At the end of three years I get back the original hundred head less the death loss plus half of the increase. The other half of the increase is yours free and clear. What do you say? It won't be easy, because for three years neither of us is going to make a dime on them. I won't get any return on my money and you won't get any return on your labor—you'll have to figure out some way to survive."

"I'm good at surviving," I said as the train blew its whistle.

"Then let's shake on it and get your horses out of the stock car before this train pulls out."

"Where will I go to get the heifers?" I asked.

"I'll be sending 'em to Chadron on the train and they'll already be branded. You'll just have to be there to get them off the train and take 'em to your grass and get 'em located before winter. . . . Yeah, that's right, I'll be sending them up on the train, the days of the trail drives are over. There was a couple went up the Western Trail this year but I'll bet they're the last ones forever. The cow business is changin' and we'll have to change with it."

We shook hands, and then Ike slid open the stock-car door and led Chip and Deuce and as good-looking a two-year-old red dun stud as I'd ever seen down the loading chute.

The train blew its whistle again and started popping the couplers on the cars. "So long, Casey," Ike said as he handed me the lead ropes of the horses and jumped back on the train. "Proud to have you as a partner—damn proud. There's not many men I would trust for a deal like this anymore. Not many left whose word is their bond."

"Thanks, Ike," I said. "Thanks for believing in me—and thanks for the opportunity."

"You may be thanking me too soon, Casey—maybe you'd better wait and see what kind of winters you have up there for the next three years."

"When do you think the heifers will be in Chadron?"

"They'll be there on the twentieth about noon—I've already checked on the schedule."

"The twentieth! That's pretty quick!"

"Yeah, I know, but I've already got 'em bought, Casey, and I have to go with 'em. I'll pay your fare to ride the train from here to there."

"No," I said. "I need to ride. But I'll be in Chadron on the twentieth to take possession of the heifers, Ike."

And just like that, on the day I got out of jail, I suddenly had more of a future than I'd had since me and Johnnie sold the Banister horses at the Oklahoma land rush. And it was going to be a busy future, too, at least for a while.

It had been over a year since I had been on a horse—the longest period in at least thirty-five years—and it sure felt good to feel one moving between my knees again, especially one that felt as good underneath a man as a Holt horse did.

It was a beautiful fall day, with no wind, a nice nip in the air, and geese honking their way overhead. A beautiful day for a man to get his freedom and ride toward his future.

The first norther of the season met me a couple of days south of the Niobrara about the time I reached Snake Creek, and spit a few snow flurries. By morning the sun was shining again and the wind had died, but there was frost on the horses' backs and on my blankets and it only warmed enough all day to allow me to unbutton my coat for a couple of hours in the afternoon.

A half-moon had already risen over the sand hills by the time I stopped on top of a ridge overlooking the Niobrara, and the air was cold enough to bite a man's ears and nose and make him snuggle deeper into his mackinaw.

I could barely make out the layout of the ranch on the other side of the river at the edge of the stand of cedars. But what I could see made me feel good, feel proud that I was the one who had built it all—the pole corrals, the log barn, and the little log cabin all under the same long tin roof and . . .

And the gray smoke curling up from the cabin?

Somebody was there!

But Calder said that Gower said that the land agent said . . .

I spurred Chip off the top of the ridge with Deuce and the dun stud stretching their necks out and following as the slack came out of their lead ropes.

When I was halfway down the slope a horse nickered from the corrals and the young stud answered.

Just before I kicked Chip off the bank and into the

Niobrara the soft yellow light of a lantern appeared in the windows of the cabin.

The stud nickered again and was again answered by the horse from the corrals.

Surely, whoever was there had not filed on the place but was squatting or just someone passing through. Surely.

The water in the Niobrara was chest deep, and I pulled my feet up to keep my boots from getting soaked as the horses splashed across it.

As we came up out of the water and onto the north bank the cabin door opened and lantern light streamed into the dog run.

A shadow passed across one of the windows, took a few steps toward the river, then stopped.

"Hello!" I yelled as the horses came up out of the water.

The shadow was silent as I rode closer.

Then I was close enough to make out the outline of a dress. The shadow was a woman, but I couldn't tell anything beyond that.

"Hello!" I said again, walking the dripping horses closer.

Chip snorted.

Then suddenly something about the woman's outline, the way the dress fit her, the way her hair was pulled back, how small she was, how unafraid she seemed, something about her made me lift the reins and stop. I think my heart stopped, too.

The woman was walking slowly in my direction again.

"Hello, ma'am," I said, straining my eyes in an attempt to see her better.

"*Bonjour,*" she said softly as she stopped.

Bonjour! "My God . . ."

I wrapped the lead ropes of the halters around my saddle horn and slowly stepped to the ground.

I dropped Chip's reins and took three steps forward and stopped again, staring in wonder and disbelief at who was before me in the dim moonlight.

"*Bonjour* . . . Casey."

"My God . . . Miroux . . . !"

For a few seconds neither of us spoke. I was too stunned to speak.

"I . . . I never dreamed it was you down here!" I said at last over the lump in my throat.

"I never dreamed it was you coming across the river!"

She took two small steps forward and stopped an arm's length away. I could now see her features in the moonlight, features I'd been sure I would never see again. Features that five years had done nothing to but make more beautiful.

"Why are you here, Casey?"

"I came back to live," I said. "But not until Sheriff Gowers said you and DuPont had moved away."

"That was three years ago."

"I just learned it a few months ago—and I also learned that no one had filed on the place. What are you doing here, Miroux? Is DuPont here?"

"DuPont died in Montreal two years ago, Casey. Of consumption—he never got over being forced to work in the Gibraltar mine."

"DuPont died?"

"*Oui* . . . But I was a good wife to him, Casey."

"I'm sure you were, Miroux. I really am sorry about him dying."

"You gave him three years he would not have had."

"*Mommy!*" A child's voice came from the cabin.

"And a daughter."

"A daughter? You and DuPont had a daughter after . . ."

"She was born fourteen months after you saved his life and brought him back. She would not have been born had it not been for you, Casey. Her name is Ona and she just turned four years old. . . . Ona, come out here, sweetheart!"

A thirty-inch bundle of energy came scampering from the cabin to her mother's buckskin skirt. "Ona, this man's name is Casey Wills."

"Hello, Ona," I said, tipping my hat to her.

"*Bonjour*, Casey Wills," she said.

"You're a beautiful young lady, Ona, with your mother's dark hair and eyes."

"Thank you, Casey Wills," she said shyly.

"Why are you and Ona here?" I asked. "How long have you been here?"

"We just got here this afternoon, Casey. I had no idea you would be here. We have been staying at a place in Montana called St. Peter's Mission, a mission operated by Jesuit priests. I needed such a place after DuPont's death. But it seemed like it finally came time for us to leave. I came here to see if anyone had moved into our old homestead—and maybe to see if I still felt I belonged here . . . but someone is in our old place."

"So you came here to stay awhile?"

"When I saw it empty, I thought we might stay a few days. . . . I spent all afternoon cleaning it up. But I never dreamed you would be here, Casey. . . . Did you bring a wife?"

I laughed and shook my head. "When a man is running from a woman's memory, a wife is the last thing he needs."

"Casey . . ." Miroux was looking up at me.

I squatted down in front of Ona and said, "If your mother will let me, would it be okay with you if I kissed her?"

Ona looked at me with her big dark eyes for a second and then craned her neck to look up at Miroux and said, "Mommy, do you want Casey Wills to kiss you?"

"Yes, I do, sweetheart," Miroux whispered. "I want that very much."

"Okay, Casey Wills, you can kiss my mommy."

I stood up and let my eyes explore Miroux's face for a few seconds. Then I lifted a hand and let a fingertip gently run the length of her slender nose from a spot between the eyes filled with tears, over the hard crest, and off the soft tip. Then our lips touched and the kiss was warm and sweet beyond belief.

"Stay, Miroux," I whispered after I found my voice. "Not just the night, but stay a lifetime with me, you and Ona."

"Casey . . . This is all happening so quick!"

"Life happens quick, Miroux—before you know it, it's gone. Help me turn this abandoned homestead into a home. I'm staying here with or without you this time but—"

"No, you're not, Casey," Miroux said, "you're not staying one single night here without me, but tonight you *are* sleeping in the barn. And tomorrow we'll go see the preacher." Then she laid her head against my shoulder and said, "You are home at last, Casey."

I looked down at her and said, "*We're* home at last, Miroux." Then I picked up my bridle rein, leaned over, and picked up Ona. Then, with her in my arms and Miroux at my side and three good horses following me, I walked toward a future I would never have allowed myself to dream of.

"Mommy, why do we need to go see the preacher tomorrow?" Ona asked.

Miroux looked up at me for a moment with a twinkle in her eye and a knowing smile on her lips and said, "So we can make an honest man out of Casey Wills, sweetheart."

And across rhe Big Lonely, not much was changed. The cold north wind would still moan through tall cedars and lonesome cowboys would winter alone in far-off line camps, thinking about spring and branding and about the sweetheart they left behind. Coyotes would still howl and prowl and drifting sand and snow would blow across many forgotten cowboy graves. But one thing about the Big Lonely *had* changed and I hoped this time forever—the long drift of Casey Wills upon it was finished at last.

Like Casey Wills, Sam Brown has worked most of his adult life as a cowboy on Texas ranches, with occasional stints in the classroom as a teacher. For the past few years he has been a modern-day drifting cowboy, working on ranches from New Mexico to Wyoming. Now Brown works indoors as a district manager for the *Amarillo Globe News*. His most recent Western, *The Big Lonely*, was a 1992 Spur Award finalist. Brown lives in Adrian, Texas.